A STAR DIES. . . .

There was no mistaking the body among the curtains. I'd seen her hounded to death in *Dark Streets* and dragged screaming to the guillotine in *Madame du Barry*. Now she was hanging in the hotel curtains, her eyes staring down at me with mild surprise. . . .

There was no question about whether she was dead. In death—as in life—she did dead very well.

MURDER ON LOCATION

"Engel keeps the plot moving along at a good clip, deftly building suspense, scattering the requisite red herrings while zeroing in on the real criminal and the real crime which is right at the heart. Howard Engel writes with great facility. He is clever and funny and his firsthand knowledge of what goes on behind the cameras is entertaining."

—*Edmonton Journal*

Murder
on
Location

A BENNY COOPERMAN MYSTERY

Howard Engel

SEAL BOOKS
McClelland and Stewart-Bantam Limited
Toronto

For William and Charlotte
and in memory of Ted Adams
and Prynce Nesbitt

MURDER ON LOCATION

*A Seal Book / published by arrangement with
Clarke, Irwin & Co., Ltd.*

PRINTING HISTORY
Clarke, Irwin edition published September 1982
Seal edition / January 1984

ISBN 0-7704-1824-4

*Seal Books are published by McClelland and Stewart-Bantam
Limited. Its trademark, consisting of the words "Seal Books"
and the portrayal of a seal, is the property of McClelland and
Stewart-Bantam Limited, 60 St. Clair Avenue East, Suite 601, Toronto,
M4T 1N5. This trademark has been duly registered on the Trademarks Office of Canada. The trademark, consisting of the word
"Bantam" and the portrayal of a rooster, is the property of and
is used with the consent of Bantam Books, Inc., 666 Fifth Avenue, New York, New York 10103. This trademark has been duly
registered in the Trademarks Office of Canada and elsewhere.*

PRINTED IN CANADA

COVER PRINTED IN U.S.A.

U   0 9 8 7 6 5 4 3 2 1

THE CAST

Benny Cooperman: a licensed private investigator from Grantham, Ontario

David Hayes: an aspiring actor-writer who drinks by himself

Wally Skeat: a card-carrying member of the fifth estate

Ned Evans: a local director who plans his shows in the beverage room and then almost forgets to put them on

Dawson Williams: film actor, durable star of the silver screen

Peggy O'Toole: vulnerable, gamine-like budding star of *Ice Bridge*

James A. Sayre: veteran director of Hollywood films

Neil Furlong: local writer now riding the big-time

Miranda Pride: as much a part of Hollywood as Taylor, Hepburn and Lassie

Adela Sayre: she'd cut throats for Sayre if necessary

Marvin Raxlin: a film producer with more than movie problems on his mind

Ed Noonan: local casting director who can't keep his hands off his work

Billie Mason: a beautiful runaway wife who brings trouble for more than Benny

Lowell Mason: a real estate dealer who deals from both ends of the deck

Monty Blair: an uncoverer of talent in unlikely places

Martha Tracy: there isn't much she doesn't know about where the money comes from around Grantham

Norman Baker: a one-time CBC TV producer, now independent and sitting on hot footage

Anthony Horne Pritchett, Tullio Solmi, Mordecai Cohn: the less you know about their shady dealings the healthier you'll be

Sophie and **Manny Cooperman:** Benny's long-suffering parents

Linda Levin: the divorcee who came to dinner

Harvey Osborne: a drunk with a grudge against Furlong

Staff-Sergeant Chris Savas: a good cop from Niagara Regional Police

Claudia Horlick: Peggy's mother

Dulcie Osborne: a name from the past that people would rather forget

Hatch: he looked like Mr. Punch behind the bar at the *Surf Lounge*

Ella Beames: Grantham librarian who has helped Benny on more cases than she knows about

Pete Staziak: a cop who remembers Benny from high school days

one

I was sitting in the lobby of the Tudor Hotel in Niagara
Falls on the Canadian side of the river, looking at the
back section of the *Star-Enterprise* and glancing up from
time to time to catch who was coming in and going out the
revolving front door. Perched behind a potted palm I felt
like a hotel dick as I read for the sixth time about local
births and deaths. When I ran out of cigarettes, I bought
a pack in the smoke shop just a couple of doors away, and
was back at my post before my quarry could have come
and gone more than a dozen times. Private investigation
is an imperfect craft and my methods are hit and miss. It's
doggedness that pays off in the end.

The lobby was more crowded than usual that evening:
couples checking in, noisy groups going up to the top-floor
bar or to the convention rooms. A uniformed policeman
stood chatting with the bell captain. Some of the movie
people had started to arrive, so there was more than the
usual amount of bustle on the part of the staff. Those who
weren't staying at Butler's Barracks — the local, unofficial
name for the posh Colonel John Butler Hotel — were
booked here at the Tudor. The Colonel John was bigger,
running for most of a block across from the river, but the
Tudor was more exclusive. I wondered how David Hayes
had managed to afford the Tudor. Maybe he'd landed that
big movie job he'd set out to get a week ago.

I was chewing on that when the light of the lobby
chandelier was cut off by a body getting in the way. For a
minute I thought it would go away, so I didn't look up.
When it wouldn't move on, I guessed it was looking at me.

"Well, if it isn't Benny Cooperman, my favourite private eye. How's it going, Benny? You making a buck?" It
was Wally Skeat from the Falls TV station. He used to be
a disc jockey in Grantham before he got fired, and now

7

he was a working journalist, a card-carrying member of the press. I'd seen him reading the evening news.

"Hi, Wally. You hustling too?" He tried on a tortured smile to show how I misjudged him, pulled over a high-backed chair with dark corkscrew legs and settled down opposite me. I could still see the door over his shoulder.

"This is the big time, Benny. Are you trying to land a part in the movie?"

"You know better than that. I do all my play-acting looking for strayed or stolen spouses."

"Come on. I remember you were in Ned Evans' *A Midsummer Night's Dream* in Montecello Park last summer."

"Yeah, my Starveling really stole the show."

"Never mind," he said letting his bass notes tumble down to the rug and roll around heavily. "Experience is experience. Don't knock it. And from what I hear, *Ice Bridge* is going to be a great flick. Remember where you heard it first. It's got everything going for it: there are stars like Dawson Williams and Peggy O'Toole, the director's James A. Sayre, and the local boy himself, Neil Furlong, working on the script. Now is that a winner or is that a winner?" For a second, I thought I heard some treble notes sneaking into his voice, but I don't think Wally'd heard about treble. "And," he continued, "it'll all be photographed against the background of one of the seven natural wonders of the world. It can't miss. Nothing since Marilyn Monroe made *Niagara* here in the 1950s can touch it. I hear it's got a budget big enough for two pictures. That's a lot of chips and gravy, Benny." Wally stopped to breathe at last.

"How long will they be here?"

"Three weeks on the nose. Every minute planned. The stars have started arriving. Miranda Pride is here. She was a star when they were still cutting them out of pure gold. And Dawson Williams. Damn it all, it's exciting. And all happening right here." He sat with a smile on his shining moon-face, probably thinking of Williams as Robin Hood back in the fifties. I was. Then he leaned over, shortening the gap between us. "Look, Benny, are you looking for a part? There are extras to be picked locally, and a few bits with lines. Say the word and I'll talk to Ed Noonan, the local casting director. I'm serious, Benny. You know, for you, it's up to here." He made a chop at his left arm with the edge of his right hand.

"You ever hear of a Grantham girl named Billie Mason? She might be trying to get a part."

"Her and a thousand others. Why, even Ned and his gang from Grantham are here staying at the Clifford Arms, that old firetrap. Noonan's a hard guy to see, Benny, but just say the word, just say the word." In another minute, after reciting the names of other actors who were coming out from Hollywood to be in *Ice Bridge*, he took his leave to go back to work. Wally worked in the Pagoda, the newest of the tourist towers overlooking the falls. The TV station rented studio space near the top, and a revolving restaurant turned once an hour just above Wally's newscast.

I should explain that my interest in being at the Falls was only indirectly connected with the movie. Wally was right, I'd been a pretty good Starveling in *The Dream*, but it was bread and butter that brought me from my Grantham office to Niagara Falls this frosty first Monday of the year. It was then about eleven at night. Nine hours earlier, I'd been sitting in my office on St. Andrew Street wondering where I was going to get half a big one to renew my licence, when in walks a living, breathing client, with slip-on rubbers and an astrakhan collar on his coat. He was a man of forty with a solid, tanned face topped with short, greying hair that looked like you could scour pots and pans with it. Solid was the word for the rest of him too, except for his belly, which pushed the front of his coat through the door ahead of him. He held in his hand one of those furry fedoras that look like the offspring of private doings on a crowded hat shelf in the dark. His yellow eyes were worried and gave the lie to the smile pencilled in with no great conviction.

We fooled around sparring for a few minutes, then I began to find out why he'd dropped in. His name was Lowell Mason, he ran a real-estate organization on King

Street, and his wife, Billie, had gone missing just after Christmas with no warning. After giving me the life story of both of them, and a quarterly report on his business, he showed me an eight-by-ten picture of a good-looking woman in her mid-thirties with ash-blonde hair.

"What are you most afraid of?" I finally asked him.

"To tell you the truth," he said to the coat rack, "I think she's been murdered."

"Murdered" was not a word I heard across my desk every day, and it took a minute to develop and print it. "That's serious stuff, Mr. Mason. Who would want to kill your wife?"

He shook his head helplessly. All I could come back with was the usual drill about how few people get murdered. I was sure that she would be found in one piece. Then I told him that it sounded like a missing-persons job and that the police were still front-runners in that market.

"I've got connections with the police."

"So?"

"So, it was a friend of mine there that gave me your name."

"Come on, Mr. Mason. Look, cops can get thick in the head too. I'm not the Mounties. If you ask my friends at the cop shop they'll tell you that they do all my work for me. They're not kidding. I . . ."

"I'm asking you to take the case, Mr. Cooperman."

"Why?"

"Because I want her found."

"And?"

"I don't want her to get hurt."

"And?"

"And I miss her, and I can't stand the place without smelling her burning something in the kitchen."

When he left, I had the eight-by-ten glossy of his wife and a fair-sized retainer. He told me the make of her car and gave me a lecture about the unpaid parking tickets she collected on the dashboard before telling me the licence number. The big piece of information he left with me was that Billie was stage-struck. She had played Stella in *A*

Streetcar Named Desire for the Grantham Little Theatre last October.

I put in a call to Robin O'Neil at CXAN. Robin had been an announcer long before Wally Skeat breezed in and out. On the side, he still ran the Little Theatre with a lot of arty flair that got on Ned Evans' nerves. From Robin I learned that Billie Mason had talent, that she was a malleable actress, but that she had made a cheap success of the part of Stella. He told me that the CBC had interviewed her about her acting two months ago, although he had to admit there were other actresses in town just as talented. When I asked whether she was particularly friendly with any other members of the cast, I heard the name David Hayes for the first time.

"What about David Hayes?"

"David was a great Mitch. He *was* Mitch. He was very good. And he's not even a serious actor. More interested in writing. Works at the *Beacon*. He was one of Monty Blair's protégés." I learned that Hayes had driven Billie home from rehearsals a few times in his beat-up classic Jaguar with a cracked windshield. When I called the *Beacon*, Grantham's long-lived daily, I found out from an editor that Hayes hadn't been seen at his desk in a week.

From there I floundered around talking to Hugo Shackleford, who serviced the Jaguar, and to Hayes' landlady, who let me see his room only when I told her I was trying to deliver a summons. Hayes had cleared out about the same time Billie'd disappeared. I took a flyer and guessed that they had both headed to the Falls to get bits in the movie. It was a pretty limp theory, but it stiffened up when I discovered a cracked windshield on a broken-down Jaguar Mk VII in the parking lot at the Tudor Hotel. From the hotel desk I learned that David Hayes, newspaperman from Grantham, was registered by himself in Room 1738. He wasn't in when I rang the number. I had no better luck in the bar, the restaurant or the snack bar. So that's when I settled down among the sheltering potted palms and waited . . . and waited.

two

I didn't get back to my over-heated room at the City House in Grantham until about two in the morning. As I pulled my damp shoes off, I felt that I'd already given Lowell Mason value for money. The snow-plough coming along King Street moved a blue flashing shadow up a wall and across the ceiling of my room, and I fell asleep to the alarm clock threatening me at each tick with an early wake-up call.

By the time I was fit to talk on Tuesday morning, I was beginning to sort things out. First I wanted to see about Mason's business, and when it comes to real estate I always go to Martha Tracy for information. She works for Scarp Enterprises, the biggest real-estate and property development outfit in the Niagara district. As secretary to the managing director there isn't much she doesn't know and for the price of a beery lunch she'd always given me excellent advice. I asked her about Lowell Mason. Off the top of her head she was able to say that he was one of the five biggest operators in the area and the fastest growing. "He's a real old-fashioned hustler, Benny. You know: rye and ginger ale in the back office. They say that he leans heavily on his wife's looks in hooking his clients. She helps him land the fish and she enjoys the fuss men make over her. She's over twenty-one, and her husband encourages her. She's the out-going type. Now, I happen to be the in-going type, but what good does it do me?"

Just before I hung up, she asked what all this was in aid of, and I told her.

"Well, one thing's sure," she said.

"What's that?"

"A let's-pretend blonde like that is going to have to get professional help. She'll need to find a good hairdresser, Benny. It's all in the packaging." Martha had a brilliant future as a detective that she wasn't going to hear about from me. She then invited me over to have a cup of her instant hot tap-water coffee. I think she meant it as a sign of growing intimacy, and so far I'd managed to slow the growth right there.

I spent an hour running up my long-distance bill, and when I'd finished I had the name Norman Baker, former CBC television producer, who had dispatched a crew to interview Billie Mason and was currently in hot water with the network brass about a film he was doing, or refusing to do, depending on whose version you went by. I couldn't locate Baker himself, but the very sound of his name made a lot of secretaries giggle and several producers growl. I tore off the page with Baker's number on it and put it in my pocket.

It was nearly noon, so I left the dusty mess of my office to grab a bite of lunch at the United Cigar Store on St. Andrew Street. They make the best chopped-egg sandwiches in town. The waitress made no wisecracks about my cowardly eating habits, she just ordered my usual for me. The mad scribbler was sitting a couple of stools away, with his shaggy head bent over his furious writing, and Mrs. Prewitt from the drug store was mining a guilty fudge sundae with a long slender spoon.

Half an hour later, I took a drive out to the north end of town to look in on my parents. When parents are getting on in years, it's easy to forget them. I parked in front of the condominium and let myself in with my key. They never hear the two-toned chime.

"Who's that? Benny, is that you?"

"Hello, Ma, how are you?"

"How am I? How should I be? My doctor's in the hospital and his locum-shlocum isn't minding the store."

"You're not feeling well?" She was standing in a wine-coloured zip-up housecoat with pink feathery slippers. Her hair was still tangled from sleep and her face was still upstairs in the bathroom.

"I'm fine, Benny. I just want people to stay in one place. It makes me nervous when my doctor's in intensive care. I hope you've eaten lunch."

"I just had a bite uptown."

"I suppose I could make you an omelette. You want me to make you an omelette, Benny?"

"I just ate, Ma. Thanks anyway."

"I know how you eat," she said rolling her eyes, "I know what you put on your stomach."

"Where's Pa?" I asked.

"Gone to the club. Lately he's been going early. I think he's got a gin game, but I don't ask. If his life is a card game, I'm not going to criticize. You've been busy?"

"I've been doing some work at the Falls."

"Don't tell me. I don't want to know. Your work makes me nervous, Benny. I wish you'd find something safe, something solid."

"Like Sam?"

"What's the matter with Sam? You could do worse than being a doctor, believe me."

"I could be in intensive care this minute."

"Don't make jokes. Dr. Bannock is a wonderful human being. You hear?"

"I believe you. Do you want me to do any shopping for you? I've got the car."

"You're coming to dinner tomorrow night?"

"Sure."

"Good, then I don't need anything. In the freezer, thank God, I've got everything I need."

"Fine, I'll see you around seven." She saw me to the door. "Ma, why don't you do something about that chime? If I didn't have a key, I could die of old age ringing the bell."

"That's why you've got a key."

"But what about other people? I'm sure you don't catch half the people who come to the door."

"Half is plenty. What am I going to do with the others? Inefficiency makes the world go round. A new chime! I'll give you a chime." Ma opened the door for me, took in

14

yesterday's mail and last night's *Beacon* and waved me off. I always liked to check in on Ma once in a while. It interrupted the patches of guilt.

The drive to the Falls is short enough along the Queen Elizabeth Way, just twenty minutes with a tail wind. The highway lifts above the Welland Canal just outside Grantham and for ten miles offers a free view of prime real estate under snow drifting up to red snow fences, with the dusty line of the Niagara Escarpment framing an old-fashioned picture. Once the canal is left behind, the road gently climbs the height of land, flies over a few frost-bitten cloverleafs before coming down for a landing beside the Rainbow Bridge, which straddles the US-Canada border, just across from the Colonel John Butler Hotel.

I drove around the corner to the Tudor Hotel and parked so that I blocked David Hayes' Jaguar in its parking lot. I checked at the desk: he hadn't been in his room. I left another message for him, just to tag his movements. I bought a pack of Player's and walked back around the corner, into the lobby of the bigger hotel.

The mezzanine floor at Butler's Barracks was more acquainted with travellers, buyers and sellers, and Shriners on convention than it was with the movie business. I looked for abandoned drinks in unlikely places without finding them. Noonan's girl read my card and then took it in to him on five-inch heels. I didn't have to stare at the plastic ferns for very long; Noonan saw me almost at once. As I took the chair he indicated, I got the idea that he was seeing me not because he wasn't busy but because he was so disorganized it was easier to take on new problems than deal with old ones. He sat behind a desk with watermarks on the wood and on the faded green blotter. There was a stack of four filing drawers, with a pile of expense-account red filing folders close at hand.

Noonan's face was puffy and forty. Curly hair made a widow's peak not very far above his heavy eyebrows, but the fleshiness of his face took away any hint of the diabolic. His eyes were heavy-lidded, and he looked like he hadn't seen a shower or a bed lately. I told him my business.

"Billie Mason, eh?" He got up and visited his files. In a minute, he came back carrying a folder with a copy of the same picture I had. "Nice-looking girl," he said, and he was right. It was a three-quarter view with the right side of the face in shadow. Shadow sculptured the planes of her cheeks and brow, and out of it two big eyes looked up at me. They whispered to me. There was loneliness and promise written in them. The rest of the face echoed the twang of the eyes. The mouth was frank and sensual, the hair arranged to make you think of satin pillowcases. She was wearing a man's shirt with the buttons at the top unfastened. The results were not in the least masculine. I tried for the second time to get the face filed in my brain and the drawer slammed closed.

Noonan read through the *curriculum vitae* that was pasted on the back of the photograph and examined the mimeographed form that completed the file. When he'd looked his fill, he passed it over the desk to me. There was nothing about her husband, but she'd mentioned her performance as Stella in *Streetcar*. I made a note of the address and phone number in town where she was staying and passed the file back to Noonan. I asked him if he remembered her and he shook his head. "I must be getting too old if I can't place a face like that, but some of them just mailed in their stuff. Sorry I can't be a bigger help. If anything comes up, I mean if Mrs. Mason comes in, where can I get ahold of you?" I pointed at the card in the middle of his blotter and picked up my hat. Noonan saw me to the top of the grand staircase.

From the lobby I tried the number in the Falls I'd got from Noonan: Billie Mason had been there two nights, but hadn't been seen since. I went back to the Tudor through the parking garages that connect the two hotels. It saved me going out into the slicing wind blowing off the falls. Up in the lobby, a mob scene was going on. The elevator doors opened on about fifty people, some with cameras, some with tape recorders, some with notebooks, all crowding around an elderly tanned giant with a string tie like a rancher in a movie. When he saw the doors open, he called out: "Hold that car!" I pushed the rubber sides of the door so it wouldn't close. A battery of portable floodlights added a silver edge to the man's profile.

"When I got back from Italy," he said into a bouquet of microphones, "I got a call from the studio about doing *Ice Bridge*. I told them I could give them until the middle of March, when I have to go to Dublin to do *Parnell*. I'm goin' to enjoy doing *Ice Bridge*. I've always liked comin' here."

"You've visited the Falls before, sir?" asked a journalist with dark racoon-like eyes.

"I know the Canadian west. I've worked in the Black Hills country and the coast. Look, I'm talked out. Have a heart. Dick," he called out vaguely into the glare of the lights, "Dick, you see that the boys are looked after. You'll excuse me right now. I'll see you later. I'm not goin' anywhere for three weeks." That didn't stop the questions, but he shook his head, and made a sudden leap in my direction followed by a bellhop with a truckload of suitcases. "Hold that car!" he repeated, and crossed the rest of the lobby with a few long strides between the exploding photo flashes. The mob tried to follow, except for the curious hotel guests, who stood frozen like lawn animals watching from the sidelines. I pushed the rubber edges again against their repeated spasm and the big man climbed aboard, moving well back so that his luggage could follow. "Much obliged to you," he said, giving me a full grin of false teeth. "I think we're goin' to make our getaway after all." The reporters crowded us right to the closing stainless steel doors. I didn't make good my escape; I was trapped inside with a Texas Ranger and his wardrobe.

"Push the button for the penthouse," he said and I did it. I got another look at his remarkable teeth as he tried to explain: "My plane got in at Buffalo, and they were waitin' for me with their cameras and sixguns. Followed me here and I guess they'll make camp in the lobby and set up a siege. Name's Jim Sayre," he said. "I make movin' pictures." He shot out a hand at me, and I heard myself telling him my name and that I was a private investigator. I don't usually volunteer that last part without my arm being twisted, but Jim Sayre had an authority about his long, lean rawboned proportions that made me confess.

"Well, it's right handy you were standin' by. I'll have to thank the hotel for thinkin' of everythin'. Well, not quite everythin'. I'm about five drinks below par and I haven't got a drop in all them bags." He turned to the bellhop. "Could you get me a quart of sourmash liquor, son?" The bellhop explained Ontario liquor laws as the car ascended, and the big man's eyes rolled in the direction of the penthouse. "I don't want to know the rules, son, I want a quart of sourmash liquor and I need it soon." He looked at me for support. "Can you do anything, Ben? This fellow's studyin' for a lawyer. I don't want to know any more rules. How much should I give him?" I suggested twenty dollars, and the bargain was struck then and there without further palaver. Here the elevator doors opened and the three of us and the wagonful of baggage headed to the suite marked Penthouse Two. Sayre hadn't stopped talking or I might have stayed aboard the car. He carried us all into the suite without stopping to breathe.

"I've made movin' pictures in three or four dozen countries and they all have their rules. I don't give a sweet sufferin' shrug about rules. I don't want to know them, I just want a quart when I need it. I'll study up on the rules later. I'm savin' them for when I retire." He stood in the middle of the room, which was about the size of a small ballroom, without looking to the right or left. The bellhop opened a pair of French windows giving on a balcony. Jim Sayre looked annoyed. "Yes, I know the falls are out there. I'll take your word for it. Close the doors and get your ass down to the liquor store or package store or whatever they call it in this state before I take leave of my senses and join the parade to Alcoholics Anonymous. Scat."

The bellhop caught a five-dollar bill growing off a high limb and disappeared. "Brr," said Sayre, "I like the weather, but I like it outside with the sun shinin' on it. Now, tell me Ben, did the hotel sign you up to look out for me, or did the company? I want to be clear about this, if we're goin' to get along." I told him that I hadn't been hired by either, that I was just trapped in the elevator as he had been by the reporters. His face cracked into a grin, which spilled into a generous laugh and then he started to cough. Once he started, he had trouble getting stopped. Under his tan, he turned pale. I made for the nearest tap and brought him a glass of smoky-looking water. He took it in his hand, then sat down hard on one of the six or seven velvet sofas that didn't begin to fill the room. Slowly he caught his breath and smiled to show that he was all right. We both listened to the silence for a minute. Then he was talking again.

"You travel a few thousand miles and when you get off you're back in the same hotel suite you left behind. Look at this place. How could anybody design a place like this? It doesn't come from life but from movin' pictures, like everythin' else. Ben, you don't happen to have a flask on you, by any chance? No? Well, it doesn't matter, our native runner will be back with the goods before we dry up and blow away." He placed the glass of water on top of an elegant end-table. I guess it was elegant, it looked all wrong with that glass from the bathroom sitting on it. Sayre was still talking: ". . . They had the governor of the state out to the airport to meet us, but I couldn't hear a thing on that tarmac what with the wind and all. I just got feedback from the speaker system and the sounds of the jet engines." He took a breath and began patting his chest, prospecting for cigars. He found one, rolled it around between his thumb and forefinger, sat back and lit it with what looked like great pleasure. "My back gets a lump in it every time I cross the Great Divide. And for me that's just east of Fresno." He laughed again, but watched himself. He didn't want to lay down another coughing barrage. Then his big head shook at the pictures on the wall behind me. "Hotels are all alike. I asked for a quiet place near the main hotel. Is that what this is?" I nodded, and told him that the Colonel John was just behind the Tudor.

"Colonel John? Who the hell was he: some frontier

hero?" I told him that he'd led a band of irregulars against the Americans during the Revolutionary War. It didn't seem to take much to keep Sayre going, just a little priming from time to time.

"I made a picture about Benedict Arnold. That was the Revolutionary War. I guess he's a big hero up here?" I shrugged. Traitors to one side didn't automatically make heroes for the other. "I've done a peck of war pictures," Sayre went on. "After a while you leave history to the costume department." He looked a little lost for a second. His mouth moved like he was trying to decide whether to fish for a crumb on his lip with his tongue in public or not. He decided against it. Then there was a noise in the hall and a big-boned silver-haired woman in an Irish sweater and lemon trousers was standing in the doorway at the head of an army of bellhops and flunkies.

"Just leave everything," she told them, sloughing a sheepskin jacket on a chair. Sayre glanced at her as she collected a few valuables and paid out rewards to the virtuous.

"So, you didn't get lost? By the good Lord Harry, I thought they had me that time." A man in a three-piece suit and a knitted tie handed Sayre a file marked "Telephone Messages" and another marked "Telexes".

"These are just the urgent things," he said. "Mr. Raxlin wants you to phone him right away." A blond man in a powder-blue leisure suit came into the room with an artist's portfolio under his arm.

"Fine," said Sayre, scanning the messages quickly. "How are you, Skip? I hope that motel's practical by tomorrow. I want to use it starting with the afternoon set-ups."

"We're nearly finished landscaping. I want you to look over . . ."

"Just drop it on the table, Skip, I'll get to it as soon as I catch my breath. See you in an hour and a half. Leave your number on top. Dick, get yourself settled and don't worry about a thing until you're fixed up. You didn't bring that Jack Daniels by any chance?"

"That's long gone, Mr. Sayre. I'll see about getting another."

"You do that. Now take all of these people out of here while I unpack. Not him," he said, pointing at me. "He stays."

Sayre got up and brought the woman centre stage with a big arm across her shoulders. "Ben, this is Adela. And Adela is my heart, my mind, my spirit and my one true love. She deserves better than an old reprobate like me. Adela, this is Ben Cooperman. He's a detective. Just saved me from the mob downstairs." Adela put down a small blue flight bag on the broadloom and gave me her hand. It was cold, and I wasn't sure whether I should kiss it or hold it, but I decided she looked more American than anything else, so I shook it. She smiled at me, took in Sayre's mood and cocked an ear to the sound of the falls coming in through the balcony door, which the bellhop had failed to close tightly.

"Oh, Jim," she said. "It's them. The falls!"

"I know, Adela. They keep up that racket twenty-four hours a day — like a broken-down air conditioner. I've sent the bellhop out for a bottle, hon." Then the phone was ringing. "If that's Raxlin, tell him I'm in the shower." Sayre waved Adela to the phone, and sent me a conspiratorial look.

"Miranda! Why yes! We just walked in this minute. I haven't even taken off my coat." I could only think it was Miranda Pride at the other end of the wire. She wasn't hard to imagine and I enjoyed doing it. She seemed to fill up the empty spaces, turning it suddenly into a crowded room. I got up and mimed to Sayre that I'd better be going.

"Say, Ben, you don't know where I can get me a good rub in this town, do you? I have a regular fellow in Los Angeles, but I'm going to need a good rub in the mornings or I won't be fit to tangle with." I gave him the name of a masseur who'd just left the physiotherapy department at the Falls hospital. Adela was letting out small shrieks of pleasure and annoyance as Miranda Pride recounted a

21

long story. The conversation was too one-sided to listen in on, so Sayre went on talking with his usual enthusiasm. "Shot a picture about the falls once in Culver City with Danny Vickers and Victoria Wilcox. Danny's a senator now."

"Oh, Miranda, you shouldn't!"

"Adela and Miranda are great friends," Sayre explained as though I was deaf. "They're always burnin' up the wire whenever they're in the same town." He glanced for a second in the direction of the noise from the falls, got up and walked to the window. "My friend Marilyn's goin' to get a kick out of seeing the falls. She's just wild about nature in the raw. She should have been a Victorian, I keep tellin' her. Maybe that rich boy-friend of hers will buy it for her." I didn't know who he was talking about.

"Well, let's get together for dinner tonight. The four of us if the men can make it," Adela was saying into the phone. "You bet your boots, kid. Well, if they do, we'll make it a twosome and find the action. Good? All right, settled. See you then."

"I wonder where that bellhop got to? It won't be the first twenty dollars I've lost in a good cause. Say, Ben," Sayre said, looking serious for a second and cranking a smile higher on the left side of his face, "if you've got business, don't let me chew your ear off. I've got nothin' to do but study the latest draft of a script. It's a whole lot more interestin' talkin' to you."

"I'm sure the bellhop . . ."

"Don't give it a flicker, Ben. Adela always comes prepared for emergencies. Is that right, Adela?"

"It leaked out during the flight. Damn it, I'll have to have everything dry-cleaned.

"Well, let's have a drink tomorrow night if you don't get stuck. Nobody to talk to around here but picture people. It'll be good to see a friendly face. Say down in the bar in the other hotel around eleven. If you don't have rules about bars."

"At the Colonel John, you go up to the bar. They're peddling the view of the falls."

"So, there's a falls?" he said raising his eyebrows with

mock interest. "I heard tell." I climbed to my feet and inched to the door through holes in the talk. Finally at the door: "Well, Ben, see you at eleven then, tomorrow night. I suppose that boy's gone clear over to the next county to find that liquor store."

three ───────────

I found David Hayes at last. But when I got to him he
wasn't much good to me. I guessed that he'd been
holding up the bar in the top-floor lounge of the Tudor
since the place opened. He was perched on a stool, his left
arm propped on the dark mahogany and supporting his
head. His long, lank brown hair nearly touched the rim of
his glass, which he hugged with his free hand like a kid
with a blanket. He was a tall man, about thirty, with a lot
of youth still written all over him: his socks drooped on
his ankles, his shirt was buttoned down, his tie slung to
one side, the leather patches on the sleeves of his tweed
coat were about to drop off.

I took the next stool to his and ordered a rye and
ginger ale. I wasn't much of a booze-hound, but when I
was working I had to make up the rules to suit the cir-
cumstances. Hayes didn't look up. It was a good face with
a friendly ski-jump nose I couldn't imagine him wearing
at eighty. His neck was skinny and his chin looked like he
would stick it out when a more life-weary veteran might
shrug. I asked him if he was the owner of the Jaguar
blocking me in the parking lot. He nodded and offered
me a drink to cool my annoyance. The bartender ignored
him on the grounds that he'd just served me one. He took
his responsibilities seriously, that bartender.

Hayes wasn't much of a talker to start with. It was the
drinking he was working on. Behind me, from one of the
tables near the view over the illuminated falls, I heard a
voice raised in the attempt to tell a funny story. When the
voice came to the punch line all the others at the table
laughed, the way people do when they are all on the payroll. I looked over my shoulder and was surprised to see
it belonged to Dawson Williams. For a minute I forgot all
about young David Hayes sitting beside me. I was suddenly

back in the Granada Theatre on Saturday afternoons with Sam, my brother. Together we'd watched Dawson Williams fight the evil sheriff of Nottingham and follow the Khalifa's forces up the Nile to the Fifth Cataract. Nobody could swing across a fight-filled room on a crystal chandelier like Dawson Williams. Nobody could jump with such accuracy from saddle to stagecoach. Dawson Williams!

I sipped at my drink and tried to get my head back on business. For instance, how could I get David Hayes to tell me about Billie Mason. The rye and mix had become sickly sweet after the ice melted. Hayes looked over at me with glassy eyes.

"It's the pits," he said.

"What?"

"Life is the pits. Look at anybody you like. Hemingway, Shakespeare, Faulkner. It's the pits. That's what I think. What do you think about that?" I couldn't follow him, but bobbed my head agreeably. "It wasn't the President of the goddamned Immortals that was sporting with Tess, it was that gimlet-eyed Hardy, that's who it was." More nods, and another pause with the solo drone of Williams' voice behind us. Hayes picked up the tortured ends of his argument. "How many years have we got before the big bad nuclear war comes along? Twenty? Thirty? Maybe only five?" He was getting rather loud, and the voices at the tables around us lowered their own volume to take in what Hayes was saying too. " 'We'll live and be forgotten with the rest . . .' " he sang not badly off key, considering. I never thought I'd live to see it, but Dawson Williams sniggered. That's the only word for it. Hayes may have been a couple of fathoms in drink, but he recognized a snigger when he heard one. He turned in his place and looked at Williams. Williams looked at the other faces at his table in turn for some support. I tried to put my hand on Hayes' arm, but he brushed it off.

"You and me, friend," he spat at Williams, "are nothing. Bugger all. You know that? We are nothing but grape seeds from somebody else's feast. Left-overs. Signatures in the air, that's us, friend." There was a nervous laugh from

25

Williams and his friends, three pale young men with the tell-tale signs of recent expensive barbering. Williams hadn't followed what Hayes had said any more than I had, but he'd taken exception to the word "left-overs". That must have sounded a little too close to "has-been" to suit the aging hero.

"Steady on, old sport," said Dawson Williams.

"Steady yourself, sport," said David Hayes, dropping off his stool, managing to hold himself upright and actually take a step across to Williams' table where he supported himself by gripping tightly to the back of a chair. I saw real fear in Williams' eyes that did in the slightly bemused smile he was wearing, and I was suddenly glad that at least my brother Sam was spared the sight. I saw the actor's face cave in around his mouth for a second, and then he recovered.

"Why don't you and your friend join us?" He was Dawson Williams again, with lots of smiling friendly teeth showing. A place was made for the drunk at the movie star's table, but Hayes didn't move. Maybe he couldn't.

"The bastards will get all of us, if we don't take cover," he shouted, and I shrugged at Williams when he threw me a look that asked was I the idiot's keeper. I got up and put a hand on his shoulder.

"Hands off, friend. I have words for the great stone face." So, Hayes had recognized his victim at least. "You think you're an actor? You think you count for something? Well I bring tidings, friend. It's all dust and ashes, dust and ashes. There goes What's-his-name. We're all What's-his-name." I heard one of Williams' friends putting a label on Hayes.

"Just some crazy local actor. Friend of Miranda."

"I'll go fetch the manager," said another grimly.

"Hold your ground," said Williams, a little more like himself again. I remembered the next line: "If they don't come out, we'll go in after them." But he didn't say it.

The bartender had come around from behind the bar and shot me the same look that Williams had a few seconds ago. I pleaded bystander status, and the bartender moved in. "Look, Mr. Hayes, we got guests and you're talking kind of loud. Why not come back to your stool and finish up your drink, pay the bill and push off before I have to call a cop? Come on." Hayes turned around, looked at me and then at the rest of the people in the lounge, who had given up all pretence of having affairs of their own, and then moved his mouth like he was going to say something memorable. Instead, he vomited on the table. The bartender grabbed him fast.

"That's it," he said. The four men at the table had all got to their feet and stood against the panoramic window looking as though they thought Hayes was going to do it again. "I've been expecting this for the last two hours," the bartender said, as Hayes doubled up and fell into me. I grabbed him, and he went limp.

"Well, you should have given him marching orders two hours ago," said one of Williams' pals. "Don't you know who he is?" He and his two friends shouldered the burden of indignation that rightly belonged to all four of them. But Williams was looking at Hayes with some sympathy and shaking his head.

"Does anybody know where he lives?"

"Don't you bother your head about him, Mr. Williams," said the bartender. We'll look after him. He's been drinking double Scotches since I come on, and he had a tab before that. Here," he said to me, "hold him a sec." I took his full weight, while the bartender leaned over and found a damp check near Hayes' glass. He looked at it, then picked up his share of David Hayes' one hundred and sixty pounds again. "He's in 1738. Help me get him to the elevator. Harry," he yelled to the busboy, "watch the cash. I'll be back in a minute."

We hefted his dead weight out of the lounge, and the last I saw of Dawson Williams was hidden by the scowls and ruffled dignity of his pals. We dragged Hayes along the carpet, leaving heel marks in a twin track. On the way down in the elevator, I fished around in Hayes' pockets for a room key. I would have given him a proper frisking, but it wasn't such a good idea with the bartender standing there. The double door opened on the seventeenth floor. We dragged the weight along the corridor about fifty feet and found his room. I got the door open without any trouble and between us we moved the body into the room and onto the double bed. I pocketed the key.

On the way back to the lounge, the bartender looked at me with a humorous grin. "If you can't hold it, you shouldn't drink it. Young lush. His old man used to be one, but he straightened out. I haven't seen this one for a donkey's age."

"So he's no stranger?"

"He grew up in the Falls. His father was a druggist." He must have caught some sign of more than usual interest on my part, so he stifled further comment. When I got him going again all I got was: "That's the way it is in a small town: everybody knows everybody else."

"Have you seen him with a good-looking blonde in the last week or so?"

"Naw. He's the lone ranger; drinks by himself. He was in just after New Year's, though, with Miranda Pride. Is she good-enough-looking for you?"

"For anybody. But I was looking for local talent."

"Well, I get paid for serving drinks, I don't pay too much attention to who's holding them."

By that time we had returned to our starting places: he was polishing a glass behind the bar and I was paying my tab and collecting my coat. The Williams table was deserted.

"The movie stars have run out on you."

"They'll be back. Peggy O'Toole is coming into town to-morrow. Things are looking up in the old burg. All week business has been as silky as a mouse's ear. Williams is playing the big lead opposite O'Toole. I hope he brings her in here some night. I'd like to have a real close look at her." I agreed and said goodnight. I could feel the key in my pocket as I waited for the "down" elevator. It began to itch, so I went back to Room 1738.

Hayes was still dead to the world. I rolled him over on the bed, fished out his wallet and went through it fast without seeing much. I guess I was getting sleepy myself. To tell the truth, I didn't much like the smell that kept Hayes company on the bed. As a matter of fact, I didn't like my own smell all that much. I looked over at the sleeping man and discovered that his eyes were open and that they were fixed on me. The hand with the wallet in it dropped.

"Take the money, pal, and leave me alone." His voice was thick and his words came slowly with some effort.

"I'm no burglar," I insisted, throwing the wallet to the bed. "I was with you when you passed out. The bartender and I brought you back to your room. I was just returning your wallet. You remember giving it to me don't you?"

"Sure," he lied. "Passed out, eh?"

"After sounding off to a star of the silver screen."

"So, I passed out and you carried me home." He waved a crooked finger at me like a court-appointed lawyer who wasn't sure of his client's name. "I gave you my wallet."

"That's right. How do you feel?"

"Terrible. Could you go away, please? I don't feel well." Even dead drunk he'd never say "good". That's class. He was lying full length on the hotel's idea of a contemporary bed cover. His jacket and pants were stained. His collar was still buttoned down; which made him look more alert than he probably felt. I turned to go. But he called me back.

"I think I remember you from the bar. They used to give you peanuts. Do you like peanuts?"

"You were telling me about Billie," I said.

"I spared you nothing. Billie hated peanuts. Otherwise an admir . . . admir . . . a very fine woman. Sorry I lumbered you, friend."

"What are friends for? Easy to see she meant a lot to you."

"Well, she did and now she doesn't. Time past and time present . . ."

"Don't kid a kidder. Nobody heals that fast. You want some coffee? It might clear your head." He nodded, and stared down at his long legs like they had recently been added to the ensemble. I picked up the phone and called room service.

"Billie was a friend, she was sweet Stella for Star, Stella for Star. Oh, I knew she was married. All's fair in . . . But where is she now? I need her right here." He banged the bed with the limp back of his hand. "I've got her face stuck in my head." I nodded with as much sympathy as I could manage.

"Where's Billie now?" I asked. I tried to let it fall as casually as you please, like a gum wrapper on the sidewalk, but it didn't work.

"Who wants to know, pal?"

"I'm interested in the end of the story."

"So why do I get the feeling you're pumping me? Who the hell did you say you were?"

"Don't get hot at me, Hayes. I brought the body home. Remember? I'm the guy whose car you're blocking. Remember?"

"A regular nursemaid," he said. "You got all the instincts of a baby sitter. Like Monty. He couldn't take care of himself, so he looked after other people. An Anglican saint, that's what he was." He lurched himself upright, waved in the wind like the last leaf of summer, his ski-jump nose wrinkling, then he started to stagger to the bathroom. I followed to the open door in case he needed support. He was staring absently at the white porcelain like he'd forgotten to read the instructions on how to use the facilities. He caught my eye in the mirror. "God a-mercy, old heart," he said, and I couldn't attach that to anything, except maybe a line from a play he'd done. Then he looked in the mirror again, experimented with his arms in suiting large theatrical gestures to his talk and at the same time trying not to lose the focus. "I know what you're thinking. I'm a wet bastard, young behind the ears. Spoiled rotten. Enjoying grief to the hilt. Well, friend, I'll have you know, announce it throughout my host, that I spent the day in toilsome labour. I'm not cadging a free ride; I'm working my passage. Put that in your copybook and blot it. Who the hell did you say you were? I keep letting it fly away."

I told him my name again, and when it looked like he remembered about bathrooms, I left him alone. He came back into the bedroom muttering about trading in his kidneys.

There was a loud rap at the door, which startled both of us, although I was a couple of seconds faster off the mark. I guess we were both expecting a genteel tap. The waiter wheeled a rattling cart into the room and uncovered the coffee. I took the bill and paid it. What's the sense of getting expenses if you don't have expenses? The waiter made the tipping process as awkward as usual, standing there as quietly assertive as a parking meter. I guess it goes with the territory, like the tan pants with maroon stripe and ill-fitting white jacket with the hotel's logo over the breast pocket. I pulled the trolley closer to Hayes. He crawled higher on the bed with his elbows. I poured him a cup then one for myself, added my regular four lumps of sugar and stirred, watching Hayes sip and spill alternately.

"Billie," he whimpered into the half-filled cup. "Billie."

"You both went to see Noonan about the movie?" He looked across at me, remembering that I hadn't left with the waiter.

"He took one look at her, one look, and I haven't seen her since. Took her to meet the assistant director. Now she's . . . oh, what does it matter? They deserve each other. Perfect casting. Both a couple of fakes, I say. Both consumers of people."

"The assistant director?"

"What? The assistant director? Don't make me laugh."

"Who then?"

"The assistant director's gay. He wasn't interested. And now he's gone back to California to direct. Not interested in Billie. It's all the pits. You and me. The whole world. Life is the pits."

"You told me. I've heard that part. Tell me who Billie's with. Noonan?"

"What's the difference. You and me, friend. We're nothing. Less. You gotta do it big." He put the cup on the edge of the bed and let his head lie back on the bolster.

He kept whispering "It's the pits" a few times, then closed his eyes. I tried to keep up my end of the conversation, but after a minute I was talking to the bedclothes. I finished my coffee, put down the cup and moved both his wallet and coffee cup to safer places, then left, taking the key with me. Hayes wasn't going anywhere that night and I was beginning to think fondly of my hotel room in Grantham. I should have played the scene differently of course. There were questions left unanswered because they hadn't been asked. But right then a hot shower looked better to me than a whole room-service trolley full of answers.

four

I awoke from a dream in which I led a small British force of the Royal North Surreys through the Fuzzy-wuzzy lines to the Nile. In the dream I looked a lot like Dawson Williams, and the Khalifa, wearing patched robes, looked like David Hayes. I tried to keep away from him, but, as it is in dreams, wherever I looked over a bit of scrub, there he was, looking like he was about to vomit at me and what was left of the North Surreys. When I opened my eyes at last and with relief, I was where I wanted to be: in my own bed looking up at the familiar crack in the ceiling and seeing the sun shine through the same old dusty curtains. I got up and showered and shaved, vaguely aware that one aspect of last night and my dream was still sharing the room with me. I rolled my suit into a ball and threw it near the door, promising myself I'd take it to the cleaners on my way out. I had another pair of pants under the mattress and found a jacket that I hadn't used for at least six months. I couldn't discover why I had abandoned it, so I put it on.

Outside on the street, the sun was shining, melting the snow on cars parked overnight at the curb, and allowing a little drainage from the gutters to the sewer gratings. There were a couple of sparrows fighting over something by the Harding House back door. I made my way by them without looking too closely, searching for breakfast myself. As usual *Bagels* was out of bagels. I looked at the Toronto paper over coffee and an English muffin at the counter. There was a picture of Dawson Williams on the front of the Entertainment section with an interview by the regular theatre critic. Williams said how happy he was to be in Canada, how he was looking forward to making a film in the Falls and working again with director James A. Sayre, who made *The Legion of the Hanged* with him ten years ago in Mexico. He was also looking forward to shooting scenes with Peggy O'Toole, who was due to arrive in Buffalo later that day. Although they had never played in a film together, he was a great fan of hers. She was a new kind of beauty for a new age. And her last film, like his own, had already grossed its first eight million. Williams was quoted as saying that being type-cast as an athletic adventurer in most of his early films hadn't bothered him. He enjoyed doing romantic pictures too, because they didn't break as many bones. He then went on to describe his various fractures and related each to the scene in which it had occurred.

Seeing all that in the paper made me feel close to the centre of things. After all, less than twenty-four hours before, I was practically having a drink with Williams. It also reminded me that I should be on my way back to the Falls to be there with a few more questions when David Hayes woke up.

So, it was up and over the canal again, a twist around the colour-coded exits until I found myself on the riverfront once more. As I got closer to the falls, a fine mist hit the windshield and froze. I sprayed a couple of jets of deicing fluid, and ice came free in chunky cakes, the wipers moving them around on the glass. There were few tourists watching either the American or the Horseshoe Falls. Anyone standing around too long ran the risk of being turned into an ice sculpture.

I made a right turn and pulled up the steep hill through a double line of sideshow attractions. On one side a waxworks with assassinated heads of state on life-like display, and on the other an exhibition of the automobiles of the famous. At this season and in this temperature the few red noses walking by looked neither to right nor left, heading for hot-buttered rum indoors. The whole street looked shabbier than it did during the summer. Even the life-sized figure of the French tightrope-walker, Blondin, balanced on a wire crossing the street and peeling from frost and sun, looked like he wanted to take the winter months off. I pulled the Olds into the Tudor's parking lot, blocking

Hayes' Jaguar again, and went into the Tudor with my galoshes jingling like sleighbells.

The lobby had the look of hotel lobbies in the morning: discipline renewed after a long night, the ashtrays empty, and the carpet clean and unscuffed. I headed straight for the elevator without getting the fish-eye from the men at the desk. Double doors opened and I was back in the corridor on the seventeenth. I still had Hayes' key, but I thought better of using it. I'd drop it on a table when he wasn't looking.

I knocked and waited. I tried again. There was no answer. I knocked louder, thinking I might have caught him in the shower. Again no answer. I tried a few more times, until the weight of the key I was carrying got too much for me. I opened the door of Room 1738.

David Hayes had flown the coop. His still smelly clothes lay crumpled into a ball on the floor and the bed still showed stains of coffee and other things. I was about to close the door gently behind me when the telephone rang. I scooped it up and grunted like I was half asleep.

"David? Can we meet tomorrow afternoon in the coffee shop on the basement level of the Colonel John?" I grunted again, and she hung up after telling me to be there at five o'clock. If that was Billie Mason, she hadn't been murdered and all I had to do was tell her husband to be at Butler's Barracks tomorrow at five and I could write "Closed" on another skinny file. I couldn't assume, on the other hand, that I knew Hayes' only female friend in his own home town.

I went through the revolving door of the hotel and saw the doorman decide I didn't look like I wanted a taxi. I turned left and walked down the hill. The wind was still blowing up a fine freezing mist, but it wasn't bothering sight-seers so far downwind. I walked across the Niagara Parkway and along the stone and metal balustrade past the coin-operated binoculars encrusted in an aspic of ice, to get a good look.

There they were: Niagara Falls, like on an oversized

box of Shredded Wheat. As familiar as your big toe, only now they were vallanced with ice. Ice above the falls, ice on the sides, ice retail and ice wholesale down below. In all of Hudson's Bay, I thought, there can't be so much ice. In one place it was stacked forty feet high. There was so much of it, you couldn't see water except on the falls themselves and ugly-looking pools of dark froth below. A few hardy cedars that lined the banks had their branches blown back to the cliff-face and frozen there. Up near the Rainbow Bridge the *Maid of the Mist* dock and loading platform that in summer sees thousands of tourists on and off the four midget steamers had been covered by a mass of glacial ice. But from where I stood, with a stout wind blowing off the falls and down the gorge, all was bright, calm and quiet. The forces pushing and pulling inside that mass of ice showed not a ripple on top.

Back in the last century and for over a decade in this, tourists were allowed to climb down into the gorge and walk out on the ice bridge, drop their jaws in awe of the falls, then buy a drink from the illegal bars that had been set up in shanties on the ice to stoke the internal fires. It had been found impossible to make a liquor offence charge stick on these bars, because the culprit always claimed his shack was across the international line from whichever jurisdiction had made the pinch. After an accident in which three tourists lost their lives, visitors had had to look for other amusements and the hotelkeepers, who had found the ice bridge a winter bonanza, had had to grit their teeth and wait for spring.

In 1938 the ice was so bad it pulled down the Honeymoon Bridge, right under the watchful lenses of cameras from the leading newspapers and wire services of the world. It was a tremendous scoop. Unfortunately the hands that should have been on those shutter releases were hugging warm coffee cups across the street, and the only picture of the collapse was snapped by a passing amateur.

I walked along looking over the railing at the river below — log-jammed with ice floes. It was an eerie sensation. They say that in the spring of 1948, when the ice blocked water getting over the brink of the falls, the suddenly silent cataracts woke sleepers and caused dogs to bark at the unfamiliar stillness.

I know all this stuff because, when we were kids, the Falls was the favourite place of my older brother and me. It was close to the border and coloured comic books (during the war) and movies on Sundays. Going "over the river" was a minor miracle. People who don't live near a border lose a free lesson in just about every subject they teach in school. People who grow up surrounded by more of the same for hundreds of miles on either side of them end up international yokels, gaping at strange licence plates or looking suspiciously at a foreign coin.

I stepped into a restaurant across the street from one of the big railway bridges that run over the Niagara gorge. Grade level was high above the road and the damp and rust of the tracks had stained the stones of the abutments. The restaurant had been let into a space between the bridge supports, a hole in the wall almost literally. There was a short counter with pedestal seats and several booths. The walls were a shiny yellow that reminded me of flypaper. The coffee, when it arrived in a white stoneware mug, was both hot and a credit to the railwaymen who had kept the place in the black over the years. I was sitting at right angles to a couple of middle-aged Ukrainian women who were sharing a sandwich and talking about property values. I ordered a chopped egg on toasted white and a glass of milk. The egg salad was a little tired, but the toast was just the way I like it, noisy.

Along the street a crowd had gathered in front of an appliance store. I joined it. Inside the window, a bank of TV sets showed a woman receiving flowers from an official who held a homburg in one hand. The setting was a large hotel lobby. A second camera gave us a close-up of the woman. It was Peggy O'Toole, in glorious colour, pushing her gamine face into the flowers, smiling and shaking hands. She should have got an Academy Award nomination for smiling through an interminable speech of welcome. Beside me, sidewalk critics and fans were addressing comments through the glass at the face on the half-dozen screens.

"Isn't she gorgeous. I love her hair!"

"Did you see her in *Needing People*? She was wonderful."

"I heard she bought John Barrymore's castle in Hollywood."

"She could afford it. Is she still seeing that baseball player from the Mets? Slinger Bone?"

"Ancient history. She's after bigger bucks."

"Bone's got a million-dollar contract. What's bigger?"

I walked a chilly block and found a public phone. When I was about to feed it change, I discovered that it had been disembowelled of its working parts. I had better luck across the street in the entrance to a gift shop that specialized in English bone china and spelled shop the long way. My answering service had no messages for me.

From the phone booth, I wandered down along the riverfront toward the falls, where I could see in the distance the film crew at work. A crowd had gathered on one of the strips of park land between the hotel and the river, and half a dozen cops were trying to keep order. It wasn't as hazardous as a rock concert, and too cold to stand watching for long. Grips were busy laying track across the street on a slant. Beyond the cops, a clutch of crew members were holding up giant reflectors; several others crowded around a dolly which would eventually be lifted to the tracks. Those not busy stood near one another drinking coffee from Styrofoam cups. A group of extras huddled for warmth in the lee of one of the customs buildings attached to the Rainbow Bridge. Dawson Williams was there beside the parapet overlooking the gorge, wearing a pigskin bomber jacket that looked like he'd inherited it from Charles A. Lindbergh. Jim Sayre, in a yellow Anorak of nylon that looked none too warm, was puffing suggestions at him as they looked down to the ice below. The cameraman joined them. Nobody hurried, but I didn't see many wasted movements.

The hold-up was the laying of the track. It had to be lifted with shims and blocks so that the camera dolly could move smoothly from road level to sidewalk level in one easy uninterrupted motion. The man in charge of the dolly looked doubtfully at the track. He didn't want to risk the camera until the track tested perfect. I wondered why the rest of the crew not involved in railway work didn't go inside and unthaw their noses.

A little farther along the curving icy sidewalk, with the mist of the falls sometimes obscuring it, the front of a motel was done up in rustic stone and advertized vacancies from its large sign. Workmen were adding touches to the windows. A painter was adding daubs to the stonework. Just as I was wondering why I'd never noticed a motel this close to the falls, I could see that behind the front there was nothing but masking canvas. A piece of scenery with landscaping.

Disillusioned with the mad make-believe of show business, I got in my car and called on several local hairdressers. I'd tried making this kind of check on the phone before and decided that you're never sure you have the storekeeper's full attention unless you're standing in front of him. The driving ate up a lot of time, but I came away from the last of my calls, Anton's Salon on Centre Street, with the information that Billie Mason was expected for a touch-up and set on Friday at 2:15. That was better than a kick in the head, and I felt like I was earning some more of Lowell Mason's money. I returned the car to the rear of the Tudor, but went into the Colonel John for a routine look around.

There were flower petals on the floor of the lobby. A bellhop with a long-handled dustpan was sweeping up the left-overs of Peggy O'Toole's reception. The crowd had found other business. I did a fast tour of the bar and all the snacking and eating places. In the restaurant, a dim place with a suit of armour waiting to show you to your table, I spotted Adela Sayre. She was sitting with Miranda Pride.

Miranda Pride had been away from the screen for

about ten years, but nobody could ever forget her or fail to recognize her. She was as much a part of Hollywood as Taylor, Hepburn and Lassie. She was adjusting a pair of enormous sunglasses and scooping cigarettes and lighter into her bag as Adela's smile of recognition dragged me over. In that light, Miranda looked about thirty-two, but I knew she was that and half as much again. She had the kind of face and figure that seems to shine in the dark.

"Miranda, I want you to meet a detective friend of Jim's: Ben Cooperman. He lives here in the Falls. Ben, this is Miranda Pride, one of my oldest friends." We both said how-do-you-do, and I got a full blast of the Pride smile, which I'll leave to my grandchildren. It was like a week in Palm Beach with all expenses paid. Her mouth was as famous as Leo, the M-G-M lion, and at times it had roared as eloquently.

"So, you're a local boy too, Mr. Cooperman?" And without waiting for an answer she continued: "When Adela calls me one of her oldest I feel at least eighty. Why don't you say I'm your niece from Bryn Mawr or something?" She was straightening a cloche hat over her dark hair, and then went on to service a series of silk scarves of the same colour and finally smiled with sudden delight at her tailored linen suit that whispered of sunshine and balmy days. "If you are planning to eat here, I'd work around the Chef Salad: I think he's just discovered spinach."

"Why did you say 'So you're a local boy too?' Miss Pride?"

"Miranda, please, Miranda. 'Why?' Because my husband comes from the Falls." She examined my face like it was a part she was learning and when she saw no kindling of the lamps of recognition she added: "Neil Furlong. He wrote the script of *Ice Bridge*. There isn't much about the Falls he doesn't know."

"Yes," said Adela, "and it's all in the script."

"That's not funny, Adela," and the maître d' hurried over to help Miranda into her mink coat. "They're still battling about that. If you're not good, you won't get your T-shirt."

"My what?"

"Thank you, Costas. You haven't heard? Neil's had *Ice Bridge* T-shirts made for everybody."

I didn't get my tongue working fast enough to make the big impression I'd been planning all these years. I didn't even get to tell her that I lived in Grantham not the Falls. Somehow the details of my life were the fine print of this meeting.

"Where to now, Adela? She's been leading me around by the nose since she arrived. We've bought out all the English china in town. And there's real wool in the stores. It makes me almost wish I'd learned to knit. But someone would come along with a camera and catch me at it and that would be the end of me. I'd embark on a new career playing mothers. Oh, I don't want to think about it!" Miranda managed to look as though she was unaware that everybody in the restaurant was watching her every move. "I hope to run into you again, Mr. Cooperman," she said extending a gloved hand in my direction, and then in a swirl of furs the two women were on their way again. I lacked the courage to follow, to confess that I wasn't really hungry, but I saw just outside that David Hayes, looking tall and sober in an old yellow sweater, had been stopped by Miranda. She took him by the arm and introduced him to Adela. A waiter offered to find me a table and when I next got to look around, the women had gone. Hayes came into the restaurant alone. I gave him a big grin, but he looked right through me. The next time he ties one on, I thought, let him crawl home by himself. The waiter sat him at a table for two just beyond mine. I wondered whether he was there to meet with Billie Mason. My instinct to go over and begin a conversation was overruled by the chance that I might learn more by keeping my mouth shut.

I wasn't hungry, but I ordered a sandwich and a glass of milk, just for sitting privileges. Hayes, on the other hand, was starved. I watched him through a shrimp cocktail, salad, top-sirloin steak, spumoni ice cream and coffee. Between courses, he made notes on the back of the paper placemat under his knives and forks. Through all of this he nursed a bottle of Danish beer. I had to give him full marks as a reformed character. He wiped his chin and paid the waiter with two American twenty-dollar bills. He did it with enough flourish to tell me that he wasn't used to paying out that kind of money without so much as a burp of protest.

He was about to get up, when he looked right at me. I was signalling my brain about some response when I realized the smile was for someone behind me. It was Miranda again. She rounded on him before he quite got to his feet. He looked startled, she was out of breath and in the middle of her argument. Hayes sputtered excuses, but Miranda sailed through them nearly upsetting his empty beer bottle with a long impatient finger. It was a difference of opinion, certainly, but I couldn't get a sharper focus than that on it. It now looked like they'd agreed to talk further, because Hayes left a tip under his saucer and got up. Neither of them seemed to notice me as they left the restaurant. The only words I heard sounded like "ingratitude" from Miranda and "I'm sorry, I was working" from David.

I counted a minute after they'd gone, and then I collected the abandoned placemat. The front told me all about the rich variety of wildlife to be found in Canada. On the back, where he'd been writing, it was more of a puzzle. Here a group of names was confused with arrows leading from one name to another. Alden Cory pointed an arrow at Karen Brophy, who was pointing in turn at Chris Fetterley and Rosemary Beattie. They sent arrows back at Karen. Two names, Tony D'Abruzzi and Hyman Shatz, were circled several times, and arrows going off in all directions made them into a sea urchin. The only name on the page I recognized was the Pagoda, the tourist tower on the rise up the street and overlooking the falls. The sea urchin was tied to this with a heavy black line. And that was all. I put it in my breast pocket, paid my bill and nodded to the suit of armour on my way out. I might not know at that moment where to find Billie Mason, but at least I had a pocketful of brand new leads. Then I remembered that one of the places they might lead me was to the morgue.

five

A rmed with a handful of change and a fresh pack of Player's, I tried once more to locate Norman Baker, the CBC television producer who'd sent a crew to interview Billie. I couldn't help feeling that when a professional outfit like the official Canadian broadcasting network points its lenses at you, it might turn your head if it happened to be as pretty as Billie's was. At the very least, Baker should know the trouble he'd put me to.

"Norman Baker here," said a voice with an English accent as sticky as a hunk of Brighton rock. I told him who I was, that I was trying to locate Billie Mason, and that I knew about the film his crew had done in Grantham.

"What else do you know?" he said in a voice that had suddenly lost its friendly edge. "Who did you say you were again?" I ran through my story again and hoped that he was now tuned in with both ears.

"When is that piece of film going to be used?" I asked.

"Well, that's up in the air at the moment. We've technically been fired from the project, but we've got an injunction against the CBC cutting the film themselves. It's a no-win situation."

"This isn't just about a small-town actress. What's all this about?"

"I'm sorry but I can't talk about it. It's part of a project that has been kept highly secret. And now we are in a very sticky bind with the Corp. Sorry, I'd like to help."

"What's the CBC trying to take away from you?"

"For over a year now we've been collecting information in a certain area. That actress was just one of the people we talked to. She's small potatoes, really."

"Small potatoes to you, maybe. But her husband thinks she's been murdered. How big do things have to get before they catch your interest?"

"Hold on. Whom does he say he thinks is responsible?"

"He won't say. But I can guess that it doesn't have much to do with acting."

"Of course not."

"If she gets killed, and you know something that could have prevented it . . ."

"I hear what you're saying, Mr. Cooperman. I know all about being an accessory after the fact. I'm thinking."

"A woman's life is at stake here, not just ratings."

"Point well taken. I'm still thinking. Do you think there is a potential for media attention here?"

"What? I can't understand you. If you mean is there a story here, I'm guessing that there is."

"Good. That might give me the leverage I need with Kellogg."

"You've lost me again."

"And then with Kellogg siding with me against the brass . . ."

"Hey! Will you please tell me what's going on?"

"I think you may have just put me back in business, Mr. Cooperman. I don't know how to thank you."

"Well I do. Tell me what this is all about."

"I suppose it can do no real harm. I can tell you the part that affects your case. The rest is too hot to carry around. You'll see it all explode on television in less than three months unless I miss my guess." He took a breath, and paused to find a place to start.

"Billie Mason's husband is laundering money for the mob. If she's disappeared, it's probably mob-connected. In our film we tricked her into talking about this side of her life, as she thought, between takes in the interview about her career. She knows quite a bit about her husband's connections in Atlantic City. But it looks as though none of it will ever be seen, unless I can make a deal with Elwood Kellogg, the assistant general manager. For nine months I've had his help. He's covered me in all the right places, but the lawyers and brass are leaning on him. . . ." He went on about his troubles, and I let him. Then, when he stopped to restore his fires, I asked:

"Why would the mob want to kill Billie Mason?"

"Well, they aren't playing touch football. Piccadilly isn't a bunch of amateurs."

"Tell me about it."

"Piccadilly fronts for a group trading as Morden Realty. Behind Morden lurks Anthony Horne Pritchett. He's the kingpin. Now, through Morden and Piccadilly he pumps money into Mason's smallish business. Mason's probably one of many such outlets. He invests their money all dressed up to look like his own. Nothing overtly crooked; all legitimate schemes."

"And you're planning to blow the whistle on them on your program?"

"Given the chance."

"Does Pritchett have interests in Niagara Falls?"

"Ummm," he muttered through his teeth, "I can't think of anything. The syndicate is too big in those parts. We covered that in another program. Our research isn't as fresh there, but the last time I looked the syndicate had things sewn up, and I mean everything: prostitution, drugs, loansharking, liquor, you name it, and at the same time they're dealing with legitimate businesses: tourist stuff, vending machines, small businesses."

"Does the name David Hayes ring a bell anywhere?"

"It doesn't feedback on me. If you want names, the best is Pritchett. That's the start of everything in the mob."

"And in the syndicate?"

"There you've got a pair of twins: an Italian and a Jew."

"Let me guess. How about Tony D'Abruzzi and Hyman Shatz?"

"Never heard of either of them. No, the boys in charge are Tullio Solmi and Mordecai Cohn. Where'd you get those others?"

"In a lottery."

"Solmi's gang hangs out at that Chinese tower at the Falls."

"The Pagoda?"

"That's the place. The front's called Cataract Vending.

46

There are a few other spots in upper New York State too, but his main organization is located there."

"But this isn't new material?"

"New enough. I hope you get a chance to see the program. The Corp's sunk too much money into it to shelve it. It's just a matter of settling who gets final cut. What you've just told me suggests we may be sitting on more of a time-bomb than we thought. Now I know a way to get Kellogg off the racketball court and back to business." He started leading me around the corridors of the CBC brass again and I got off the phone as soon as I politely could.

I don't know about other people, but when I hear about the mob, I want it to be in a movie or a thriller. I don't want any part of a non-fictional mob. Unfortunately, as I was thinking on my way back to Grantham, mob-tracks cover the Niagara Peninsula running back through the Depression to Prohibition. Prohibition hit Ontario in 1916 during World War One. That's when, for a choice few, the illegal liquor business became fun. When the States went dry in 1920, it became big business. After 1925, Ontario went wet again, but there were still big bucks to be made in bathtub gin and hijacked bonded rye. For the most part, the Canadian authorities winked at the illegal traffic. The laws were unenforceable and bootleggers were as popular as Robin Hood's little green men of Sherwood.

That's all ancient history now. Water over the falls. But successful bootleggers are clipping coupons today; the unsuccessful ones are wearing cement galoshes at the bottom of Lake Ontario.

I parked my Olds next to my father's rust-pocked Cadillac convertible in front of the condominium. I let myself in.

"Benny, is that you? Is that you, Benny?"

"That's right. You weren't expecting Sam were you?"

"Your brother's too busy to get away during the week. You know that." Sam is the chief of surgery at Toronto General, a top position, my mother never tires of reminding me, in a hospital that isn't even a Jewish hospital. We all had to give Sam full marks. Ma was wearing a bright fuchsia gown or housecoat. She was quite blonde again. She presented her cheek and I grazed it with a kiss.

"You've been to get your hair done."

"Yeah," she said, rolling her eyes with pleasure, like she was a little girl accused of coming top of her class again. "You like it?"

"Very nice. Very nice."

"It was getting so I couldn't look at myself in the mirror any more. I had to get it done to preserve my sanity. It gets me out of the house. Better I should go to the beauty parlour than to my doctor. That's the only other reason for going out."

"What's this about your doctor? I thought he was in the hospital."

"It's the locum-shlocum. He gave me a prescription."

"You didn't tell me you've been sick. Ma, what's going on around here?"

"Don't ask."

"Who's asking? I'll be screaming in a minute. Give."

"I had a little infection and it's clearing up. I shouldn't even mention it."

"If you're keeping secrets from me . . ."

"Your father's downstairs."

"That's right, don't listen."

"Open the wine it should breathe before you go down."

"Stop changing the subject."

"I'm just a juvenile delinquent, that's what I am," she said, batting her eyes like a fourteen-year-old. "Open the wine." I opened a bottle of Macon and placed it on the dining-room table. It had been set for four.

"Who's coming for dinner?"

"What?" She had her vague voice on, and was trying to lose herself cutting bread.

"Never mind." I went down the broadloom-covered steps to the television room. Pa was wearing his blue cardigan and watching the local news. I handed him the paper. He gave me a dirty look like I was personally responsible for all the bad tidings it contained. "Who's coming to supper?" I asked. Pa grew pink at the corners of his cheeks.

48

"An idea of your mother's," he said with a shrug.

"An idea is coming to eat with us?"

"It's Linda Levin. Wilfred Levin's sister. You remember her. She's back from New York. She's divorced now, making a new start, has a nice settlement, and your mother thought, well . . ."

"And she's coming to supper. No sweat, Pa. I know Linda. We used to watch Rabbi Feingold kill chickens."

"What?"

"He used to interrupt our Hebrew classes to do a job for a customer. You could hear the trussed-up chickens outside the door. He used to pretend he didn't hear them, then he'd excuse himself for a few minutes. Linda and I followed him down the cellar steps to watch."

"Well, what do you want? We're a small community. In New York a rabbi doesn't kill chickens on the side."

"Who did Linda marry? He was a broker of some kind, wasn't he?"

"Import-export or export-import, something like that. She has a boy, Paul-David. He plays drums. That's all I know about her. Ask her yourself when she gets here." We both watched a uniformed attendant close the back doors of an ambulance, which then drove away from the camera. It's for shots like that that I love the local news.

"Pa, do you know anyone in the mob?" I asked without a build-up.

"What kind of question is that? You think I'm a crook, or you want to enlist? Which is it?"

"I'm working on a case. Tell me what you know about it."

"There are a couple of guys in town you can place a bet with. Is that what you mean? There's the Big Deal club over at the hotel. The club gets a rake-off on every hand."

"I'm talking about the mob, the Mafia, Cosa Nostra."

"They say that Lou Tannenbaum was close to that fellow, what's-his-name, Greenblatt from Detroit. But I never . . ."

The doorbell rang upstairs, then voices at the door like jingling crystal. A moment or two later, my mother, transformed by a dinner dress of soft milky-coffee-coloured material, ushered Linda Levin into the television room. In her honour, Pa turned the knob down a couple of notches, so that you could no longer hear the announcer talking about the arrival of Peggy O'Toole in the Falls.

Linda Levin was a slender woman about six feet tall. She shivered. Her dark hair was cut in bangs across her forehead, and the rest, in two even plaits, fell to her shoulders. She was dressed in a black cocktail dress with a peek-aboo, low-cut top, covered by dark net. Her lips were very red, her earrings very green. She didn't look as though she'd been closer to New York than the North Pole. She smiled a nervous smile of recognition and shook hands with my father, who half-lifted himself from his over-stuffed chair. I could still see in her the skinny girl who crouched with me on the rabbi's cellar stairs.

"How are you, Linda?" I asked, and pulled a news-paper from a chair for her. My mother excused herself in order to complete her serving arrangements upstairs and warm the canned peas.

"Just fine, Benny. You're looking well." She smoothed her hem at the knees as she sat between my father and me. It was an awkward grouping now that Ma had broken up the composition. "Wilfred ran into your mother and she invited me. Wonderful to see you after such a long time." I could see that she was nervous. I don't think I've ever seen knees pressed so tightly together. I'll bet she had bruises. And I found that I was sweating a little too.

"So, how are things in New York?" Pa asked, not much liking the whole business, but trying to be polite. After all, although Linda was one of Ma's ideas, she was also a person in her own right. Pa saw that.

"Very busy," she said. "Traffic, muggings, hold-ups, looting, you name it. We didn't go into Manhattan much. Just for dinner and a show. The last time, Benny, we were caught by a blizzard and had to find a hotel."

"So you didn't live in New York?" Pa looked disappointed.

"Hightstown is just a short drive, except in a snow

storm. And it's close to Trenton and Philadelphia too. Do you know the States, Benny?"

"Some. I was in New York on a case a year ago."

"And he didn't look up my brother, his own uncle."

"Princeton's miles from Manhattan, Pa."

"You could have phoned."

"He's right, I could have. Tell you what, Pa, let's phone him right now. I mean it."

"What are you suddenly crazy or something?"

"I have this urge to hear Uncle Max's voice."

"You could do with some of his class, believe me."

"Do you know the street number? I'll get it from Information."

"Sit down. Don't talk foolishness. A long-distance call you can make on your own phone."

"But your own brother, my Uncle . . ."

"*À table, à table!*" my mother shouted from the top of the stairs. On the way up, Pa gave me a wounded look. I guess I'd laid it on a bit thick. Linda went into the kitchen to ask if there was anything she could do, and was returned promptly to the table. I pulled out a chair for her, and took the one opposite for myself. Ma brought in the soup.

The meal went without incident as far as I can recall. All the little family rituals were observed: Pa asked where my mother's soup was, and she explained to the company and to my father, as though for the first time, that she never ate soup. Pa quizzed me about brands, bottles, sizes and temperatures of wine until I wanted to sit the next course out in front of the TV. Linda kept her eyes on her plate and smiled at everything. Ma kept rolling her eyes in Linda's direction, so I wouldn't miss my last chance this side the grave to have a well-rounded family life.

"Pa, you were telling me about the mob before supper. What else do you know about it?"

"Suddenly I'm an authority."

"Such a subject for the table," said my mother.

"I've got a case," I explained to the three of them, "and the mob might be involved."

"Paolo Nigri used to hang around with them, I remember. He disappeared just after the war."

"Benny," Ma said leaning toward me, "why don't you take part in plays any more? Remember when you did Shakespeare in the park?" And then she added to Linda: "He was wonderful in my green hat and the gold belt from my Paris Star suit. I couldn't take my eyes off him."

"From what I hear," my father said, "there are two mobs: the Italian mob and the Jewish mob. They used to fight all the time. Now things are more businesslike. But it's not just gambling, drugs and prostitution — excuse me, Linda — it's loansharking and . . ."

"More pie, Benny? Linda?"

"Thank you."

"Today, the mob dress in business suits and put up money for charity. Diversified, that's what they've become. They take an interest in politics, they are big in real estate, property development, telephone-answering services, soft drinks, ice cream, fruit juice . . ."

"Import-export."

That last contribution had come from Linda, who was looking at her pie plate. When she became aware, because of the silence, that we were all staring at her, she looked up and gave each of us a share of the same wan smile. "That's why I left Jason. I couldn't go on living like that: not knowing anything, not being able to find out where he was, or when he was coming home. That's why I took Paul-David and caught a plane out of there. You asked about the mob, Benny. They are wonderful, friendly, family people. And then suddenly you don't see someone anymore, and your husband tells you to shut up when you ask why. I left, Mrs. Cooperman. I just up and left everything."

It took a minute for my tongue to recover. Ma was rubbing crumbs into the tablecloth. Pa looked at Linda like she'd dropped out of the crystal chandelier. "What about real estate?" I asked, playing it as calmly as I could.

"In New Jersey a lot of them are into fast-food chains. You know the one that specializes in breast of turkey sandwiches. They also get someone very low in the ranks to buy up a lot of property cheap, then sell it to the mob, under one of their front corporations, at a much higher price. That way they can clean up some of the dirty money that they can't declare as income."

"They call that laundering," my mother added, getting into the act at last. "They do it all the time on television."

"The mob is made up of all kinds: Italian, Jewish, even English. They're all trying to move into more respectable lines, as Mr. Cooperman was saying. I know of an amusement pier near Atlantic City, some apartment buildings there, and a few weeks ago I heard that one of them was investing in a movie being shot at the Falls. They get into all kinds of things."

I spilled my brandy, and Pa poured salt on the spreading stain. Ma made Nescafé and served it in her silver tea-service, which usually lives under a tent of Saran-wrap. Pa and I lit up cigars. I like a good cigar after a big meal, although not well enough to keep a supply of my own. Linda looked a little happier. She took out a package of Egyptian cigarettes and offered one to my mother, who I'm sure rejected it thinking that it contained either opium or marijuana. The night had been heady enough as it was.

We retired downstairs again to watch television. After an hour of this, I drove Linda back to her brother Wilfred's house, and thanked her for a very unusual evening.

"**M**y old man was a stunt man. He could do anythin' with a horse or on a horse. In his heyday, if they couldn't get Bud Sayre to do the shot, they changed the shot. I had a stunt man's point of view on Hollywood from the cradle." Jim Sayre was leaning back in his chair in a dark corner of the roof-top bar at the Colonel John Butler. For about the last half hour he'd been telling me about his early days in the movies. I was slowly sipping a Jack Daniels he'd insisted on buying me. He was on his third since I'd arrived. To hear him talk, you could see that he was still in love with the movies. His stories were lightning fast and I often missed the point because some name slipped through my fingers. He liked stories about his father.

". . . Hell, he pulled all the leather there was to pull, and she nearly throwed him. When they got back to the corral he found a burr as big as your fist under the blanket!" He told me that he had played in a few westerns before trying his hand at doctoring bad scripts. "I showed them how they could make a few changes and turn two scripts into four. Same dialogue, practically, same actors and locations. Hell, I don't know what they thought of my writin', but they sure as hell liked my economics . . ." He was wearing a checkered Viyella shirt with a string tie in a tooled silver clasp. His head was large, senatorial, with sparse white thatch on top and heavy glacier tracks down both sides of his pug nose. The nose, and the cowlick, helped touch everything he said with humorous irony.

The waiter hovered near. "Excuse me, Mr. Sayre. I don't mean to interrupt, but I've got a collection of autograph books back of the bar, and I wonder if — I don't mean now — but if sometime you could see your way clear to . . ."

"Sure thing, Walter. Just hold on to them until I get a spare minute." Walter agreed with a nod, but was prevented from turning by one of Sayre's big hands on Walter's near elbow. "Tell me, Walter, what's that all about?" Sayre tipped his head in the direction of a clutch of photographers at the door.

"Them. They'll be here every night you're here, I guess. You want I should get them to shove off?"

"No, Walter. Won't be necessary. We all have to make a livin'. Some of us are horses and some of us are sparrows." Sayre ordered two more drinks like he was ordering a seven-course dinner. His precise instructions were relayed to the bartender, who shot a glance under his eyebrows in our direction. Jim had been going on about Fields and Chaplin and about how he'd been called an "oh-toor" by the French film critics. I never caught up with that one. The waiter poured my old drink into my new one without comment. For a minute Sayre and I sipped quietly. From where I was sitting, I could see the outline of the nearest of the tourist towers overlooking the falls. There were several of them, but this was the Pagoda, and I looked at it in the rising mist with new meaning.

"Damn it, Ben, look at the way that man's pawin' that poor girl. You'd think he'd get her home first." I shifted to see what he was looking at. The man was probably a branch sales manager on a toot, and she looked like she knew all about sales managers. This was a funny quirk in the battered old director, a bit of the white-hatted cowboy hero left over.

I sipped my drink between my teeth, wondering where Billie Mason might be and why wasn't I out looking for her. Sayre was in the middle of another of his stories. He was a good host, but he took a lot of listening to.

". . . so he came from New York and we shot the scene twice. It was terrible. So I went over to him, put my arm around his shoulder, and told him: 'Clyde, you just say the lines. We put the acting in later.' " I smiled on cue, and he enjoyed his umpteenth telling of the story.

"But I don't have to go into the manure pile to dig

up funny stories. When I picked up the phone this morning, it was the mayor of Niagara Falls, New York. Somebody'd told him that a body gets swept over the falls in *Ice Bridge*. I told him, 'That's right.' And he wanted me to promise him that any bodies that go over the falls will go over the Canadian falls. I told him I'd look into it. This afternoon I got a call from the head of the Chamber of Commerce on this side. He wanted me to keep any evil-doing on the American side." Sayre drained his glass and stretched expansively.

"Ben, I want to thank you for recommending that masseur. He's a first-rate fellow. You know, I get these knots between my shoulders and they can tie me up all day." For a minute, I thought he was going to pull his shirt off to let me see, but before he got the chance, the face I'd seen in the papers for the last couple of days pushed its way into the conversation.

"Neil! Sit yourself down, boy!" Neil Furlong, the writer. Neil Furlong, the big success story of the Falls.

The man who joined us wore a generous boyish grin under a shock of wild uncut, or at least uncombed, dark hair. It was a calculated effect but he got away with it in spades. He was a lean man of medium height, about forty-five or a little younger. As he leaned over to shake Sayre's big hand, I could see that his face was as smooth as a painting. There were no warts, moles, or freckles. Not even wrinkles. He looked like an actor standing in the wings in his pancake make-up waiting for his cue to go on.

Jim Sayre introduced me as a friend and Furlong took my hand and looked me in the eye. After that he called me by name and seemed to remember what I said. I don't ask much of friendship and Furlong made me feel that I wasn't keeping the chair warm for the next comer. Maybe he took his lead from Sayre, who was easy to be with. Furlong was wearing a leisure suit that made him look like the great white hunter. It was beige, with a belted twill jacket over similar trousers. There was a key on a thong hanging around his neck, and a gold bracelet with flat chunky links which he waved into the air to attract a waiter. By the time one came, and Sayre had ordered one of his meticulous rounds, Neil Furlong was telling us about Port Richmond, where he'd been born. Port, as we called it, was Grantham's look at Lake Ontario, the "Port Said of the Great Lakes", as Neil Furlong described it. "But," he said, holding a tanned finger in the air, "Port is the home of the only merry-go-round in the world that still charges a nickel a ride." When I told him that I was from Grantham, the old inter-city rivalry was reflected in a mock-angry frown. "Port is like Anaheim or Encino to someone from L.A. I won't say the harbour is polluted, but you don't have to be a believer to walk across the water in mid-summer. There's a risk of bubonic plague, of course." We all laughed. I was a real Granthamite where Port was concerned. "So, you're from Grantham." Furlong shook his head in disbelief, as though nobody in this day and age could be from Grantham. "When I was in my early twenties, and still working in a garage greasing cars, I met Monty Blair who pulled me away from the gas pumps. I owe Monty everything. And Ned Evans? Is he still around?" He told a funny story about Ned and Monty. Sayre had slipped into his one-sided sleepy smile, which creased his face from his hairline down.

"I remember," Furlong was saying, "Monty turned to Ned, it was at the dress rehearsal of *A Doll's House* at the Collegiate, and he said, 'You know, Ned, we are the only people in this whole county who have ever heard of *The Yellow Book*.' "

"Neil, remember, fella, I'm an illiterate maker of movin' pictures. I grew up on the back lots. What the hell is *The Yellow Book* when it's at home?" Neil shrugged and I turned a little pink, because I'd laughed without understanding any more than Sayre. Furlong took out a silver cigarette case and took and lit a long, tipped cigarette after waving the contents at both of us.

"You wrote the script of this movie," I said. "Have I got that straight?"

"Guilty as charged. It's an original, not based on a book. Jim's trying to find a kernel of sense in my gangland melodrama."

"Lots of good action, Neil. Nothing to be ashamed of.

I'm looking forward ..." Sayre was cut off by another interruption.

"Hi, Mr. Sayre, can I join you?" We all looked around. It was a girl in jeans; she looked about eighteen and as though she'd just discarded a school uniform. The words on the T-shirt read *Ice Bridge*. Sayre was the first to break into a grin.

"Marilyn, my dear, Marilyn. For the love of Mike. This is wonderful!" He got up and they hugged one another like she was his long-lost grand-daughter. "It's good to see you, girl."

"Hello Peggy," said Furlong. "Did you have a good flight?" He sat up straight in his chair.

Before she could answer Sayre said, "This is Benny Cooperman. He's a hard-boiled private eye. Honest, he's real. Benny, this is Peggy O'Toole." I nearly dropped my teeth, naturally. I'd been seeing her in the papers and on television for the last two days — you couldn't avoid her even if you wanted to — but I was completely surprised. She was so tiny, smaller than life. I couldn't believe it. And the Marilyn bit I didn't even try to deal with. Peggy turned and waved at a couple of women just settling at a table nearer the bar, flashed her smile with the chin tilted up slightly, then she sat down. Sayre fussed, moving glasses, and Neil tried to scare up a waiter. I tried to reconcile my picture of a flick-siren with the half-grown child in front of me. Neil glanced over his shoulder at the women, who were smiling in our direction.

"Wherever Peggy goes Lynn and Nicole cannot be far behind."

"That's right," said Peggy. "I have two shadows."

"I can understand about Lynn," Sayre said. "She's the best coach in the business — although I won't have her near the set — but that Nicole ... Agents are nothing but meat hustlers. Why's she here?"

"It's in the contract, Mr. Sayre. They both look after me. A girl can be taken advantage of."

"Nicole wouldn't hear of it," said Neil with a smirk. "She's tough."

"Adela can handle her. I've seen it happen."

"I'm drinking green stingers tonight," Peggy announced, deftly changing the subject. "In case I get sick, it'll match the rug. They put me next to you, Mr. Sayre. Isn't that cosy? We can roll from one suite to the other. I hope you don't mind about my having Penthouse One, Mr. Sayre? Nicole said it was part of the arrangement. Oh, have you seen the falls? Aren't they perfect? They give me goose-bumps. It's all so wonderful!"

I gave Sayre a look that said I should be running along, but he answered it with one that told me to hold my ground and enjoy the company. Maybe I was reading a lot into a look that lasted only two seconds, still they say more with looks in his movies than they do with the dialogue. Peggy O'Toole was staring at me.

"You're not a detective, Benny. Tell me what you really do." She leaned across the collection of empty and near-empty glasses, so that I could see her freckles and the fine lines around her eyes, just beginning to testify against her.

"Marilyn, are you accusing me of mendacity?"

"Shush, Mr. Sayre, you sound like Tennessee. I'm talking to Benny."

"Why don't you think I'm a detective? We don't all look like Robert Mitchum or Humphrey Bogart. Come up to my office and I'll show you my licence."

"And a bottle of Scotch in the second drawer from the bottom in your filing cabinet?"

"Last time I looked, there was a dried-up orange and a couple of apricot pits."

"Have you unravelled any murders, really?"

"A few. My share."

Peggy O'Toole was looking at me with the eyes of a ten-year-old trying to decide between two jaw-breakers and a piece of bubble gum. Sayre was resting his chin on his rust-spattered hands, while Neil Furlong sat back expansively, like he'd arranged the entertainment himself.

"Why do you call him 'Mr. Sayre', when you obviously know him better than anyone else in the room? And why does he call you Marilyn?" She took a deep breath.

"Well, first of all, Marilyn Horlick is my actual name. I was born two years after the real Marilyn made *Niagara* right here. It gives me goose-bumps just to think of it. She was wonderful. I've seen all her pictures. I came from a show-business family: my mother was a secretary at Paramount in the Writers' Building, and my father . . . what are you laughing at, Neil?"

"Your father came from a long line of circus people. Your grandfather told you there was a Horlick in the circus when Quick and Mead first started doing a show under canvas." Peggy's eyes widened and then narrowed as Furlong continued. "You don't know how long ago that was, but you do remember that they had four wagons, nine horses and one hurdy-gurdy."

"That's eerie! How do you know that? Stop teasing."

"It's all in your biography. Something the company's put together. You can read about all of us."

"But you read about me. And remembered it."

"I'm a quick study. Always have been. I know that Jim is a country squire in Ireland when he chooses to be."

"Right now I owe too much money to horsetraders to be seen there. That's why I'm here making a movin' picture."

Peggy still had a look on her face such as she might wear when taking a bath in a room with no lock. I asked her to explain the name.

"Mom named me Marilyn, but Dad called me Wink. I guess that's what I call myself. 'Wink,' he'd say, 'we're off to see the clowns!' Mom didn't like the nickname, so Dad only used it when we were alone. In school half the other girls were Marilyn too. Then Mom got religion and they moved to La Jolla. When I did my first picture, it was for Mr. Sayre. He was the first one to take a chance on me. By the time the movie was released, I wasn't Marilyn any more. My first agent, Johnny Crowe — like in the children's book Dad bought me — Johnny dug up the name Peggy O'Toole. He wouldn't tell me where he got it at first, I had to worm it out of him: Peggy O'Toole was the name of a racehorse!"

"A winner, I hope."

"That's exactly what I said! Everybody said it suited me, and Johnny and I were the only ones who knew about the racehorse. Now, everybody calls me Peggy but Mr. Sayre, and everybody calls him Jim, except me because I'm a professional." She caught her breath like she'd just recited a long speech all the way through without a mistake.

Sayre bent his big head into the centre of the table and lifted his arms to Peggy's and Furlong's shoulders. "Careful, my children. Here comes Mr. Raxlin. I don't think he'd care to hear anything real or honest. The dude prefers plastic to wood and reproductions to the real thing. Ah," he said, turning around, "Mr. Raxlin. We were just talking about you. Sit down. Come join the party."

Raxlin was a man in his mid-thirties. He looked like a chartered accountant candidate who'd not made the grade. He was dressed from head to toe in imitation fabrics, the kind that never wear out, they just turn yellow and roll over. He didn't sit, but stood right next to Sayre. He enjoyed being close to Peggy O'Toole, judging by the shy ogle he gave her.

"My father was a streetcar driver," Furlong said. "Fastest temper in Port Richmond's north end. Step out of line and it was off with the belt and who started it. We were talking about origins before you arrived, Mr. Raxlin. Did I ever tell you that my father drove the longest electric run in the world at one time?" Raxlin shifted uneasily. Furlong's charm seemed to have an edge to it. "This part of the world is full of history, you know. A few miles down the river the British beat the Americans hollow at Queenston Heights."

"First Vietnam, and now this. Soon you'll be saying we never once won a war, Neil." Raxlin's thick neck turned pink above the pink collar of his polyester shirt. "Anyway, I didn't come in here to join your party. There are some problems to talk over, and I hope you'll spare me an hour in my suite in a few minutes. You'll excuse me until then?" Then he looked at me for the first time. "Hello, I'm Marvin Raxlin. Your friends didn't introduce you." I jumped and so did the others. Sayre and Peggy fell over each other getting my name wrong, and Raxlin looked worried when he heard that I was a detective. He nodded shyly to Peggy O'Toole and slunk off.

"Mr. Raxlin is our producer, Benny. He holds the hoops, sets them alight and we jump through them."

"Tonight he was calling problems, problems. Yesterday he said we only had challenges," Neil said with a wink at Peggy.

"The producer," I asked Furlong, "he's the one that pays the bills, isn't he?"

"Sure, he pays. And sure, he does have problems. But a man like that is always out of his depth in any artistic endeavour. He turns to lead every bar of gold he touches. He would get three hacks to rewrite *Hamlet* in a week. Now there are other producers who'd do that. I'm not kidding myself there. But Raxlin is the only producer in the business who'd say he was making it better." Sayre snorted appreciation. Even Peggy laughed.

"Benny," Sayre said, trying to make disliking Raxlin all right, "when I made *Donnybrook* at Paramount in 1954, there were two producers assigned to the picture. Neither of them could read as far as I could tell, neither'd had the education or the background to enjoy reading for its own sake. But Sam Bruzer and Mort Skulnick, two lovable, dear men, went to their graves wishing they'd had the opportunities I'd had. And I'm no scholar. I bought my last promotion when I socked the principal in my senior year of high school. But Raxlin and his kind, they think it's queer or soft to sit down to a good book. They grew up on television. What I dislike about him isn't his ignorance, we're all ignorant one way and another, it's his goddamned complacency. That bothers me. It makes me mad."

Peggy hadn't said anything for some time. She wasn't taking sides. From the look of her, she didn't like to watch people doing battle, unless maybe it was over her. When the silence made it clear that it was her cue, Peggy said to Sayre, "I loved *Donnybrook*. Naturally, I didn't see it when it came out — that was the year I was born — but I've seen it on TV. It stands up wonderfully. You got the Irish background so wonderfully authentic. And the scenes!"

"Back-lot stuff and in the hills around Malibu. But we were workin' from a first-rate script by Fergus Kelly. He's in the Irish Dáil now, but he used to be a pal of Brendan Behan and Louis MacNeice, the poet."

By now Furlong was beginning to look nervous. He and Peggy had been taking turns burning holes in a paper napkin held drum-tight across the top of a glass. A dime in the middle of the lacy tracery looked about to fall at the next turn. "Shouldn't we?" he asked Sayre when he passed the cigarette to Peggy. Sayre laughed and nearly started coughing again. He caught his breath and looked fondly at Peggy, who had just tumbled the dime into the dregs of a green stinger. Sayre was well along the way to feeling first-rate and he had courage he hadn't used yet.

"Sit down a minute. He isn't goin' to bite your ear off. He only wants to play around with your script. Probably has a plan to show an airline logo in close-up. That's a way to hold the story up and pay a few bills."

"Still," said Neil, getting closer to the edge of his temper, "he does pay them, including your piece and mine."

"What's the hurry? I've seen the schedule. We've got plenty of time. Some people never feel they're in charge unless they're callin' you in the middle of the night, or flyin' you in from Rome or Athens. The more money he wastes, the bigger producer he is."

"Yes, Jim, but that's my script he's playing with!"

"Exactly. You're goin' on like he's fussin' over a script that's only slightly better than a second draft. We're on location, boy. I can shoot around any rewriting that has to be done. That's why he got me on this goddamned picture. This isn't the servants' hall. You don't have to jump when the bell goes."

"I want this picture to work, Jim. I need that bad."

"It better finish on schedule, Mr. Sayre, or I'll be in England," said Peggy.

Furlong got to his feet.

"Sit down for God's sake! Tell you what. We'll go in another minute." Furlong sat reluctantly and fingered his empty glass. He looked for a sympathetic eye in Peggy's direction. Peggy was looking at the table. I tried to get the conversation rolling again.

"What came after *Donnybrook*? I have them all mixed up." The others looked relieved.

"I did *Donnybrook* in the early winter of '53–'54. I was finished and scouting locations in Monument Valley by February. Let's see, in the autumn I was in North Africa doing scenes for *Devil Catch the Hindmost*. Then I went to England and Ireland for *Moll Flanders*. I didn't do another picture in Hollywood until *The Dain Curse* in 1958. I wanted to do *Red Harvest*, but they thought the title sounded too political. That was 1960. Then I collected my Oscar for *Blood of John Dillon* in '62. I was always lucky in my Irish pictures. My father was in *The Legion* in 1964. Did it on a dare. Year before he died."

"Jim, I think we'd better be on our way."

"Oh, I guess so." He took a last sip of Jack Daniels and let out an exaggerated sigh of pleasure. He got to his feet a second or two behind a relieved Furlong. "This is my party, Ben. The waiter knows. Good night, my dear. See you in the mornin'." He bussed Peggy and walked off tall and without a sign of a stagger after Neil Furlong.

I watched them for a couple of seconds as they made their way among the tables and had just turned back to Peggy O'Toole when I heard a woman scream and glass break. Suddenly flashbulbs were popping and whole rolls of film were squeezed off in seconds. With everybody else in the room, I got up and looked in the direction the noise came from. All I saw were backs of people, some moving away from and some getting closer to the action. Above it all there was Jim Sayre's big head, looking calm but looking down toward the floor. As I came closer I could see that he was reaching down into the gloom of the rug-covered floor for Neil Furlong's hand. Furlong was sprawled on his back with one leg straddling an overturned pedestal table. Ice cubes caught the light, what there was of it. Sayre helped him to his feet. He dusted himself off and rubbed his jaw.

The bartender arrived about then and told everybody to sit down, but he might have as effectively written a letter. Everybody was looking at the little, fat red-faced man in the brown sports-coat, the one three men were holding back.

"Let go, you guys. I won't hit the bastard again." He pulled himself free, picked up a drink and hurled it at Furlong, who managed to escape most of it. The little man was grabbed again and dragged toward the door by his friends.

"Remember me, Furlong? Remember Harve Osborne? Remember us? That's just to show you that we remember you, you son of a bitch!" His friends were urging him away before a cop came. Around me everybody was talking at once, while Furlong rubbed his jaw.

"He just stood up and let him have it."

"He moved like a boxer, I never saw anything so fast."

"What happened?"

"A guy just hit a guy that's all."

"We were sitting right beside him, and he up and bopped that guy right there."

"Why do I always miss everything?" Lynn and Nicole were standing on the edge of the gathering crowd like two black birds in their dark dresses. I moved closer to Furlong.

"Who was he?" I asked.

"Never saw him before. Some crank, I guess."

"Jaw hurt bad?"

"He didn't get a direct hit. I'd better get out of here before we attract a crowd. Shit," he said, feeling his chin.

"I never saw a fellow's face turn from white to red so fast. Just a little fat hombre," Sayre was saying to no one in particular. He took Furlong's arm and led him toward the door which he managed without further incident. The bartender picked up the fallen table and I returned to mine and Peggy O'Toole, who hadn't even got up to watch. My blood was thumping in my arteries even though I hadn't fired a shot. Peggy's face was placid.

"Was he hurt?" she asked.

"Not bad. He'll have a sore face in the morning."

"It gives me goose-bumps," she said and hugged herself. "I hate violence."

"What do you think brought it on?"

"How should I know? Maybe it was a member of the crew who didn't get a T-shirt. People in crowds can love you and tear you to pieces at the same time. You have to figure out every move ahead of time."

"If it had been Jim not Furlong that had been slugged, would that have excited you more?" I asked.

"I guess so," she said after thinking it over. "But nobody's big enough to hit Mr. Sayre. Not even Hamp."

"Hamp?" She looked at me over the top of her glass.

"Fisher," she said, naming the newspaper tycoon as though his only test of strength was the preservation of peace and a woman's fair name. Hampton Fisher was the latest of a wild and wealthy family to try to keep the Fisher chain of papers going. Besides being rich, Fisher was an eccentric food faddist, adventurer, health nut and crank, but easily the most eligible bachelor in North America. He was possibly too fastidious to share a bathroom, and two years ago the papers, at least the non-Fisher papers, were full of the story of his breaking off an engagement to some writer when he learned that she'd been living with a poet when she was in university.

"Does Hampton Fisher usually look out for you?" I asked.

"I can see you don't read the gossip columns."

"Not when there's a Corn Flakes box handy."

"Well, the columns have had Hamp and me eloping to Mexico, flying to Nantucket, and absconding to Nice three or four times. He's a nice man: a little boy all wrapped up in a grown-up physique. He's so shy you wouldn't believe it."

"Especially shy of germs, I hear."

"You mean the way he always bundles up? He just gets chills more easily than most people. That doesn't stop him going through the ice at the North Pole. He flew down to see me in his own plane. He's a typical Capricorn. He's wonderfully sad sometimes, and oh, you should see him when he doesn't get his own way. What sign are you, Benny?"

"Pistachio."

"Another cynic. Honestly. A lot of world leaders were Capricorns." She pulled at my wrist and read the time. "I've got an early call," she said, sighing through a sad smile.

I offered to walk her back to her hotel after we finished our drinks. In spite of her threat to drink green stingers, she'd only managed to finish one. Peggy talked a good drunk, but wasn't going to embarrass the bartender's supply of *crème de menthe*. She did know about how to slice through crowds, though. Like the Hollywood veteran she was, she led the way to the freight elevator, and then through the kitchen of the Colonel John, which backs on the Tudor's rear door.

"I hate it when those men claw at one another. It's usually over money, or billing or something. Why do people have agents if they still want to mess in all those details just for the sake of a wrangle. It's stupid. I wish Mr. Sayre would stay out of it. I wish he wouldn't drink so much." When we got to her door, she patted my cheek. "When's your birthday, Pistachio?"

"Won't give up, will you? March first."

"Pisces, the fish. I'm Sagittarius. I think we'll get along. I think you're sweet, Pistachio." And Peggy O'Toole kissed me good night. That's what you get for being good.

seven

The highway was nearly deserted as I sailed back to Grantham and my bed at the City House. I dropped at once into a dream written and directed by a maker of Technicolor musicals. Peggy O'Toole was my leading lady and Neil Furlong was my best friend. From time to time Jim Sayre had a scene in which he told me what it was like in the big world outside.

When I woke, I thought of prolonging the night artificially by rolling over away from the light, but I knew I was still on Lowell Mason's payroll. With any luck I was going to see Billie at five, but I decided the first thing was to beard David Hayes again when he was sober and not on his guard. I got showered and dressed and launched again onto the open road before my eyes were completely open. I was still carrying a key to Hayes' room, which was giving me ideas as I parked the car. But I wasn't Superman. I needed coffee first. As I came in, Marvin Raxlin came out. He was in a hurry and looked like grim death. The cheekbone on the left side of his face was bruised. I decided then and there that there were easier things to be than a Hollywood producer.

On my way up to the seventeenth floor, I wondered whether it was Sayre or Furlong who'd hit him. Sayre looked like he sat on a large temper which sometimes got away from him. Furlong didn't strike me as the violent type at all, but he came from Port and that counted against him. I knocked at Hayes' door. It was a replay of the day before. I thought of problems hearing the door from the shower and the same other thoughts from twenty-four hours ago. I decided to edit out a loop and used the key faster than I had last time. I opened the door of Room 1738, and found myself looking straight into the big face of Staff Sergeant Chris Savas of the Niagara Regional Police. Savas

68

was a friend of mine, but not what I expected. Beyond him I could see David Hayes lying on the bed. He wasn't in the shower after all. In fact, he would never stand in the shower again. The next wash he would get would be the kind they give you on marble slabs in the morgue.

I considered turning around and walking back to my car. There was still a lingering smell of vomit in the room, but it was overlaid with the more lethal smell of cordite. Savas' eyes widened for a fraction of a second and he slipped a tight smile on for size. "Join us," he said, moving back from the door.

I didn't like looking at dead people. The shine had gone off Hayes' surprised open eyes. Apart from the stains on his shirt and bedclothes, he looked a lot like the drunk I'd put to bed on Tuesday night. That was the hard part, and that's when I had to beat it to the bathroom. I parted a couple of fingerprint men bending over the toilet, and they got out of the way not a second too soon. One of them frowned when I washed my face and dried it on what they were treating as evidence. I returned to the bedroom with my face stinging from cold water and a too-vigorous rub. Savas was waiting for me.

Chris is a massive man who just made it to the required height with no change to spare. His big hands were dangling from thumbs tucked into his belt, and his steely eyes were focussed on me. He was one of the best policemen in the business, a complete professional. We'd crossed paths before and we both had a fair idea of how the other's mind worked. I counted four uniformed men in the room and two others in shirt-sleeves going through drawers.

"Benny, why didn't you tell me you were branching out? Since when are you working so far from home? I assume you are working. Is that right?" Chris turned his eyes toward the bed for a second. "Was that the client? Or are you just taking in the natural beauty of the falls?" There was no malice intended, it was just professional banter. I'd get the same thing if I called around at his office to borrow a cigarette. When Savas got rough, you didn't just prickle from the indignity of it all. Sometimes he had the warmth of a Sunday roast of beef in his face, and sometimes all you could see were those eyes like steel ball-bearings.

I tried to answer the question I knew was on Savas' mind. "I don't know who would want to bump Hayes. I can't think of any reason for taking a swing at him. He was an ambitious kid who thought he was going to remake the world." Savas lifted a bushy eyebrow. "No, Chris, it wasn't political. It's just when he got drunk, he cried out about how we were all going down the drain. He was more interested in theatre. He was trying to get into the movie, *Ice Bridge*. He was a serious actor; quit his job at the *Beacon* where he was freelancing up until last week."

"How come you know so much? You hanging out with the post-graduate crowd, Benny?"

"I was talking to him in the upstairs bar Tuesday night. Ask the bartender. He helped me carry him down and tuck him in."

"That's when you forgot to return the key. Just slipped your mind. Come on Benny, don't ration it. You're not exactly feeding the multitude with information."

"Well, if you don't believe me, and you don't want to bother the bartender, ask Dawson Williams."

"Dawson Williams! Was he there?"

"Yeah, big as CinemaScope and cutting up with the swordplay."

"Cut the bull. Where was he?"

"Sitting behind us. Hayes was getting a little loud, and Williams thought it was funny. Hayes turned around, made a little speech about how we are all heading for hell in a handcart, and puked on Williams' table. Williams was with three other guys. It's easy to check."

"Cooperman, when you tell me something's easy to check, I know I've been asking the wrong questions. How'd you run into Hayes in the first place?"

"He played Mitch in *A Streetcar Named Desire* at the Legion Hall in Grantham a few months ago. Terrible place to hear a play."

"Go on, Benny. You think I'm some kind of whisky

cop can't remember I'm not in uniform anymore? Who is this Hayes and what's your interest in him?"

"It's business, Chris. I'm looking for somebody and I heard that maybe Hayes knew where this somebody went. That's all I'm saying. I'm nearly one hundred per cent certain that this somebody had nothing to do with Hayes getting knocked off, because I know that this unnamed person had a date to meet Hayes later today. I'm not stringing you, Chris. There's an outside chance that the person making the date wasn't who I think it was, but it's an outside chance. I'll eat your shirt at the end of your shift if this somebody's involved."

"I don't give a sweet and sour rib what you think. I'm running this investigation, not you. I'll decide what's good goods and what's garbage. Now, I want you to open up on this."

"I can't help you, Chris. Not about that. Anything else including my right arm, you can have."

"You know what you can do with that. Shit, Ben, you're a bloody marvel. I got a murder on my hands and you're protecting some woman who maybe killed this guy."

"You think I haven't thought of that? Besides, who says it's a woman?"

"All those somebodies and unnamed persons always point to a woman. Besides, we've a witness who says he saw a woman leaving this room around the time of the murder." Savas looked like a cat lapping cream I'd paid for.

"He saw a woman, not necessarily the someone I'm looking for."

"I'll be glad to check that out for you."

"Damn it, Chris, you know I can check out an alibi as well as anybody. If there's anything fishy about it, you'll be the first to hear."

"You're goddamned right, and the time has come."

"Chris, don't push me."

"Benny, it's my warrant card that's pushing. I'm not going to wait around for press releases. Let's have it. Right bloody now."

"Give me forty-eight hours, Chris. Then I'll tell you anything you want."

"Are you crazy? What if your client has been following you? Have you thought of that?"

"You honestly think I'm going to get caught in a squeeze that old? If my client was following me . . ."

"It wouldn't be the first time."

"Twenty-four hours. Let me have that much time. And if I turn up anything that links what happened here with my business, I'll call you at three in the morning if necessary. Come on, that isn't asking much. I'm not asking for gold bricks."

Savas sucked at his teeth for a minute, and as soon as he scowled, I knew I'd won. But I waited for him to say so, and acted surprised, so he wouldn't change his mind.

"What have you got besides Hayes, Chris?" I was taking a chance that he would throw me out of Room 1738, but I thought I'd give him an opportunity to show me how efficient the professionals were.

"Hotel dick found him when he investigated his not answering a wake-up call at 7:30. Looks like he's been dead since about six. It was around then that William Blacklock of Detroit saw a woman wearing big round sunglasses and a tailored suit leaving the scene: dark hair, between thirty-five and forty, five-feet three or four, hundred and twenty, hundred and thirty pounds. I've got a man on that. Sound familiar?" It did, but I decided to let Chris' boy run it down without my help. To make up for that I filled Savas in on all the things I knew about the case that didn't run across my territory and I was back on the street around noon, starving. In a glorified hamburger stand between a wax museum devoted to the history of crime and a parking lot, I ordered French fries, a glass of milk, and vanilla ice cream. The best thing about the place wasn't on the menu: there was a pay telephone in a place where the wind didn't freeze your ankles.

I dialled the number of my client and listened to the electronic buzzing while watching a freight train crawl between the legs of the Pagoda across the street. The tower straddled the main track of the railway which crossed Clifton Hill at this point.

"Mr. Mason?"

"Yes." I could imagine a salesman's smile on his face. And I made it go away.

"It's Benny Cooperman. I thought I'd better give you a report about what's been happening around here."

"Glad to hear from you. Where are you calling from? I've left word with your answering service, but . . ."

"I'm at the Falls. I've managed to trace your wife to a writer-actor fellow from Grantham called Hayes. Name mean anything to you?"

"Not off-hand. Is it important?"

"Important enough for somebody to shoot Hayes this morning. Billie left Grantham with Hayes and came here. Then she ditched him."

"Mr. Cooperman. This thing has gone too far. I want out, and I want you off the case."

"Okay, you're calling the tunes. But how is that going to look to a judge? You hire me, I trace Billie to Hayes, and then suddenly Hayes gets dead and you tidy me away telling me to keep the change. It stinks, Mason, and you're smart enough to see it. You're the aggrieved party in this. So far I've managed to keep your name out of it, but I can only stall the cops so long, and then I'll have to come clean. I'd make sure I knew where I was around six this morning if I were you. You've got the oldest motive in the world for shooting Hayes, and the sanctity of the home is no defence."

"You've already talked to the police?"

"They insisted."

"And next time you'll have to tell them about Billie and me?"

"I still have a few hours. Meanwhile, I want you to come clean with me about why you were worried about Billie disappearing. The real reason."

"I don't understand."

"You understand fine. We don't have time for parlour games. I'm coming to see you at your office around 6:30

tonight. And when I see you, I want to have a real heart-to-heart about lots of things besides Billie's acting career."

"As for instance?"

"As for instance why you were worried she might have been murdered. As for instance why you're letting me play with less than half a deck. I want you to tell me the whole story when I see you, without skipping any chapters this time."

"Look, Cooperman . . ."

"Save it until 6:30." I may even bring you some good news. You never know."

eight

At five o'clock I was sitting in the basement coffee shop of the Colonel John Butler Hotel. In a nearby booth an old woman, her red hair covered by a chiffon scarf, shot a disapproving glance at two skinny youngsters in T-shirts who were playing with, rather than eating, large ice cream sundaes. The woman's features were hard and set, her gloved hands rested stiffly on the leather handbag on her lap.

The Colonel John did everything on a bigger scale than the Tudor. Everything looked as though it was expected to be handled by more people and stand up to less discriminating use. The coffee shop was called "The Guard Room". An attempt had been made to carry a military motif from the cash register to the salt and pepper shakers. On the wall crossed muskets hung benignly. Powder horns, battle prints and campaign maps extended this theme, but the waitresses were a sop to those for whom history was either rough or controversial. In their blue and white checked uniforms, with criss-cross lacing at the waist, they looked less like camp followers and more like Mother Goose's little girls. I sipped a coffee slowly.

Billie Mason walked into the restaurant alone, looking more attractive than her eight-by-ten glossy three-quarter view. I've never seen blue like the blue of her eyes and her neck was like a note held at the end of a song. She wasn't the sort of woman who could kill conversation dead when she walked into a room, but you could hear the level drop for a moment and there wasn't a man in the place who didn't lose the drift of his wife's monologue for a minute. She was about five-feet seven and weighed under 120. There was a confident glide to her walk that made the women look up from their cottage cheese as well as the men. She was obviously looking for Hayes. She hadn't heard, then, unless she was playing some kind of elaborate game that happens only in mystery novels or on television: he knows that she knows that he knows that she knows. She frowned prettily and stood in the aisle wondering what to do next. I got up, crawled over my bunched coat on the padded bench beside me and went over to her.

"Mrs. Mason?" She didn't like the *Mrs*. It was clear warning. "My name's Benny Cooperman. I'm a detective from Grantham. I'm sorry, but your husband has asked me to find you. He's been very worried about you." I kept talking, but I could see as her face darkened that she'd stopped listening. Her smile went inside the house.

"I knew he'd try to find me," she said, tilting her head away from me. It looked like a summer squall had hit her features. "The creep. Why doesn't he leave me alone?"

"Let's talk about it. I'm sitting over there."

"I can't. I'm meeting somebody. You'd better leave me alone. I don't want a scene."

"That's right. Nobody does. Let me buy you a cup of coffee."

"I told you. I'm waiting for someone."

"I know. He won't be coming. Please sit down, have a cup of coffee and I'll tell you all about it." I started toward the table and she followed. I pulled out a chair and climbed over my coat again.

She was wearing a fawn-coloured suede jacket and skirt with a soft blue blouse under it. Her hair was ash blonde and as unreal as angels.

"You're not big enough to take me back to Grantham," she said rather awkwardly, getting used to the face across the table. I checked myself in the mirror behind me. It was a good enough face, the eyes hazel and fairly honest. I made them look sympathetic.

"He's worried," I said.

"Worried about my commissions. Worried because I'm not there putting out for his friends. Where'd that ever get me? Maybe he'd give me another Salesman of the Month award. He could fix it. He could fix anything."

"I think he cares about you apart from your sales record."

"In a doughnut, he cares! Oh, all right. So he cares. I feel sorry for him, but he's *so* . . . Lowell. I can't describe it. If I told him I'd dreamed of a Spanish castle in the clouds, Lowell would start talking about plumbing and upkeep. Don't get me started on Lowell. There's no way I'm going back to that." For a minute I thought the storm was passing over. Her brow smoothed out, and she stopped fidgeting. She then looked up at me suddenly: "Have you told him where I am?"

"How could I? I just found you. You're the first to know."

"Hell, Mr. Cooperman, I didn't even know I was lost."

"He thought you'd been killed. That's how worried he is. Why would he think a thing like that? Do they play rough, those real-estate pals of his?" The beginnings of a smile died at the corner of her lips.

"They'd grind my bones to make their bread. They can't find out where I am. I'm finished with all that. In a week I won't even remember any of their names. I'm next door to the biggest break an actress ever had. Don't muck it up for me, Mr. Cooperman."

"I'd do a lot to please a lady, Mrs. Mason, but it's your old man that's paying the bills. I'll have to turn you in."

That didn't please her, but she accepted it as reasonable. And she didn't take it personally. From time to time she looked into the mirror to see if David Hayes had come into the restaurant.

"David won't be coming," I said flatly. She looked up at me with something of a challenge in her face.

"Is that a clever detective guess? How do you know about David anyway?"

"I was in his room when you called. In fact, you spoke to me, not David." I let that hang there between us for a few moments before I went on. "David was out."

"You make me sick. Why don't you get an honest job in a factory or greasing cars? I don't know how you can touch yourself after the things you've done. I'm going. Please don't try to follow me."

"Sit still. I'll tell you about David. About why he can't come."

"It's because he's drunk again. Poor David. He's not really a lush. It's just that . . . Anyway, I have news for him from Ed Noonan. Why are you looking at me that way? Why don't you say anything? You make me nervous."

"David's dead," I said simply. I could see that it hit her, but it was a glancing blow; she didn't fully take in the news.

"That's not funny, Mr. Cooperman. What were you doing in his room? He doesn't know where I've been. Where is he, and why didn't he come himself?"

"I told you. I'm sorry. David's dead. He was killed this morning in his room at the hotel." Her eyes suddenly had bigger whites, and then she looked disappointed, as though David's death was a dirty trick someone was playing on her. She looked cross, almost sulky. By now, though, I think she believed me. She didn't say anything, she just sat there watching me play with the empty cream container. I took my wadded paper napkin, pressed it down inside the fluted plastic and bore down on it with some force. When I removed it, the napkin had taken on the shape of the empty container. Billie Mason watched and neither of us said anything.

After about three minutes her hand reached across to mine and took the creamer away from me, as though I was her child. "Tell me," she said. "Tell me, please."

I told her about Tuesday night, about coming back this morning and finding him dead. "I'm sorry," I finished.

"I just can't believe it. People like David don't just die."

"He didn't just die. He was murdered. Can you think of anyone with a reason for killing him?"

"This is a B movie. I can't believe what I'm hearing. Why do you say it was murder?"

"That's what the police are calling it. I saw him, and that's what I'd call it."

"It's like somebody strangled a teddybear," she said.

There were tears in her eyes now, and she tried wiping them away with a table napkin. It was unequal to the work, so I handed her an almost clean handkerchief. She blew her nose in it like it was her own and I told her to keep it.

"I was so very fond of him," she explained, trying to smile over the tear tracks on both cheeks.

"I heard." The smile went indoors again.

"Lowell. Did Lowell tell you about David?"

"No. As far as I know, he knew nothing about that."

"It's just as well. Things are complicated enough."

"He wants you back."

"I know, I know." She was nibbling at the end of a long fingernail. "I just need a little more time."

"Time for what? Time to strike it rich in the movies? Come on. You should know the odds on that." She held up all ten manicured fingers like redcoats on parade and reviewed them like a stern field marshal. "Where are you staying?" I tried to slip that in.

"I can't tell you that, Mr. Cooperman. Don't be silly."

"But I can always get to you through Ed Noonan, right?" The redcoats scattered off the parade ground and the field marshal glared at me.

"No! I mean, why do you say that? I hardly know him."

"But he knows you well enough to cover up for you. Nowhere in your file does it refer to your marital status, but he called you Mrs. Mason when I talked to him. Maybe you know him better than you care to say." Red-tipped fingers were crawling up over the edge of the table and hiding behind the coffee cup and saucer.

"Ed Noonan? You should make a comedy, Mr. Cooperman. Ed's just a little man with hot coals where his eyes should be. I hate a man that slavers. But, yes, you're right; he will get a message to me if you need me." Fingers were now on the ramparts of her hair, patting, flattening, reshaping a curl near her left ear. "Are you going to try to find out who killed David?"

"Mrs. Mason, I'm just a peeper. I'm good at tracing people like you for their husbands. I do divorce work when

I can get it. I work for a couple of lawyers when I can, I do all kinds of things, but, when I can help it, I stay clear of murder. The cops are a hard act to follow. They know their business."

"Poor David. Why would anyone want to kill him?"

"Actors are funny people."

"David wasn't an actor. Not a *real* actor, I mean. Sure, he was a wonderful Mitch in *Streetcar*, and he could read well, but he could do it because he didn't take it all that seriously. Not like me. I'd kill for a part." She bit her lip. "Well, almost." She took a breath and tried to be helpful. "David was more interested in writing, really. He's written some wonderful TV scripts and plays. I suppose now, nobody will ever produce them."

"Then why did you two take off together?"

"We both hoped to get bits. For the experience, you know."

"And for 'the experience' you broke up your marriage? That's pretty hard to swallow, Mrs. Mason."

"Call me Billie. Everybody calls me Billie."

"Well?"

"Well, it was a long time coming. I could have taken off a year ago, but I stayed. I tried to make it work."

"Maybe you didn't like your husband's business friends from Atlantic City? Maybe that Piccadilly bunch made for a crowded bed."

"Where did you hear . . . ? What has that got to do with this? I didn't leave because of them."

"Let's not forget poor David. You say he wrote plays for television. Did he show them to anybody?"

"I guess he showed them to Monty Blair. Yes, as a matter of fact, Monty was quite excited about some of them. He thought David had real talent and tried to get him launched. I met Monty when I was in high school. He presented a best actress award to me for Portia in *The Merchant*. He took an interest in me too, until his sister put an end to it. She was always jumping to the right conclusion where Monty was concerned."

I tried to picture Monty Blair. For an instant I could

hear his languid drawl as he ordered up more amber and fewer magenta lights on stage. Grand and portly he was standing halfway back in the empty auditorium of the Grantham Collegiate. That was back in Grade Nine and my introduction to both theatre and Monty Blair. His death at the end of the seventies robbed Grantham of its greatest cultural resource and most memorable character with one snip of the shears. I tried to fade the lights on that and get back to business.

"David told me he'd been working. Would that have meant writing?"

"I guess. There haven't been any scenes with bits yet, just extras."

"Can you think of any reason why his writing could have got him into trouble?"

"Of course not. He's never had anything produced, and he's only published theatre reviews in the *Beacon*."

"What about your husband's pals, the ones who'd like to grind your bones to make their bread?"

"They're a pain for me, not for David. He doesn't know anything about all that. It's all over anyway."

"You say it's over. It's what *they* say that matters. What if they killed David? Try to give that some thought."

"Oh, my God! I didn't think! They wouldn't! Oh, poor David! Do you really think they did it, Mr. Cooperman?"

I can't remember very much about the rest of that conversation with Billie. My imagination kept over-acting. I saw myself trussed up like a Christmas turkey with a dead canary in my mouth. I remember that for a long time we just sat looking at each other. She was crying. The coffee was cold and the room seemed empty. I was holding her hand tightly. Her nose and knuckles were pink, like she was shaking off frostbite. I got her to agree to meet me at noon the next day, Friday, in the same place. I promised that for the time being I would leave her husband out of it. Then I remembered my 6:30 appointment in Grantham with the very man I was double-crossing. I would be late — but Lowell Mason wasn't holding my hand.

nine

I crossed the parking lot to collect my car. Moving from hotel to hotel, it was easy to forget it was January out there, where the weather was making a pitch to be noticed. I had the motor going, and was about to start on the road to Grantham, when I saw that the headlights fell on the cracked windshield of David Hayes' Jaguar, and, more important, on someone sitting behind it. I turned off the key, listened to the disappointed sound of the motor dying, then went to investigate.

In spite of her head-hugging hat and miles of silken scarves, I recognized Miranda Pride's head resting on the steering wheel. For a second I got that nasty sensation in my stomach, but it went away when I saw her shoulder heave in a sob. She raised her head and blew her nose into a balled handkerchief. She tilted her glasses up to her forehead when she saw me looking through the window at her, but put them back in place to hide the red eyes and stained face.

"Oh, it's you," she mimed through the glass, leaning across to unlock the door on the passenger side. I walked around the car and got in. I stared at Miranda and she stared at the crack in the windshield. "I wasn't going any-place. I just wanted to get away for a few minutes. The police want to talk to me about David. I don't think I can do it. Usually, I'm my own favourite subject, but . . . Have you got a cigarette?" I dragged out my pack of Player's and she took one without using her eyes. I had matches and did the honours. Her face, in the flickering flame, seemed to shimmer. The shadow of her nose darkened her cheek and showed off the good bones beneath that sculptured well-known face. She held her head like a monarch on her way to the scaffold, proud and contemptuous. I burned my thumb, and she became a silhouette lit only by the mercury lamps of the parking lot. Her coat had slipped off her shoulders, but she didn't seem to feel the cold.

"He was so young," she said. "It's a dirty trick." Her voice was hoarse and husky, and she looked straight through the glass at nothing. "We took a walk by the falls. I only met him a little over a week ago. I thought about him at a terribly sad party in New York. You know parties that go brittle and break? It was that kind of party, and all I could think of was David here by the falls. We walked there again when I got back. The trees, even the twigs, were encrusted with ice. He was enchanted. I remember all the things he said. We talked all night and I remember it all. That's the way I am when I'm with a person. I am there one hundred per cent. Oh, Mr. Cooperman, why? Why?" I didn't say anything. We just sat and finished our cigarettes. It was like it had been with Billie, only with less talking. She seemed fragile, as though anything I might say would only hurt her. After a few minutes, she shivered, pulled her coat around her and looked at me closely for the first time. "I was in love with David," she said. "Funny, isn't it? I loved him and I'm not even sure he liked me. Why do I never come out even?" She got out of the Jaguar and walked through the back entrance of the hotel without looking back.

This time I didn't like the looks of Lowell Mason. I didn't like the way he kept me waiting, staring at a bunch of bad photographs of over-priced bungalows, I didn't like his taste in office furniture, which ran to cigarette burns on blond wood finish, and, when he was finally sitting across from me, perspiring and ingratiating, I didn't like the wiry curl in his hair. He may have been my only client, but I would have traded him in for a little tidy legal work.

"Well, then, Mr. Cooperman, how are we getting along?"

"I told you we were up to our armpits in murder. That's not getting along at all. I have to talk to Staff-Sergeant Savas by Friday noon, so we haven't much time to shoot the breeze. You didn't know Hayes, you said. Has anything come back to you since we talked?"

"Sorry. I may have met the fellow after a performance. I went to the play and to the cast party. But, honestly, I don't know where he fits. Terrible thing, I mean, a thing like this."

"Yeah, I know. It cut Billie up pretty bad when I talked to her this afternoon too."

"You saw her? Where? How?" His eyes flashed an angry warning. "Why didn't you let me know?"

"Take it easy. I've got some answers for you. I saw her in the Falls at the Colonel John this afternoon just after I talked to you. She's all right. Nobody's murdered her. She just isn't ready to come home yet. From the way she's talking, she doesn't want to come home at all. She's on the brink of an acting career that she thinks is going somewhere. There's a lot of hot air down at the Falls this week, a lot of promises are being made and most of them will be broken. The movie company's here for two more weeks. I'd say her acting career will be over in fourteen days. I think she's latched on to somebody who said he could do her some good. I'm sorry. But that's the way it looks to me."

"I see." His lips made a prissy straight line. "Thanks for being direct. Any idea?"

"Not even the bad breath of an idea. Tell me: you didn't look very relieved when I told you she hadn't been killed. Is that my imagination?"

"Of course I'm relieved. What do you think?"

"I think you're gelding your information, Mr. Mason. I can't get full results with partial facts. I may be a genius sometimes, but a magician I'm not. Tell me about it. Tell me."

"If I could. Ha! Oh if I could tell you half of it."

"I know it has to do with the mob. You can level with me. That's what you're paying me for."

"Where did you find out about the . . . what do you think you know?"

"A CBC film unit doing a film on organized crime did

an interview with Billie. They claimed to be interested in her acting, but that was just a come-on. What could she have told them? Come on, Mason. Open up." Mason's face went white around the nostrils and pink at the cheekbones. I read that as agitation, although he just sat there with his hands neatly folded in front of him. He started a couple of sentences but broke them off after a few words. They didn't have much life in them so he let them die. He got up and walked across to a cupboard, looking back at me as he went.

"You take a drink, Mr. Cooperman?" He pulled out a bottle of Canadian Club and added a few ice cubes from a half-melted tray that had been out of the pint-sized fridge for about half an hour.

"I'll have a short one. With water," I said. He did the pouring, the mixing and, for the next couple of minutes, the drinking. I tried to see where the cracks were.

"The CBC, you say?" was all he said. Cool, I thought, very cool.

"Yeah. Some sort of special unit. I've talked to the boss. He told me about all the fun you're having."

"There's nothing I can tell you, Cooperman. I've said all I can say."

"You haven't said a word. Okay, let me do some guessing. You've got some partners you don't talk about. People who don't want their names in the paper. They're publicity shy, but they're bright and brassy in the money department. They have sweetened the business for you. Let you in on a few good things. Told you when to bet and when to fold. Just as long as a little of your money mixes in with theirs, they're happy. Silent partners. Only they haven't been so quiet since Billie left home. They've noticed. They've asked questions. They don't like it. They want things to go back the way they were: you and Billie keeping house and your mouths shut. They don't know about that CBC interview?"

"God, no!"

"All right. So you brought me in to get her back just to make them happy. They're calling the tune. Do they know about me?"

"Of course not."

"You're a terrible liar, Mason. Who did you tell? I've got to know that much. Did you tell Pritchett?" He was jiggling the ice so noticeably he put his other hand over the top of the glass. He was looking at everything in the office but me. "Easy stages, now. First, you told them that Billie went away. Did they buy that in the beginning?"

"Yes, to start with. Then she was seen. In the Falls. I don't know who saw her. But they were asking again. I told them that it had to do with her theatrical ambitions. They didn't like that. They wanted her with me, where they could keep an eye on her."

"Where they could watch the pair of you. Just a small laundry. When they got itchy, you threw them a bone. Me. You had to show that you were moving heaven and earth to get her back."

Now Mason flared. But it was all show. He was like an inflated paper bag, puffed up with anger, just before you burst it. I said nothing, until he wore himself out.

"Well, what would you have done in my place?" he finally asked.

"You don't pour a strong enough drink for me to answer that one."

"What are you going to do?"

"I'm going to try to do what you're paying me to do. She's a tough woman, Mason, and she'd do all right on her own. So whether she comes back or not depends a lot on you." I put down my glass on a stained, gritty window sill and got up to go.

"Where did you find out about Pritchett? Did . . .?"

"No, Billie didn't tell me about Pritchett. You can pass the word along. If she ever starts to talk, it will be because you've run her into a corner. Pass the word back to your boss. And try to brace up. Look at yourself. You're scared of Billie, scared of me, scared they're listening, scared they're hiding under your desk. I bet you weren't so grey when you were just running a real-estate business."

I walked out, letting the door slam behind me. The fresh air hit me like another shot of rye. And I didn't need the first one. I was muttering wisps of fog at myself as I walked up the street to where I'd left my car, slightly tilted on a snow drift gone black. I felt I was being looked at by about fifty short-barrelled handguns. When I started the motor I didn't expect it to turn over, I expected it to explode. I was getting close to the edge, close to something bigger than Billie, and Mason, and something that made me wish I'd taken a quick peek behind Lowell Mason's bleached desk instead of just talking about it.

When I got back to the Falls I went around to the Clifford Arms, the hotel overlooked by the guide books, to book a room from the bartender in the beverage room. He looked suspiciously at my overnight bag. I found Room 209 without help, one of those places where there is nothing over 40 watts above ground level. It was a bed, a chair and a wash basin at the crowded bottom of a tall slot. Turned on its side, Room 209 would have been something you could almost stretch out in. Coffee-coloured tattered curtains ballooned out below the sash overlooking Lundy's Lane. I could see a spaghetti joint across the street tripping a sputtering neon sign from pink to blue and back again. Looking into the room, with my back to the light, I told myself that it was fine, no better or worse than the place I live in in Grantham except that they charged two dollars a night more. That was probably because the fire escape here at the Clifford had knots tied in it at regular intervals.

The beverage room was about half full of men dozing or droning over draft beer. There were no women. Ladies and Escorts had a room of their own next to this one where the floor was cleaner and the atmosphere more animated. The room behind the door marked Men's Beverage Room was reserved for serious drinkers.

On the colour TV over the bar, Wally Skeat was giving a newscast. I found a paper on one end of the service bar. There was nothing in it about David Hayes. This far from Toronto, the news doesn't break, it crumbles.

ten

In spite of evidence to the contrary, I try to get a decent night's sleep and eat regular meals. When I left Grantham it was with the double notion of securing a pillow and getting a bite of dinner as soon as possible. I'd managed the first half, but a telephone in the lobby of Butler's Barracks recalled me to duty. I pulled out the piece of paper where I'd written the name of Furlong's attacker: Harvey Osborne. There was only one in the book.

"Hello?"

"Is that Harvey Osborne?"

"That's right. Who's this?"

"My name's Cooperman. I want to talk to you about what happened last night."

"I'm sorry. I don't. I've had the newspapers calling all day. I want no part of it. What's your interest in this?"

"I'm not sure. But I'd like to know why you took a poke at Furlong."

"And connected. I sent the guy sprawling."

"That's right. Somebody said you moved like a professional."

"Go on, it was just a lucky punch."

"I'd like to talk to you."

"Some other time. I'm busy."

"I can be there in ten minutes."

"Don't trouble yourself. Some other time. I got nothing to say."

Next I called Ed Noonan, and got nowhere after talking to him for five minutes. He wasn't going to tell me who Billie's friend was, and I couldn't make him. So I went into the restaurant.

By now I was beginning to recognize faces belonging to members of the film company. Peggy's two women were pulling apart a club sandwich. I was glad to see movie people ate on the cheap when they could, like everybody else.

"Good evening, Mr. Cooperman." I turned around wondering how I'd got so famous all of a sudden. It was Raxlin, the producer. Tonight he wasn't sitting with his problems, he was half-way through a pink grapefruit. He waved his hand at the empty seat opposite him and I took it.

"I hear that I missed some excitement last night." His smile looked a little shifty as he bantered. I wondered why he was eating grapefruit so late in the day. Was this breakfast in movieland?

"I don't think he was hurt. He walked away."

"Sure, I fixed him an ice-pack in my suite. We had story problems, otherwise I'd have let him get to bed. We didn't break up until three a.m. He took some sleeping pills I gave him. Regular prescription. What else could I do?" He looked at me for sympathy, so I shook my head at the crazy things people will do for a few million bucks.

"It can't be easy keeping things afloat these days."

"Things never float. They do everything but float. I've got backers on my neck who don't go for the international stuff, investors that want the crime element played down, others that don't like the sex angle. As far as I'm concerned, I can live with the sex, but what are backers if they don't try to spoil your appetite. I've got a new assistant director, who may have to return to L.A. to testify in a dangerous driving case. So what if he's never worked with Sayre before. Furlong, poor Neil, dies every time I talk of changing one comma in his script. Peggy's agent wants the part 'modified'. Victoria St. Omer doesn't like working outside. Dawson Williams is drinking. Sometimes I think that Sayre doesn't want to make this picture at all. If he wasn't the best there is, I'd be worried. Everybody wants something. Everybody knows exactly what he doesn't want to see in this picture, but can't tell me what he does." I thought he was going to pop a couple of pills about now, but he didn't. Give him another year or so.

"I spent four years putting this package together. When

I picked on Furlong, he was a TV writer, a non-starter in the picture business. Now he's a name, with a play running on Broadway. Did you see it? Terrible cast. I don't know what they were doing up there on the stage. And the girl: she was an embarrassment. You know her agent tried to get her a part in this picture. Honestly, I tell you, you try to be polite and go backstage. Nothing would make me break up this cast. Okay, so I took a chance on Miranda. I couldn't get insurance, but what the hell, I did it for Neil. This is the most important picture she'll ever make. It could be a come-back. She needs the picture more than it needs her. That's between you and me. Neil's written a honey of a story. I'm just worried that it may be coming true."

When the waitress came, I ordered spaghetti and coffee. Raxlin ordered a soft-boiled egg of precisely three minutes to be served with dry whole-wheat toast. We both watched the bow on the back of the girl disappear toward the kitchen.

"Did I hear straight that you're a detective?"

"You've got good ears."

"So, who are you detecting? Me? Peggy? Who? What's the matter, the cat's got your tongue?"

"Nothing to do with you. It's a private matter."

"In a pig's eye. Private. Nothing's private. You want to know something? I'm impotent. I can't get it up anymore. How do you like that? I've got the best-looking girls in the world falling all over me and I'm as dangerous as an eunuch in a harem. I've got starlets and college girls crazy about me, and I'm embarrassed to say 'Okay, let's go.' So don't tell me about secrets, Mr. Cooperman. Listen. This afternoon I had two visitors. Two businessmen who very politely asked me to make changes in the script. How did they get the script? I don't know. But they had it all right. They had the parts they didn't like marked in blue pencil. Like professional editors. Only they weren't editors. They weren't asking me to make the changes, they were telling me. Like in that movie, they gave me an offer I couldn't refuse. Lawyers they looked like. Nobody raised his voice. That's why I'm asking you about your work. Are you looking for work, Mr. Cooperman?"

"First I have to find a missing wife. The husband paid me to find her. She's been bitten by the movie bug. That should interest you. She wants to get into pictures."

"Better she should take an overdose. It's quicker." Raxlin was trying hard to look twice his age, but in spite of the big city line he was shooting me, he looked like he'd been thrown out of a third-year commerce course. He'd learned to talk like a movie producer from the movies. He was going on about something called "golden time" as the food arrived.

"And this woman, the wife, are you close to finding her? How much longer is it going to take?"

"There are complications. Her boyfriend has just got himself murdered." Raxlin started beheading the top of his egg, which he did with all the panache of a real headsman.

"All I need is a killing," he said, like we'd been talking about a twist in the plot of Neil's script. "Today I had to arrange to kill a story about Peggy that would sink her and this picture. Straight blackmail, nothing in it, but I'll fight that out after the picture is in the can. So I bought time. When I'm not on the rack, I'll say 'print and be damned!' I'm in the picture business. What am I, a crusader? I beefed up security just in case. There must be more off-duty cops picking up an extra buck here than there are tourists in this town." Then he glanced up at me over the dripping opening in his egg. "Murdered? What are you talking about? Where?"

"Next door at the Tudor."

"They don't tell me anything that doesn't have to do with the picture. Who was he? Some local man? I hope they keep it under wraps. That's all I need, a killing. I'll have screaming backers." Raxlin was watching me chop up my spaghetti with the edge of my fork. "You should eat some fruit, have a salad. You're asking for trouble."

I couldn't figure him out: half the time he sounded as sensitive as a length of sewer pipe, then he'd surprise you.

"How many movies have you made?" I asked. He didn't choke, he just took a new bite of toast and chewed it thoughtfully.

"This is number eleven. My first four and my last four have all grossed between six and seven million. The other three I don't talk about. Better forgotten."

"How did you start?"

"My first picture I'm not so proud of. You know what a snuff movie is?" I shook my head.

"It's a low-budget horror-porno-sexploitation film with the rape and murder of a girl at the end. Horrible things. I've seen real ones from South America. Disgusting. But ours was only a fake. Nobody got hurt; it only looked that way. Girl called Moonflower in it. I'm ashamed to mention it. Though it made money. It made a lot of money. After that, I did *Brides in the Bath*. We did it mostly in 16 and blew it up to 35. We got a Wardour release on it and it went international. It grossed four million five in its first nine months. I followed that with *Mercenaries* with Jack Hogarth, then *Gestapo Agent*. For the last few years I've been doing musicals and science fiction. Why should I be any different? Did you see *Brother Can You Spare a Dime*? They didn't think I should leave the question mark in the title. Crazy. My last picture was *The Time Top* based on an old comic strip. Today, the funny papers is where you have to go to find properties."

"Tell me more about the thugs that called on you."

"They weren't thugs. They were businessmen. I've seen both. I know the difference." There was still a mark on the left side of his face where the businessmen had chipped their calculators. He might have gone on, but at that moment another of the walking wounded came into view. The bluish mark on Neil Furlong's chin suggested that Harvey Osborne had landed a left. He was wearing a brown corduroy jacket with a fuzzy turtle-neck jersey under it. He looked like he was going to cry. He sat down next to me facing Raxlin.

"Marvin, the police have taken Pye in for questioning."

"Miranda? You have to be joking. But why? What has she . . . ? What do they think she's done?" To me he added: "Miranda is Neil's wife." I nodded.

"She's not been arrested. But they've taken her in for questioning. It's about that shooting at the Tudor this morning. Miranda had talked to the man who was killed. If anything happens to her, I'll . . ."

"Take it easy. Nothing's going to happen." Raxlin was pumping up and down in his chair, not taking his own advice. "When did this happen?"

"A local cop, I don't remember his name . . ."

"Was it Savas?" I prompted.

"I don't know. Yes, I guess it could have been. Anyway, he said he had some questions he wanted to ask her. They talked in her suite for half an hour, and then she knocked on my door to say she'd been asked to go with the officer to assist in the investigation. That was around 7:30. It's nearly ten now and she's not back." ·

"I know Savas," I said. "He's a good cop. He won't frighten your wife. He won't hurt her."

"He hurts her and this town won't ever forget! I promise you that!" This was Raxlin. Furlong was just looking at the table. He tilted his head in my direction and nodded his thanks for the ounce of reassurance I'd given. It wasn't much to offer. I tried a question.

"How well did she know David Hayes?"

"That's the dead man?" said Furlong. I nodded. "She told me that she'd met a sensitive young man with talent. She was always meeting sensitive young men with talent. Good God, I was one of them. This one was a writer and actor and she said that she would try to help him. She asked if I could do him any good. But I've been so busy with this script and all the changes . . ." Raxlin cleared his throat.

"If that's all there is, I wouldn't worry. She might even be enjoying herself."

"Not Pye. Those things just make her anxious. Marvin, will you call up the mayor and see if he can do anything? I wouldn't ask for myself."

"Sure, Neil. Naturally, I'll get her out of there right

away." Raxlin dropped a few bills on the table and left the room. Furlong and I sat side by side without saying anything for a few minutes. The waitress bringing coffee led us back toward the here and now.

"It's a shame," I said lamely. Furlong didn't answer for a few seconds. He shook his head slowly.

"Pye picked me up when I was just trying to get my foot on the ladder. She saw me through hundreds of hard times. She tried to help this local actor too. She's always been like that."

"Don't worry about it. Savas can see through brick." Furlong glanced at me with disbelief, then excused himself. I didn't manage to out-grope him for the check. He looked like he was off to spend the evening in his room with the Gideon bible.

In a few minutes, Raxlin was back. I told him that Furlong was still very upset and had probably returned to his room.

"I'll give him a couple of minutes to get there, then I'll call him. It's amazing the doors Neil's name opens up in this town. I spoke to the mayor, I'd been at his home for dinner a few nights ago, but it was Neil's name that got his attention. It must be wonderful being the white-haired boy in your own home town."

"I don't think this is serious. Unless she really was involved."

"With Miranda you have to watch out. She's always taking a flyer on somebody. Lasts two, three days, then, poof. Neil's right. She'll tumble for a half-starved genius the way I used to go for blondes with high, squeaky voices. I'm still a push-over for a funny voice. Neil's had a hard time with her over the years. He still looks out for her. Wrote in a part for her in *Ice Bridge*. It fits Miranda like a glove."

"He calls her Pye."

"Yeah, funny. Remember her in the *Sally* pictures? That was a beautiful series. Must have been a dozen of them. Yeah, when he was a nobody, she was big. She helped him to get to be as big in the business as she was. She knew everybody. And when he got big, she started to slide. Booze did it. Drugs. Classic story. She got pushed aside by all the young stuff coming up. But Peggy O'Toole herself should look as good as Miranda does at her age. She hasn't done a picture in eight years. She's a good actress. What do you mean? When you can act, you're not finished at forty-five. Her, I'm not worried about; but most of them: poof! Who'll even remember?"

eleven

I had a vague idea of calling it a night. I'd been hob-nobbing with the likes of Neil Furlong and talking about his wife, Miranda Pride, like I was a member of the family. It was heady stuff, if you weren't preoccupied by a body in the morgue and a reckoning just twelve hours off. I went through the back door of the Colonel John, taking the time-honoured shortcut to my car. I don't know when I became aware that my footsteps were echoing and that the echo belonged to two pairs of footsteps that had fallen in behind me. It was chilly and my breath hung in the air like a balloon in a comic strip. The footsteps didn't get closer. They didn't go away.

There was a salt-stained Chevy pulled up in front of my Olds, but I wasn't seriously blocked: the driver was still behind the wheel and the motor was purring. As I was about to pass, the door opened on the driver's side and a pallid, lank-haired stringbean got out and stood in my path. I began to get annoyed. There was no way by him, and he didn't look as though he was going to alter the rate of his gum-chewing for me, let alone move out of the road. He looked like a walking definition of dumb insolence. So I turned around. One of the guys behind me had opened the back door of the Chevy. I was boxed in. Two unfriendly grins met my eyes over the open door. Suddenly I wasn't angry any more. I was scared.

"We don't want any trouble," the voice of the driver said in my ear. I was going to respond. I could already feel a big sunflower exploding to life behind my right ear. My hands were half-way up to cover my face, when I heard my name.

"Benny! Yoo hoo! Pistachio! Benny Cooperman!"

"Shit!" said the driver. I tilted my still un-sapped head

in the direction of the voices. The first thing I saw were uniforms, police uniforms, four of them. They were standing on the steps of the hotel's back door, with two other figures I couldn't at once make out. The uniforms were advancing.

"We'll catch you up later," the driver said. "Scarper." I heard shoes scraping on the gravel and skidding through the slush. Car doors slammed shut.

"We're over here, Benny. What's the matter?"

I coughed up some dust from the exhaust abandoned by the car that had been blocking me. I still had the Spearmint breath of the driver in my nostrils and his message, "We'll catch you up later," was sinking in deeper. The sunflower of pain hadn't exploded in my head, but I felt as though it had. "Benny, are you trying to high-hat us?" It was Peggy O'Toole in a lumberjack's mackinaw and knitted cap with Dawson Williams standing with the cops slightly behind her. I felt like hugging all of them. With the car of my would-be abductors pulled suddenly off the face of Thursday night, it left a large space of gravel, ice and slush between us. I cut the distance down by getting my stunned body moving again.

"I say, your friends left in a hurry. I hope it wasn't on our account." Williams was blinking a little under the mercury lights of the parking lot. They made even Peggy's golden skin look blotchy. "We were just on our way to find some low life. Want to join us? The officer here was trying to talk us out of it." I couldn't tell whether Williams recognized me from the other night or not. Maybe he assumed he knew everybody since everybody knew him.

"Hello there, Pistachio," she said, and that's all she had to say. My cheek where she'd kissed me goodnight began to burn all over again. "Dawson's heard of a wonderfully low place on the other side of town."

"It's not the safest place in the city," said one of the uniforms to me with a grim look. Dawson Williams clapped the officer on the back and assured him that they would be fine. "Well," said the policeman, with a glance at his mates, "we'll try to keep an eye on you from outside. We don't like to go into those places unless there's a riot going on inside."

"Officer," said Dawson, "don't give it a second thought. If I can't handle the situation, I shouldn't be allowed out after dark."

I slipped the cops a look of confidence and a grin to Peggy and Dawson. I joined in, flanking Peggy's left side, and following them to a compact Buick that looked clean enough to be rented. I took a fast glance over my shoulder to see if we were being watched, then slipped into the seat beside Peggy. Williams took the wheel and backed with authority out of the tight corner he was wedged into. The cops were climbing into an unmarked car parked on the street. They kept in the curb lane and followed us into traffic.

"Did you hear about Miranda?" Peggy asked. I nodded.

"They wouldn't treat her that way if she was a nobody," Dawson Williams offered. "These places are all alike. Coat-tails are for climbing on, what?"

"She's probably back at her hotel by now. The police aren't going to hold her unless someone saw her waving the smoking gun."

"Well, they *did* know one another, you know," Williams said, without taking his eye off the road.

"About as well as you did?"

He fired a look at me.

"Me? I didn't know him from Adam, old boy. Oh! A fleeting introduction perhaps. But if you're thinking of the other evening, that's as close as we ever got. Miranda was having one of her famous three-day infatuations. You know the old proverb: Hot love is soonest cold."

"Dawson, you didn't tell me you knew the dead man? What was he like?"

"Now, Peggy, don't embroider it. I met him with your friend here. He was drunk, insulting, then sick. Cooper-man here trundled him off to bed with the maître d'."

"I miss all the excitement," Peggy pouted.

"My dear Peggy, you very often are the excitement. I

shouldn't carry on about it if I were you. We're nearly there."

Outside the windows the neon-lit signs had been flashing by. I hadn't been paying too much attention, except to notice that the further we got from the parking lot the better I felt. He pulled off the main street into a side-alley and parked. "This will do," he said putting on the emergency brake.

Peggy put her arm through mine and Williams led the way down the block. He paused in a sheltered doorway and pulled Peggy and me after him. "Here you are, old girl. Try that on." When she grinned at me she was wearing a false nose which took me by surprise. It wouldn't pass a close-up test, but from where I was it transformed her completely. I was hardly used to the new Peggy when the new Dawson appeared in heavy-rimmed plastic glasses. He looked Peggy over expertly. "That will do very well. It's not perfection but in an odd way it suits you, my dear." He tweaked the nose playfully then continued the safari. "Just stay close to us and no giggling, mind. From what I've heard, this place is deliciously low. Don't give in to panic. Keep calm. These places can go off like a bomb."

I was so surprised by the disguises that I let myself be led into the droning din of the Men's Beverage Room at the Clifford Arms, the hotel with my pyjamas in Room 209. The noise and smoke surrounded us like a featherbed. Waiters dressed in white carried crowded trays of draft beer, dropping rounds into the midst of disputes and smoky anecdotes. I scouted for a table.

"Benny Cooperman, as I live and breathe! Have a beer! Have two!" It was Ned Evans, the director of *A Midsummer Night's Dream*, surrounded by his Grantham cronies. Wally had warned me. Peggy and Dawson shot me the same surprised look of alarm. They had been on the lookout for low-life, but was this stretching it? Dawson looked around the room, a little worried about being recognized and about not being recognized.

Ned hopped up from his chair, letting the weight of his parka tip it over backwards. Jack Ringer, whose father ran the bookstore, cleared coats from chairs and shifted the furniture so that Peggy, Dawson and I could settle. Will Chapman, a little dried-up man with red bird-tracks on his cheeks and nose, was staring into his beer until he felt the table rattle, then he looked up and saw the three of us without surprise. Peggy's eyes were bright as she wolfed down a draft. Dawson and I sipped ours.

"Well, I guess you're all here for the same reason," Ned said, nodding like a magistrate. "Ed Noonan told me we can all depend on at least five days' work. But there won't be any contracts. We're just casual local labour."

From Ned's ape-like bouncing up and down as he talked, I could tell that he and the boys had started their drinking some time ago. Jack eyed Peggy suspiciously, while Ned seemed to take everybody on faith. Will sat like he was sipping through a stuffed straw and could see the world in his glass.

"Benny," said Ned, "I'm thinking of doing *Richard III* in the spring. What do you think?" He hiked his right shoulder up and dropped his chin so that I'd get the idea. Peggy smiled over at Dawson, who winked at me. "I will, of course, play Dirty Dick myself, with Monica Bett re-creating the role of Lady Anne. We once did a scene at the Library together: 'Poor keycold figure of a holy king!' You know the bit."

"Ned used a dummy from Hoffman's store for the corpse on a litter," I explained to Dawson and Peggy. "Only one night Jack here took the dummy's place. After Ned pulled the sheet away, he needed a dry costume." Ned swished a swallow of beer around the front of his teeth. He smiled sleepily at the sight of us laughing.

"I remember hearing of a performance of *Salomé*," said Dawson, "that went off the rails when the tray supposed to hold the head of John the Baptist was revealed to bear a stuffed bull terrier instead." Ned joined in that time, leaning his big head back into the conversation. Jack repeated the punchline to Will. Peggy seemed to be enjoying herself, although she sometimes sniffed at Will's jacket. Her rubber nose was slipping, but it didn't matter;

in a place like this nobody looked at anything that required focussing. Even the waiters, who swam above most of the smoke like white icebergs in the flood, ignored the customers' faces. They only saw money and empty glasses.

"Benny," Ned said, "I see you as Lord Mayor of London. You could carry a cat. I think it was Dick Whittington. I'll have to look it up. Or do you want to be one of the Murderers? I've promised Clarence to Jack."

"That's right," said Jack." 'What, shall we stab him as he sleeps?' "

Now I'm not all that familiar with the *Complete Works of Shakespeare* and I've known Ned long enough to place a heavy lid of caution on my theatrical ambitions. Ned does a couple of plays a year, but he plans a new production every night. One time he was going to shock everybody by having Lady Macbeth eight months pregnant in the early part of the play, then have her do the sleepwalking scene after a miscarriage. A few months later he was hot about doing *The Merchant of Venice* with Gratiano, the pal of the leading man, played as though he was a Jew trying to pass as a Gentile, and wasn't fooling as many people as he thought. Ned was a gift to a small place like Grantham. We were lucky he could step in when Monty Blair died.

"You heard about David Hayes, Ned?"

"Yes. That's a tragic loss. That boy had talent."

"He was as tight as a Dublin tinker," added Will without looking up. "He owes me ten bucks."

"Will, the man is dead. Forgive and forget," said Ned. Will didn't even shrug.

"How well did you know him?"

"He was in *Streetcar*. That was a terrible show. The Ferret did it with scrims and loud music. He got a decent Mitch from David, I'll say that much." The Ferret was Ned's name for Robin O'Neil, his chief rival as a theatrical magnate in our community.

"Tight as a Dublin tinker. Ten bucks," said Will.

"Shut up, Will." When Will had been drinking, his conversation snagged on a line and he kept repeating himself for the rest of the night.

"The Ferret added a funeral procession at the end."

"Back to the libretto. What else do you know about Hayes?" Ned shrugged his big shoulders and looked at Williams for sympathy.

"Monty thought he was the brightest coin to pass through his hands since Neil Furlong went off to Hollywood by way of Toronto."

"Ah yes: Furlong is a local boy," said Williams. "What sorts of things did he do in his salad days?"

"He owes me ten bucks," said Will, his nose not an inch from the rim of his glass.

Ned and Jack seemed to recognize something in Will's behaviour that brought both of them to their feet at once.

"Come on, Will," said Jack, "We're going to see a man." He and Ned pulled at an arm and Will came to life, rising out of his chair like mist above a sewer. "We'll be right back," Jack said, putting a two-dollar bill on the table so we'd remember him. Together they shuffled into the smoke in the direction of a running toilet.

"Pistachio," Peggy said, "Neil Furlong was the first grown man to ask me for a date. I was scared to death, I mean, 'Why me?' Mom knew his first wife and he was married to Miranda Pride. Mom said that he had more brass than a hundred-foot yacht."

"Who was his first wife?" I asked. "I never heard about her."

"I love gossip, don't you, Dawson?"

"Oh, no, my dear. I've *been* gossip." He looked around like he was looking for an interruption with an autograph book.

"When Mom was a secretary at Paramount, Blanche Tyler was her best friend. A long time after that, Blanche was in television and married to Neil. She was executive producer on the Basil Simpson series. Remember that?"

"Basil Simpson, 'the internationally-known lawyer-sleuth'," Dawson intoned. "God, the world really was young once, wasn't it?"

"Pistachio, if you were me, would you have gone out with a divorced and remarried man? Ever since Mom got religious, I can never tell what ordinary reactions will be. And you can never tell what the papers will do with an item like that."

"He seems like a friendly enough guy to me."

"Friendly!" Peggy exclaimed. "The trouble with men is they aren't women."

"You're a philosopher, my dear," said Dawson, finishing another draft of beer and setting the empty glass down harder than he'd intended.

"And Dawson," she said to me, "is the best pro in the business."

"Oh, come now."

"It's true. You never get cross with me when I blow a line. You give me the camera all the time. Dawson, you're the best. Last summer I did *The Lion's Share*. The director treated me like an idiot, my co-star wouldn't talk to me and used every cheap trick in the book to mask me so that you needed a program to see that I was in the damned thing. And the producer kept coming on with 'sweety this' and 'sweety that'. It was torture. I think *Ice Bridge* is going to be lucky for me. You know, Dawson, I'll bet it'll be lucky for all of us."

"It's cold. Especially down on the river. I can't take it the way I used to."

"Oh, Dawson, you should see yourself out there. You carry all of us. Mr. Sayre depends on you. You're the best there is, and I'm so proud to be working with you. It gives me goose-bumps every time I think of it." Dawson looked pleased.

"Thank you, my dear," he said. Then we were listening to the racket of the room all around us. I sipped my beer. Peggy and Dawson started new ones.

"Will's cute," said Peggy. "But he should send his suit to the cleaners."

"I remember one year Ned did a history of theatre on the radio in ten weeks. Will was in it. We all helped out." I felt an urge to explain my friends. I hadn't set up this meeting and I felt uncomfortable. "Monty Blair, who discovered Neil, directed the plays."

"That sounds like such fun," said Peggy, "It must be wonderful coming from a small town where you have to make your own entertainment. Tonight's going to help me a lot with Karen Brophy. I mean, it's a whole new dimension."

"Karen Brophy?" I asked. I thought I'd seen the name somewhere not so long ago. "Any relation to Alden Cory?"

"I say, that's me, old boy," said Dawson. "Peggy's right. I'm glad we came. Have to soak up the atmosphere."

"And what about Rosemary Beattie and Tony D'Abruzzi?"

"You've got the names. Where'd you get them?" I reached into my breast pocket and waved a wrinkled paper placemat at them.

"What can you tell me about them?" I asked in a voice that didn't quite sound like my own.

"You mean you don't know who they are?" Peggy said, with a superior and sidelong glance at Dawson. I should have given her the award for answering a question with a question. I tried to withhold the look of exasperation from my nod.

"Why they're the names of the characters in *Ice Bridge*."

"That's right, old boy; I'm Alden and Peggy's Karen. Have you seen the script then?"

"Right now I don't know what I've seen." And I remembered suggesting two of the names to that fellow from the CBC. "I wonder," I said out loud, "what David Hayes was doing with those names."

From nowhere, Ned, Jack and Will were back in their places. Drinking beer edits out loops of time. Another dozen full glasses had appeared.

"This round's on me, Ned," said Dawson. "I want to hear more about *Richard III*. Will you use the usual pieces from *Henry VI*? And what about that rigmarole at the end?" Ned looked at Williams darkly. I don't think he'd ever been challenged before. "I saw a production once . . ." Ned sank deeper into his chair as Dawson began to expand, telling stories about the Old Vic, the Royal Shakespeare Company as well as funny stories about the first sound version of

Romeo and Juliet "with additional dialogue by Sam Taylor." Ned wasn't used to hearing about the world of greasepaint beyond Grantham. But stories are stories, and soon they were taking turns trading anecdotes while the rest of us drank our beer and listened.

"Well, you know your theatre, I'll say that for you," said Jack, a grin animating his blunt face.

"It's in the blood, old boy," said Dawson, expanding with sleepy eyes. "My great-grandfather played Macbeth at Covent Garden in 1857." Will made a wheezy snort.

It was now past midnight, and Ned suggested that we all go across the street for spaghetti. We got up. Ned's chair tumbled backwards again. He and Jack lifted Will between them. Peggy fumbled with the unfamiliar buttons of her mackinaw.

The walk out of a pub is always shorter than the walk into one. Before you know it the night air is nipping at your cheeks. We hurried across the street in a clump and found an empty table in the back of the restaurant. It was decorated with empty Chianti bottles and mended red and white tablecloths. The waitress was sleepy and bored. She looked as Italian as plum pudding. It was my second spaghetti dinner of the evening, but it had been a crazy day from the beginning. I needed something to sit on the beer.

"There is an excellent likeness of David Garrick in the Royal Collection," Williams confided to the company, wagging a finger in the air near Ned's half-closed eyes. "Ralph Richardson says it hangs outside the Queen's bedroom at Buckingham Palace. I assume she told him." Peggy was yawning openly, but relaxed. Jack was staring straight down at his congealed pizza and Will, sitting between them, was fast asleep, like the Dormouse in *Alice in Wonderland*. I was examining the tomato-sauce stains on my tie and wondering if they would come out with lighter fluid.

"Will youse be wantin' anythin' else?" asked the girl.

Will awoke with a start. He looked with heavy eyes at all of us, like we'd been glimpsed in a dream that had come true. He finally settled on Dawson. "Covent Garden," he said in a voice pulled thin. "Covent Garden burned down in 1856." He smiled up at Peggy. "And the new theatre wasn't finished until 1858." Then he retreated back to sleep again. And then the bill came.

It was after 1:00 a.m. when they finally said goodnight. The four cops were still parked outside. The glass of the windshield was steamed up. I walked Peggy and Dawson to their car, then went up to my room, where I fell into a deep sleep without even trying.

Some time later I awoke out of a comfortable dream and felt a minty breath on my face and heard the words in the parking lot again: "We'll catch you up later." I looked around and there was nobody in the room. I turned on the light and confirmed the fact. The rest of the night was fitful, with tangled bedclothes and sweaty pyjamas. Visions of Peggy were banished by a dark Chevy opening its doors like jaws and pulling me inside.

twelve

It was a well-storm-windowed house on Brock Street, one of those tiny bungalows that has been looked after to death. The sidewalk had been shovelled and the steps cleared of snow and ice. The cement porch was newly patched and painted; fake awnings in green stripes matched the swan on the aluminum screen door. I knocked on the brass knocker.

Harvey Osborne hardly looked like a man who would throw a punch at a popular screenwriter as he stood in his shirtsleeves in the doorway, blinking at the early morning light. He looked surprised, and well he might, since he wasn't expecting me.

"I'm Cooperman. The guy who telephoned. You told me not to bother coming around. But, you see, it's no bother." He backed his two hundred pounds out of the doorway. It wasn't an invitation to follow him into the house; not a *prima facie* invitation, but he hadn't closed the door behind him. He'd gone through the small hallway into the front room. He wasn't much over five-feet five, but his shoulders were big and his arms hadn't turned to fat. The room told me that he lived alone: a television set was crowned with an ashtray and an empty foil tray from a frozen TV dinner. Only the piano looked out of place, but the potted plants on the piano bench told me that nobody played it any more. He was shaking his head from side to side.

"I shouldn't have hit him. It was a wrong move. I want to get Furlong, but that's not the way."

"What's he to you?"

"Ha! That's a laugh! 'What's he to me?' It's my girl, Dulcie. She's dead and I hold Neil Furlong responsible. Oh, I know he isn't guilty in the legal way, wasn't even there, but I sniffed bad news the first time I heard his name." He hadn't asked my business yet, but I thought that it was a bad time to remind him. "That's her picture on the piano." I looked between a metronome and a bronze attendance medal and saw a young, pleasant, dark-haired girl looking past me into the void. "That was taken two years before the accident, just before she met Furlong." He let me digest that, then launched into a story about how his talented daughter had been lured by young Furlong from honorable paths to those that led to the stage. "In our whole family, we never held with dancing or getting up on a stage. Music's different. Music is, well . . . I told her I didn't want her acting foolish in a theatre." Harvey had reworked this tale more than once, with and without an audience. He seemed to swell like a bullfrog in the telling of it. Neil was doing public relations for the railway then and doing plays on the side. Dulcie fell in love with him. Furlong left town for Toronto. "Young kids think they know everything," he said reaching out to me to match his emotion. "Well, Dulcie was all upset. Next thing I heard was that she'd been killed in an accident on the Lewiston Road driving Furlong's old Ford. There's a bad turn between Lewiston and Youngstown."

"But it's not as if Furlong killed her."

"Well, he didn't take a gun and shoot her. But she's just as dead. It's all the same to me. If it hadn't been for him and his high and mighty ideas, I'd still have my girl. Do you wonder that I hate the man? I swore I'd kill the bastard if I ever got the chance, and I will."

I tried not to look shocked. I did it so well he settled down into an overstuffed chair beside me, sitting so close I could see fresh razor nicks at the ends of his sideburns and the frayed edges of his shirt cuffs. "Furlong's not liked in this town. It's not just me," he said, with a look at the wilted plants on the piano bench. "You ever hear of Clark Mattingly?" I shook my head. "Clark worked at the Upper Canadian Bank, assistant manager. At the time I'm talking about, he'd been there over fifteen years. He fell for a woman that worked in a bar over the river. Place called the Surf Lounge. Clark lost his senses over her. The upshot was that he took some money that wasn't rightly his to take and he served a term in the penitentiary at Kingston. The man made a mistake and paid for it. Go into any town and you can find out the same sort of thing if you ask the right people. Nothing unusual about it. The insurance people must have figures on how it happens one-point-something times for every hundred thousand population. Doesn't matter. When Clark got out, he tried to pay people back. Then one night the whole town was treated to a TV play by Neil Furlong. Oh, he changed the names, you know. He didn't say it was the Falls. He called it Cataract City. Now that might have fooled the cat if it was asleep. Clark couldn't take it. It was like it was happening to him all over again. Killed himself with a cut-throat razor. There hasn't been a television play or a movie of his that didn't make this town wince one way or another."

"But if there's been a genuine libel, there are courts to deal with things like that."

"You can't libel the dead, and Furlong was clever when it came to the living. Don't think a lot of us didn't think of it more than once. I hear this new movie he's written has things in it that shouldn't be anybody else's business. I hear that he's taken a few people he knew and put them down on paper. Oh, he's going to get it one day. I hope I get to him first, that's all."

I drove back toward the hotel. Icicles were dripping along Lundy's Lane. Merchants were digging notches in the snowbanks left by the snow-plough to let their customers cross the street. In a long narrow restaurant I had my morning coffee and a bran muffin. I hadn't noticed that there were bagels until I'd put strawberry jam on the muffin. There was a drawing of the Parthenon on the paper placemat. I started thinking of Hayes again. Everything moved me in that direction. Even the time. Savas was sitting behind his desk waiting for my call. That's what my watch told me. The man listening to the Greek hit parade pointed the way to the pay phone.

"Benny, I'm proud of you. You're right on time." Savas sounded happy. I wondered what was cooking.

"I always pay up, Chris. I was brought up in Ontario. It's in my blood."

"Well, I've cooled off since I spoke to you. We've been busy ourselves. Found out things. You know."

"You sound pretty happy."

"Oh, things are ticking along on the Hayes case. I think we've got a positive identification of the woman coming out of Hayes' room around the time of the murder. A couple of other things are pointing in the same direction. So, I'm less interested in what you plan to contribute than I was."

"So, you think Miranda Pride bumped Hayes, eh?"

"That's what you think I think. Me? I'm not speaking to the private sector until I know for sure. Where the hell are you phoning from? I know that music."

"Have you given any thought to the possibility that the mob might be involved in this?"

"It's Theodorakis. I know the words. You want me to sing it?"

"You never sing the song I want to hear. What about the mob? Somebody tried to take me for a ride last night."

"You should never take a lift with strangers, Benny."

"Okay, you've clammed up. Damn it all, Chris, I get bad vibes from this whole lousy set-up. We're only looking at the tip of the iceberg . . ."

"And it's called *Ice Bridge*, right?"

I was five minutes early for my meeting with Billie Mason in the coffee shop at the Colonel John. I ordered coffee, had it refilled, and tried some cinnamon toast. I told the waitress I was waiting for somebody and she let me wait without pushing more than a third and fourth cup of coffee on me. The place was beginning to fill up with the noon crowd. Some of them were connected with the film company and I overheard snippets of conversations from nearby tables.

". . . Charming! Well, at least I don't have to meet the cameras at six in the morning . . ."

". . . I sympathize with you one hundred per cent. It could take twelve corporation lawyers a year to figure it out . . ."

". . . It was a certified blockbuster, number three in *Variety's* list of top rentals . . ."

After the first forty-five minutes, I could feel my stomach tightening. It wasn't the coffee. She wasn't going to show. I tried the idea out from several directions, and I didn't like any of the possibilities. I kept seeing the beanpole from the parking lot leaning against the open door of his car, slowly chewing gum. The restaurant was crowded to the cash desk when I paid the bill. As I came out, sucking a free mint, I remembered that I had a fall-back position. She had a hair appointment at 2:15. Somehow the feeling in my middle didn't go away and I discarded the mint in an ashtray.

My watch was ticking at half-speed as I sat in the lobby of the Colonel John watching limos arrive at the front door to pick up and deliver small-part players. They stood inside the revolving door, away from the other hotel guests, joking among themselves. Uniformed cops stood near the door to see that nobody lifted it because Peggy O'Toole had walked through. I had over an hour to kill and I'd already spent half an hour on the first ten minutes. I took my anxiety outside to cool down. I walked the quarter mile to where the limos were parked and where the lights and reflectors were set up.

From what I could tell, there was a lot of standing around and waiting in making a movie. Nobody seemed to mind. The formula, according to Wally Skeat, who had passed me through the line of cops standing near the generator truck, was "Hurry up and wait". He didn't claim that as original, just true. The camera was being moved to a new position near the parapet, shooting back toward the park and the false front of the motel which had now been landscaped so well it looked like it lived there. Bundled up in Anoraks, minks and blankets, Peggy O'Toole, Adela and Jim Sayre were sitting around in a circle with Victoria St. Omer and some of the others in the scene. I kept out of the way when I saw some flunkies grab a skinny journalist with a tape-recorder and chat him right across the road and back to his car. He didn't know what had happened until he was back on the highway. From my corner, I could hear pretty well.

"Well, how do you like that, Dawson? Does it feel right?"

"It's just a trifle short, Jim. I'd feel better with three or four more words to get me all the way across. I've tried spreading the speech, but I sound like I'm trying to draw attention to myself. I suggest you either cut the line completely, or give me a few words to play with."

"Such as?"

"Oh, maybe a joke directed at the falls. Something like: 'We can always go look at the falls.'

"Adela, would you make a note of that, please?" Adela, wearing half-moon glasses on a black string, wrote into her big loose-leaf binder.

"Mr. Sayre," asked Peggy, "why don't I just go up to him, or take a couple of steps closer. That would make it easier."

"I think we could use the longer line, Marilyn. So far the scene has been run on looks and shrugs. You might cheat a little closer to him in the reaction shot. But we won't get there for an hour." His voice was calm and soft, softer than when he was yarning in the bar in fact. You got the idea that they could just sit there and talk things over until the ice bridge broke up and was carried away. "Well, let's read it through again just so we know where we are." And they did that. Then the cameraman came up to announce that everything was ready. Adela got up and went into the back of a truck, from which in a second I could hear typing. I felt hot breath on my ear, and, turning, I caught a big grin from Neil Furlong.

"Good morning, or I guess I should say, good afternoon. You were right, about Pye."

"What time did she get back?"

"It wasn't much after ten. That Savas is a reasonable

fellow. He said that Pye'd been a big help." When you looked at Furlong up close, the smooth skin broke down into a map of fine lines whenever he smiled. We both watched the crew move around the camera. The grips hunched over their coffee when they could, or retreated to the generator van. One guy hunkered like a wrangler at a rodeo with a cigarette held between red fingers.

"In the old days," Furlong said, "we'd have had to bring down a crew three times this size." I made a gesture to show my interest. "We'd have needed a camera blimp to protect the sound track and a crew of four men to move each of the brutes."

"Brutes?"

"The big lights. Four men each. Union rules. Lighting's changed in the last few years," he added. His eyes were lazy triangles that looked half-shut as he squinted into the scene. "We get greater intensity now with lighter equipment. Film's faster too, doesn't need the set to be so hot — I mean bright."

In silence we watched Peggy. She was now standing near the parapet with Sayre, who was talking to her steadily. Apart from occasional nods, she didn't show much animation. In fact she looked like a statue or a painting in a museum. She was wrapped in a studio blanket, under which she was wearing a mink coat over a long party dress of midnight blue. Her woollen mittens didn't go with the ensemble. She waved one of them in our direction when Sayre turned to hear from the assistant director. Then Adela rejoined the group at the parapet, delivering new pages of script to Sayre, who nodded thanks.

"Sayre owes that woman a lot," Neil said to nobody in particular. He looked a little sheepish when he realized that he'd spoken his thought aloud. "She can put him back together blindfolded, the way a soldier can reassemble an automatic rifle. They've been married and divorced so often I don't think anybody knows what the official status is at the moment."

"Can't get along without each other, eh?"

"That's the good side. Loyalty, absolute loyalty. She'd

cut throats for him if necessary. She nursed him back to life three or four times and fought her way into a faddist health sanatorium once to drag him away from snake-oil cures and a daffy broad with a nice set of knockers."

"Why aren't you writing the new lines?"

"Oh, that isn't writing, that's just blocking with words. The real writing is the conception that brings them out here in the first place. What the actors say is the least of it. It's a question of scene following scene following scene. Within the scene, at this stage the writer stands clear. Nobody tells James A. Sayre where to put his camera."

Behind me, I could hear a couple of the make-up boys sniggering. Furlong went to find out why, and came back smiling. "It's Williams. Every time he takes a poke from that flask of his, it goes right to his nose. Bluey, the make-up guy, says he's got it worked out to the ounce; so much drink equals so much pancake."

To my left, a grip was spraying wax on a highlight reflecting the sun from a car's windshield. The spray didn't help, so he tore off a length of black masking tape and ran it along the bright spot. He made a wide enough patch so that the movements of the sun during the next half-hour wouldn't require the job to be done over again. Furlong saw me looking, and smiled, before walking back to the hotel. "So now you know what goes on behind the screen."

Somebody yelled, "Quiet! *Ice Bridge*. Shot 51. Take 1."

thirteen ────────

By two o'clock I had parked outside the chain-link fence of a school yard a few blocks from Centre Street. It was deserted except for a red cap stuck in the fence. The abandoned ice slide was grey and lonesome. So were the covered drinking fountain, the brick wall and the sky. I lit a cigarette and opened the car window to let the smoke escape. A huge icicle hung from the eaves of the school where it made an angle with the street. The cold hand of mid-winter was on the small of my back. In the glove compartment I found my Alekhine. I tried to remember when I played my last chess game. I flipped through the pages, not really taking anything in. Chess seemed a million miles away, where it was possible to build a strong centre and advance with more than hope.

I hardly knew Hayes. I'd just met him, only had one drunken conversation with him. There are probably lots of people more worthy of being alive than Hayes. Looking at Anton's sign I thought Martha Tracy had had the only useful idea in the whole case. Instead of waiting for Billie at the beauty parlour, I should be phoning her husband. That's what he's paying for. So, what's the big idea of me sitting here worrying about a murder that has nothing to do with Billie Mason. Nobody killed Hayes because of Billie. Billie couldn't leave Hayes fast enough. The Hayes problem was some other can of trash, not the one I'd been paid to pick through. I put *My Best Games of Chess* back where I found it in the glove compartment.

Across the street and around the corner, a woman with blue hair under a kerchief was entering Anton's Salon. If the mink coat she was wearing was completely paid for, she could afford to have the hairdresser come to her. The large plate-glass window was steamed up and a couple of pictures showing hairstyles cut from *Vogue* and other fashion magazines were curling at the edges from the humidity. I couldn't make out more than rose and green shapes through the dripping glass, so I went in. An old-fashioned bell, like in a country general store, jangled as I closed the door behind me. It was now 2:30 p.m.

The shop was a long rectangle on two levels decorated with weathered barn siding. A horse collar, a kerosene lantern, and a few other rustic touches completed the decor. Four women and two men in green coveralls were cutting a swath through twice that many women, who were draped in rose-coloured wrap-arounds. A lean young man with a comb in his breast-pocket looked up from cutting or perming — I didn't want to look too close — and came over wearing an easy smile.

"Are you lost? I don't remember seeing you before."

"I'd like a word with one of your customers, please. Miss Mason?" I smiled. He didn't stop smiling. He didn't twitch a muscle, but the impulse behind his expression died. He didn't move.

"I'd like a word with her myself. I rewrote my whole appointment book to fit her in and now she doesn't show. Some people, honestly. She didn't phone. Nothing. She said she needed emergency treatment, so I break my back trying to accommodate her, and it's not like she's an old and valued customer."

"Do you think she may have been held up? You know these theatrical people."

"Well, you don't hold me up more than once. That's a rule I have. You want to wait to see if she comes?" I nodded. He indicated a chair and I took it. He took another squint at his watch, looked as though he could bend aluminum pop cans and left me.

"Sorry we're fresh out of *Field and Stream*," one of the girls said in a few minutes. "Sherry will be going for coffee in about ten minutes. Would you like some?"

"Sure." In my chair — a refugee from a farmer's kitchen, but rubber-padded and covered with gingham — I began my re-education when I picked up the magazines.

There were new shades in nailpolish and lipstick for the spring. That was heartwarming. And facial cleansers were penetrating more deeply than ever this season. I read two movie reviews which told me nothing about the movie, but everything about the director's post-production depression. In an article called "Dressing for Less", I discovered that it was possible to buy an Oxford cloth shirt for only $48 and a linen blouse for $105. I skipped the piece about "Acupuncture for a Younger You" and gave Sherry two quarters as she left the store with her list. A cold wind blew the nests of cut hair away from the door. The woman with the blue hair eyed me suspiciously. Under the mink she was wearing a tan twin-set over slacks in a large hound's-tooth pattern. I stared back at her and she buried her head behind *Harper's Bazaar*.

Sherry returned with a large paper bag stapled closed with a bill attached. She found my regular coffee and gave me an extra package of sugar. It was hot and welcome. The woman behind *Harper's Bazaar* sneered at me as I drank my coffee. I didn't think I was making any noise. I don't know the etiquette for drinking from a Styrofoam cup. I didn't think she did either.

When I'd put my second cigarette butt into the cup, I saw the proprietor headed my way again.

"Well, it looks like she's disappointed both of us."

"How close is she to not being a blonde any more?"

"Oh, to hear her talk last week, she was within an ace of turning brunette before your very eyes. But I don't suppose she's that badly off. She needs a set more than other major repairs."

"Oil and transmission okay?" He shrugged, and snipped the scissors in his hand rapidly. "When did she come to see you the first time?"

"Let me think. Well, I know it was more than a week ago. She came in, had the complete treatment. Then she was back a few days later for a special job. That's right: it was New Year's Eve. She said she was out to impress some movie mogul or something. Said it was her big chance. So

I gave her my personalized service, and when she stepped out into the waiting limo that picked her up she was really stunning."

"A limo, you say?"

"Hired, of course, by the film people. That's what she said anyway. But her movie mogul was a cheapskate, if you ask me. I happened to be celebrating over the river that night with a few friends and I saw the same limo parked outside the Surf Lounge. I wouldn't go into that place if they had it fumigated. Tacky-tacky-tacky."

"Well, I guess she's not going to make it this afternoon."

"Tough titty, I say. I won't rearrange my book from now on. Well, I'd best get on with Mrs. Solmi."

"Mrs. Tullio Solmi?"

"The one and only."

"Then I guess you'd better."

The general store bell clanged behind me as I left Anton's Salon feeling like I'd come up with a few loose clues. The limo, for one, the bar across the river, and Mrs. Solmi. It was a strange sort of grab-bag and I couldn't put a value on it. This line of thinking was designed to put me off worrying about my major concern. It was good of my head to try to spare me, but I had to face it: Billie was in some new and deep trouble. Had the tall guy with the chewing gum caught up to her? I tried to think of other explanations that would fit with the facts of two missed appointments. The only explanation that made sense was the least attractive. Billie was either in a lot of trouble or nothing would ever bother her again.

Noonan was up to tricks. I didn't know him well enough to know that they were old tricks, but I suspected it. A very pretty redhead sat primly across the table Noonan was leaning on with both elbows. He looked like he was going to jump the gap and finish her off with one bite. I hated to interrupt, but there was no butler around to leave my card with. And the only maid wouldn't remain one long if I didn't butt in.

"I need a word with you, Ed." I'd moved up from Mister when I caught him covering for whomever Billie Mason was seeing.

"Oh, Mr. Cooperman. I didn't see you come in. Ruby, I want you to meet Mr. Cooperman. Ruby Stevens. That's right, isn't it? There's a lot of talent in the little lady, take it from me." Noonan tried to grin at me, but it was a dark grin from under heavy eyebrows. I could almost let up on him a little, he'd been caught redhanded. Ruby made an excuse to leave after Noonan muttered something to her while patting her hand over the table. He walked her to where the door would have been if there'd been a door, and returned to the table.

We were in a low, shed-like room, part of the government set-up near the Rainbow Bridge. There were some scattered tables with mirrors and make-up boxes on them, and a dozen tubular chairs with plywood bottoms, some against one wall, the rest where they'd been abandoned by the actors and crew of the film unit, who were using the space for changing and make-up. On one side was a luggage rack with letters of the alphabet strung out to aid the Customs officials. I could hear their voices coming from the other side of a partition, which corralled an office area near the front door, *for official use only*. The windows were few and institutional. There was a coating of bureaucratic dust everywhere.

"Nice kid," Noonan said, looking after Ruby. "Lots of heart. Now, ah, you were wondering about Mrs. Mason." I let him struggle with it. Confused people spill more than calm ones. "I tried to get your office. You're not sore, I hope, because I didn't help you get ahold of Billie the first time, are you, Mr. Cooperman? A job like mine has to deal with very sensitive stuff. It's a position of trust, really." He pulled a flask from his inside breast pocket and placed it on the table. "Let's talk this over calmly." He poured a shot into the cap and pushed it toward me with a desperate smile, trying to brighten that dark comical face. I didn't look at it. I somehow had the upper hand and I wasn't going to throw it away for an ounce of rye with Noonan's sweat on it. If he had no reason to be afraid of me, then it was the other guy he was worried about. The one he was covering for could buy and sell a flunky like Noonan and Noonan's white knuckles told me all about it.

"I can't hand out addresses to anyone who wants them," he continued, with both eyes shifting between me and the drink he'd poured me. "There's a dirty word for that kind of thing. But I've levelled with you since then. I haven't heard from Billie. I swear it."

"Has your friend heard from her? The guy you're covering for?"

"She hasn't been in touch. Changed her mind, just gone off."

"If she's gone off it's probably because she's in a ditch outside town. Get this through your head, Noonan: Billie's disappeared, vanished. She's been snatched. That kind of thing can't be covered up. You'd better get that news back to your pal. There's already been one murder, so they're not kidding around. I've got to talk to the Regional Police and I'm running out of harmless press releases for them. They want to pin that murder on somebody, and I don't want to sweat it out under the bright lights protecting a guy like you, a guy who won't even level with me."

"Cooperman, you got me all wrong."

"The way I see it, you're the perfect patsy in this business. You knew Hayes and you knew Billie. You thought you could do something for Billie, but the boyfriend had to go. It's rough, but I've seen rougher. It will hold you until the movie's finished, and that'll be too long for you."

"There was nothing between Billie and me. I can prove that."

"I'm not talking about proof. I'm talking about time. Time you can't afford to sacrifice right now. Time that won't ever come around for you again. Okay, maybe it's stretching it to say that you popped David Hayes, but the cops won't take long to figure out that you're fronting for another party, someone who will let you take it and take it without coming forward and saving your skin. So, you're a patsy, and you can only blame yourself." Noonan was breaking out in a shiny forehead, and I was getting his bad breath across the table: rye on top of Corn Flakes and milk.

"You've got to be reasonable. I can't tell you what I don't know."

"Fine. Fine. Play it that way. I won't push it. It's your look-out. But after today, there will be cops around asking the same questions, and you won't be able to stonewall them. They'll have you tucked up in the slammer so fast you'll leave your shoes where they're standing. By the time they finish with you, you can advise on the re-make of *Ice Bridge* as a musical."

"I'll have to phone somebody. I hear what you're saying, Cooperman. I'm not dense. But I'll have to talk to a certain party. Okay?

"Where will you be at eight tonight?"

"Wherever you say."

"Good. Meet me in the restaurant at the top of the Pagoda, the one that revolves."

"I'll be there. I will. I'll do what I can."

"I know you will, because you're not doing it for me, you're doing it for yourself. See you at eight."

I could almost see myself walking out of there. I don't know where I'd learned to talk like that. There is something about being on a movie set that brings the ham out in everybody, and I heard an echo of Raft and Bogart with a little Edward G. Robinson thrown in.

Across the street, I phoned my answering service — Lowell Mason had called, so had my mother. I'd almost forgotten I had one. And I was neglecting my client just as badly. There was a message to call Miranda Pride. I wondered what she wanted. I called her suite. No reply. She wasn't in any of the restaurants or coffee shops. I tried the bars in both the Colonel John and the Tudor. Nothing doing.

When I walked past the office of the Colonel John's

hotel detective, the door was open, the room was empty and a burning cigarette was sending a straight line of smoke to the fluorescent tubes on the ceiling. A detective magazine was lying open, face down on the desk, the girl on its cover cowering in the back seat of a taxi. Under the magazine I found his VIP list which included the movie company's whipped cream as well as a titled nobody from a country that doesn't even exist any more. Miranda's suite number was third from the top. I tried the top drawer of the desk to see if there was an extra set of skeleton keys. There wasn't. Usually security people are pushovers. I walked over to the hotel desk and casually asked for the key to suite 1456. It was a chance. I took it and it worked. I guess it's bad business to question the guests of your guests.

From the doorway of Miranda Pride's suite, the sitting-room looked like Jim Sayre's place over at the Tudor. It commanded the same view of the falls and betrayed the hand of the same interior decorator or his twin brother. Maybe there was more gilt on the lamps and picture frames here, maybe the military prints were more authentic-looking than the Elizabethan recreations next door, but it didn't add up to much. There was a bedroom off the main room and a connecting door to Furlong's suite. I put my head to the door and heard the sound of typing. So that's how it's done. You just put down one word after the other until it's done, and then re-done and then re-re-done, or until Mr. Raxlin says you're done.

I looked in the cupboard: one thousand and one dresses for one thousand and one nights, mostly pastels. Lots of scarves in a top drawer. The three hat boxes on one of the blond wood dressers showed three well-looked-after wigs, of different lengths and styles, each one mounted on a little head-shaped cloth-covered knob. It was like running across a dead animal act. It had a theatrical side and a morbid one. I put the lids back on and opened another drawer. Underwear of all kinds, shapes and colours. I closed that one quick. In the next I found a purse and in the purse a driver's licence for the State of California and a receipt for a Hertz Rent-a-car dated Tuesday. Not much money, a few travellers' cheques, lipstick, two drinking straws and a small bottle of perfume. Very nice.

I couldn't find a diary or journal telling me why she had wanted to kill poor David Hayes, and there was nothing of interest in the bedside table drawers except prescription sleeping pills. Across the bed lay a fur coat that some women would marry for. But David Hayes couldn't have given Miranda Pride anything more than the glance of youth.

I slapped my hands down on my thighs in exasperation, just a bit more noisily than I'd intended.

I listened to the room for a moment: the distant sound of typing, punctuated with a bell at the end of every line, an occasional bang or thump from the heating system and the sound of traffic thirteen floors below. I looked up. I was right, one of the bedroom windows was open, the curtains billowed in the sunlight. I moved toward the open window. A shadow rocked gently against the light.

There was no mistaking the body among the curtains. It was Miranda Pride. Miranda Pride of *The Secret of Cynthia Carrol* and *Woman of Abilene*. I'd seen her hounded to death in *Dark Streets* and dragged screaming to the guillotine in *Madame du Barry*. Now she was hanging in the hotel curtains, her eyes staring down at me with mild surprise, and the Pride mouth, something she could have signed cheques with, hanging limply open.

For a minute I just stood there, as if the curtains would close and then she'd take a bow. The confusion of reality and fiction doped the shock. I moved backwards to a chair and sat down hard. I looked at my shoes for a long time. Shoes were real. Solid black, of the earth. The chair beside the window was real. I raised my eyes a little: Miranda's feet were bare. The hem of her red nightgown and negligée fell to her ankles and moved with the curtains in the slight breeze. I could hear the steady sound of the falls on the wind. It didn't help me to start moving. I listened to the hum, almost electric, or like a summer insect in the garden. I wasn't taking this very well at all. I fished out my cigarettes but put them back again. I forced my head to tilt up again. Her hands hung limply at her sides; I hadn't noticed her rings before. I took counsel with myself, decided that action was needed. Taking a deep breath, I got to my feet and then sat right down again. The second time it worked. I put the chair next to the wall and climbed on the windowsill. A piece of nylon curtain cord was fastened to the stout bracket holding the curtain rod. The cord disappeared into the hair and folds of a scarf around Miranda Pride's neck. Her head was tilted almost quizzically to the right. There was no question about whether she was dead. In death — as in life — Miranda did dead very well.

fourteen

*C*hris Savas is a good cop and he knows me well enough to have told me on several occasions that I'm a good detective but would make a lousy cop. After that Friday he took it all back. He had me taken apart and put back together again by three of his best men. They were good. They were smart. They tried the 'good guy-bad guy' routine and, to make matters worse, they smoked up all my cigarettes. Chris stuck his nose in the door only often enough to satisfy himself that I wasn't gaining on them, and then went back to his desk. It turned out Miranda Pride had asked Savas about me the day before. He said it sounded like she had business to throw my way.

I tried to keep Lowell Mason's name out of it as long as I could, but I'd warned him that it might have to come out, so I told them I was working on a case involving Mason's missing wife. By the time they were finished with me, I felt like I'd spent the last forty-eight hours in a Turkish bath with a busted thermostat. My legs felt like they didn't want any part of this. It was guilt by association. They didn't even know me. When I stumbled out into the hall, Savas was there, working away at what was left of his lunch with a toothpick, leaning in his doorway. He motioned me to follow him as he ducked inside and cleared a chair of files so I could try to sit down. It was a friendly gesture and much appreciated. He handed me his cigarettes and matches and then took them from me when I couldn't co-ordinate the effort. When I put the lighted cigarette between my lips, it felt like God was in heaven again. Savas was looking at the report with some interest. He'd seen most of it in rough at various stages. Some of it he knew without seeing. He was that kind of cop. For a while he left me to the cigarette and the view of Grantham from his window through dirty Venetian blinds to the county courthouse, a not unfriendly limestone building from the middle of the last century. There was something classical and restful about it. I looked at the icicles hanging from the eaves of the pediment, at the starlings clustered on the dirty snow by the fountain. I looked at the panhandlers conferring about the economy.

"You bit off too much this time, Benny." I didn't even bother to nod. "I could see it when you were holding back about Hayes. I told you. 'Course you didn't know it was going to end up with the suicide of one of the truly greats of the movies, did you?" He was calm again and I was glad of it. So I just listened to Savas sermonizing about where the domain of the peeper leaves off and the realm of the policeman begins. It was a routine thing for Savas and he didn't get personal about it or even suggest that he was taking himself more seriously than necessary.

"Tell me, Chris, was it on the up and up? The suicide, I mean."

"There's none of the usual evidence of a faked hanging. No funny business. No evidence that she was pulled up after she was unconscious."

"Did the cord tell you anything?"

"Ordinary nylon curtain cord. She put the slipknot in the middle of a twelve-foot length taken from her bedroom."

"Taken? How? Cut? Pulled? What?"

"Just untied and removed from the track. If this one's fishy, Benny, we're dealing with a clever bandit."

"Just a routine suicide, then?"

"Looks that way. But I'm not with the coroner's office. They're the experts in things like this. I've checked out the circumstantial stuff: a chair near the windowsill, and the drop."

"Drop?"

"Yeah. It was consistent with where she was standing before she jumped. In fakes you get people jumping from above where they should have been. Easy to spot." Savas was beginning to get itchy. He didn't like sitting around jawing when he was in the middle of an investigation.

"Okay, Benny? We'll be in touch with you about the inquest. Both inquests! Shit, don't find any more bodies for a few weeks. Can't you do a little honest transom gazing? Try it out." He let a heavy paw hit my shoulder in an almost accidental way. I got up and wandered out into the late afternoon. The light was gone and the nighttime cold was closing its jaws on us again.

I hadn't had any lunch, so I went up to the United on automatic pilot without taking much in except dirty cars dripping salt and rust in the parking lots and a few shoppers who hadn't yet abandoned the centre of town for the shopping plazas on the edge of the city. I ordered a chopped egg sandwich on white with a vanilla milkshake. Today I felt like climbing back to basics. A couple of girls in high leather boots were leafing through the magazine rack near the door and giggling to one another over what they saw. The salt was eating up the leather, leaving a jagged white line of slow destruction behind.

"What's the matter with you today?" It was one of the waitresses. I forget her name. "Not a peep from you. And where have you been keeping yourself the last week? Are you two-timing me or something?" I gave her a grin, but she could see there wasn't much behind it, and started to leave me to eat my crusts alone.

"How well do you know Niagara Falls, New York?"

"It's a change after this place. What do you want to know about it?"

"The Surf Lounge. Where is it and what sort of bar is it?"

"Just a bar near the tracks, that's all. Sort of a neighbourhood bar. Nothing fancy, just a joint close to the bridge. Why? Were you leading up to something? If you were, that's not the way to get there." I sipped at the milkshake and wondered whether I had a full tank of gas.

I hadn't been across the border in a couple of months. I used to go across often enough to make an annual bridge ticket pay, but nowadays it wasn't worth it. On the Canadian side I answered the questions of a skinny man in his fifties who looked carefully into my back seat and trunk, and asked where I'd been born, where did I live and how long did I intend to remain in the United States. From the Rainbow Bridge I was able to get a new perspective on the ice bridge. From here, the illuminated vault of ice just out of reach of the falls was impressive enough to make me slow down. The horn of the car behind got my mind back on business. On the American side, the guard took my bridge money and instructed me to have a good day.

I took a turn through Niagara Falls, New York, trying to stay off the beckoning tendrils of freeways which would like to scoop me up and let me off on the far side of Buffalo. The whole place looked like it had been hit by a fire-raid and the rebuilding had stopped when the job was only half done. The street of theatres I remembered from when I was young had vanished. A large deserted convention centre occupied a nearby site. I followed a street of brick and wooden two- and three-storey buildings across a railway track, with dirty snowdrifts high between the rails. More shopworn snow leaned up against the sides of dog-eared stores and walk-up apartments. Board fences showed the latest in graffiti including a backwards "N" and the word "Private" with a dot over the capital "I". At the corner not far from the railway track I saw the neon sign advertising Schlitz Beer. The sign above the door, looking faded and tired, read *Surf Lounge*. I parked the car and went into the dim interior.

A bar of dark hardwood ran the length of the tavern on my left with a few tables along the wall to my right. The place was deserted, except for a cop sitting at one end of the bar next to the wall and the bartender standing as far away from him as he could manage.

I ordered a Miller's Highlife. American beer is lighter than Canadian and doesn't lay you out as fast. The bartender served it and mopped the mahogany half-way between where I was and where he had been. He didn't look very talkative. His face reminded me of Mr. Punch. His chin and nose were conspiring to meet at a later date. I tried him on the movie being made on the other side. I couldn't get it to light. He'd seen everything and he didn't want to talk about anything. I thought I'd seen the cop flicker. So I tried again.

"I see that Miranda Pride killed herself across the river." The cop looked up.

"Just as long as she does it on the Canadian side. Geez, I never found it hard to look at her. She's a pip."

"Yeah," I said. "I've seen her a few times. I guess I liked the *Sally* pictures best."

"That's right. I forgot that. Killed herself, you say? She was one of the top stars in her day. Haven't seen her lately. I didn't see it in the paper. Was it on TV?"

"It'll be on tonight. Just happened a few hours ago."

"Geez. Good-looking woman like that."

"She was married to Neil Furlong, the writer. He used to live over the river." I watched the bartender, who hadn't said anything and didn't even appear to be listening. He stopped moving his cloth along the bar. His jaw looked like it was trying to decide whether to move. "Furlong's made a lot of money from TV, and they say Miranda Pride was worth quite a lot herself."

"You do a lot of talking on one beer, Mister." It wasn't what I'd expected him to say. Still it sounded more cautious than aggressive.

"I didn't see the sign," I said. The cop was enjoying this.

"Don't get wise. There's no sign. Talk all you want, but I'm telling you to pick something else. Furlong's been bad news in this place. I wouldn't give him a used bottlecap if he wanted one. I knew some nice people that he scuppered. He's not liked in here, so sing a different tune if you want to sing at all."

"You knew Mattingly?" I asked, looking him in the eye. He slowly took the butt of a cigarette from his thin lips and looked at me through slits.

"What's your game, Mister?"

"I'm a friend of Harvey Osborne. Harve took a poke at Furlong at the Colonel John Butler Wednesday night. I was there. It was a good punch, landed squarely where you would have planted it yourself."

129

"I asked you a question. I don't hear any answers."

"I'm just nosing around. Harve could get into trouble if Furlong lays a charge. It looks like Harve could be put away if he gets convicted."

"Yeah, and Neil'll write another play about it. Make another million."

"He used to come in here, didn't he?"

"Drink your beer and clear out!"

"Tell him, Hatch," the cop chipped in; "it might help Osborne. Assault's serious stuff."

"Okay, okay," he said, taking a fresh cigarette and lighting a match but not doing anything further about it until the match burned down to his finger. "Furlong used to come in here with his friends from the railway at first; then it was his acting friends. They came from both sides of the river. They put on a show at the Patriot Volunteer once and once at the high school. Came in two or three times a week. Always had a lot of people with him. They were always cracking jokes and playing games.

"Sometimes Clark Mattingly would be here with Flo. Sometimes they'd join in the games and get to talking. When Furlong wrote that play he had Clark Mattingly to the life, and I'm telling you as a man who knew him for over ten years. Flo was my own half-sister, for your information. Furlong should have waited a year before putting that play on TV, he could have put in the part about how Flo started drinking after Clark killed himself, Flo who never took more'n two or three drinks a night. I tried to get her straightened out, but I couldn't get through to her. Nobody could. Then she froze to death one night in the alley behind the billiard parlour. He was in Toronto by then. Probably never heard about it." His cheek twitched and he opened a beer for himself, which he poured into a tapered glass.

"Tell me about his girlfriends in those days."

"How long have you got? You got some nerve coming in here with your questions. I'm only talking because Gerry says it might help Harve. But I guess Gerry and I could tell you about Furlong's girls all right. There was Dulcie.

She was about sixteen or so. Jailbait. Geez, Gerry, she'd be nearly thirty now. Funny, huh?" Gerry smiled mechanically. "Tell you one thing about Dulcie. She was a hot little bitch, whatever Harve says. Ain't that right, Gerry?"

Gerry pulled at his chin and nodded. "Another thing: she couldn't drive a car in a straight line sober, let alone liquored up the way she was when she got killed. I caught her driving Furlong a few times. One night I nearly ran the pair of them in. But he was such a twister. Charming, I guess you'd call it. He turned everybody into a pal. He was Mister Personality when he wanted to be."

"Was Dulcie the only liquored-up minor?"

"Hell, he had women like I got dandruff. And he never listened to a word they said," Hatch observed, running a handful of fingers through his hair. "Gerry, remember the one that used to sound off all the time?"

"Have a heart, Hatch. That's a dozen years ago."

"She had a great little figure on her and could curse up a storm."

"There was one used to drink straight Scotch. Used to toss it back like tomato juice. Geez, what was her name?"

"If you asked me a month ago, Gerry, I wouldn't have been able to tell you, but it just happens I do know her name."

"That's because she was in here on New Year's Eve. Right?" I said. Hatch looked at me like I'd guessed that his middle name was Heathcliff. "Was that the first time you'd seen her since the old days?"

"First time in a dozen years. You know Billie?"

"I know her, and I'd like to find her. She hasn't been in since New Year's?"

"No."

"Well, then, that's another cold trail. Only one question left to ask. Who was she with New Year's Eve?" Hatch threw a look at Gerry, the cop, and broke into a broad grin.

"The fellow we've been talking about."

"Harvey Osborne?"

"No. I'm talking about Neil Furlong."

fifteen

As soon as I stepped back into the lobby of the Colonel John, I saw Marvin Raxlin sitting stunned on a plum-coloured velvet ottoman. He was looking straight ahead of him without seeing. I went over. He blinked his red-rimmed eyes and didn't focus on me as I sat down beside him. An executive assistant in a three-piece suit I'd seen around was hovering near a square pillar talking to the hotel manager but watching Raxlin for the slightest tremor for which he held the antidote.

"They found coke in her room," Raxlin said. "How do you like that? That's all I need: drugs on top of everything else. How could Miranda do this to me? Every minute we're closed down is costing me. What can I do? The head writer is in mourning. He's on golden time and he can't get hold of himself. Miranda's scenes, they can be fixed; but what a blow this is. I get calls from the coast: 'Is the production jinxed?' I get calls from New York: 'What's going on up there?' "

"You look terrible," I said. "Why don't you try to get some sleep? The cops won't bother you again tonight. They know where to reach you."

"That's the trouble. Everybody needs me. How many hands can I hold at once? That's why I've come down here. Every three minutes the phone rings. Alvin," he called to the man at the pillar, "show the revised production schedule to Mr. Sayre and tell him I'll talk to him in the morning." We both watched Alvin unlatch himself from the manager and head toward the elevators.

"Mr. Cooperman, you're a detective and you're working on a case, right?"

"Right."

"You ever take on other cases that may be related?"

"I might. It depends. You want to talk about it?"

132

"You were asking me about the men who came to see me. You called them thugs."

"And you corrected me; said they were more like businessmen. They wanted changes in the script."

"You were closer to the truth. I met them this afternoon and went with them to see one of the bosses."

"First of all, who met you?"

"Hoods. Hoodlums. What do you want me to say? Dressed in four-hundred-dollar suits they were still hoodlums, street rowdies. They collected me at lunch, took me to the Pagoda." He was wiping sweat from his forehead with a Kleenex. He wasn't used to being pushed around.

"So you talked to Tullio Solmi? Or was it the other one?"

"You know him? My God, he threatened me. He asked if I enjoyed living. He told me the name of the school my daughter goes to. He showed me her picture."

"What did you give him?"

"A man like that . . . there's no telling where . . ."

"What did you promise him?"

"They want script changes. You know about that. They want a piece of the picture. It's crazy. He wants a piece out of my end. He says he doesn't like dealing with the studios. He threatened accidents that won't be accidents if I don't do as he says."

"So what are you going to do?"

"I spent four years putting this package together!"

"So?"

"Four years out of my life!"

"So, you gave in. Well, at least now you have syndicate protection and syndicate money. You could be worse off: you could have no money and no protection."

"Four years into the ashcan. That's what it means. Why me? Why this picture? Because it's going to be very big, that's why."

"Tell me what you saw and heard."

"I told you. I met Solmi in his outer office. Some vending company."

"Was he alone?"

"The heavies that brought me went into another room. We talked alone for about twenty minutes."

"Why the outer office? You were having a private talk, weren't you? What was going on in the private office?"

"They said Solmi's wife was using it."

"This happened when exactly?"

"Two, two-thirty, three, who knows. I wasn't timing it."

"There's a missing piece in all this, Mr. Raxlin." He looked up with watery, innocent eyes.

"What are you talking about? I told you like it happened."

"So how did they get to see the script? How did they know about the Pagoda getting in the story?"

"They have ways, those people."

"Those people put money in your picture, didn't they? I mean *before* the threats started."

"What are you talking about?"

"In a picture you get all kinds of backers. Nobody looks at the list too closely. Money has no criminal record. It doesn't wear stripes. In fact some kinds of money go around looking like lawyers, or hoodlums in four-hundred-dollar suits." He was still for about the count of five, then his head went down so that he could see his shoes better.

"All right! Shoot me! I had to keep the picture going. You blame me for that? You think that's the only block of dirty money in the picture? Grow up. Get some education."

"If you're talking about Tony Pritchett's money, I know about that. He wouldn't care if you put Solmi and Cohn in the script without changing their names. But you've had a juggling act to see that they don't find out about one another."

"You wouldn't believe," Raxlin said. "You wouldn't believe."

"And how does Neil fit into all this? You thought you were paying for an original screenplay. Pure fiction."

"He told me that it was loosely based on fact. But I thought ancient history. This reads like a documentary. If we don't get killed we can get sued. That's why the changes. You think it's cheap to rewrite on location? With everybody on golden time? You're crazy." I tried to ease the pressure.

"I think you could use a drink." He lifted his head high enough to see a cat smile. He looked like a tire with a slow leak.

"Yeah," he said, blowing to bits the scrap of Kleenex, "I guess you're right."

We didn't talk in the elevator. Raxlin studied the imitation woodwork finish on the metal sides of the car. I found a table with a view of the American falls. We sat by the window, and both of us kept quiet until Raxlin's drink had been ordered and disposed of in a single neck-cracking belt.

"You know I'm looking for a guy's missing wife," I said at last.

"You told me. An actress, wasn't it?" I nodded.

"Her husband's my client. But I don't think he'd mind my taking a side-trip to see what can be seen from Solmi's office in the Pagoda. If I find anything of interest to you, I'll let you in on it."

"Paper you won't find. There's nothing in writing. He might have the script in the office his wife was using."

Raxlin was smiling now with a second drink in his hand. Then a familiar face came into view.

"Hello, chaps. Mind if I join you?" It was Dawson Williams, smelling of cold cream and looking rather pink. It was odd seeing his craggy jaw this close. The lines were powerful, but the skin was as smooth as a certified cheque. "Bloody cold out there this afternoon. Some are cold but few are frozen, what? Reminds me of a winter I spent in Wadsworth, Nevada on a Ford picture. Ten of us living in an unheated circus train. Say, I enjoyed your friends last night. I like his Lady Macbeth idea. I think it would go down very well." Raxlin raised an eyebrow of inquiry, but I ignored it for the moment. "Peggy was quite taken by the little fellow."

"You mean Will Chapman. Quite a man in his day.

He was once a champion singles rower when he went to Cranmer College. That's a private boys' school in Grantham. Not much of him left these days."

"Well, old boy, our Peggy was quite taken by him."

"Maybe she's trying to make Hampton Fisher jealous. He's taken over the top floor of the Colonel John." Raxlin was now restored to order, and I escaped at the first opportunity. It came after a brief mention of Miranda.

"She's just gone on ahead, old boy, that's the size of it. Stealing a march on us. She was a game old girl. Ah, well, we all come to it, what?"

"Not that way, I hope," said Raxlin.

"We have heard the chimes at midnight, we two," he said. "The readiness is all."

I changed the Colonel John for the Tudor, following the traditional escape hatch through the kitchens. From the lobby, I tried Sayre's number on the house phone. Adela answered. When I apologized for bothering her and tried to wiggle out, she told me that Jim was in the shower but would be out and with a drink ready for me when I got off the elevator. She sounded friendly enough, so I pushed the button for the penthouse.

When I stepped out of the car, the door was open; but it was the door to Penthouse One. From it I could hear women's voices soothing and cajoling.

"Peggy, come on now. Look in the mirror. You look wonderful."

"Nicole's right, Peggy. You just glow. It's radiant . . ."

"I hate it! I feel fat and fifty in this. I don't care what you say. It's how I feel that matters."

"Peggy, why won't you trust me? Why would I say you look fine if you don't? What's my motive? You believe in an honest interpretation of a character. If I lied to you, it wouldn't be consistent with me as you know me. Come on back into the bedroom and we'll look again."

"I hate being crowded this way! Why won't you let me do it my way?" The voices moved further away from the door, retreating to the far end of the suite. When I looked up, Adela was standing with her head cocked to one side in her own doorway.

"Women are like that," she said with a smile. "From the Colonel's lady to Judy O'Grady." Adela was striking. She was wearing a dark green pyjama suit of some shimmering cloth that flattered her figure in all the right places. Without the half-moon glasses I'd seen on her earlier she looked almost frivolous. "Nicole and Lynn have their hands full sometimes, but I think in the main it's clear sailing. Peggy is basically a very sweet, down-to-earth girl." As if to confirm this, we could hear laughter through the open door.

Adela led me into the suite I'd first seen less than a week ago, but it seemed like half a century. "I used to be able to judge that man's showering time, but I'm losing my touch. Maybe he's giving himself an extra rinse or spin dry in your honour." She'd made a few changes in the furniture to try to get rid of the denatured look. There were new pictures on the wall; some I thought I'd seen before. A couple of tables had been pushed together to make a large desk area. At one side, a portable typewriter had been set up, and near it lay piles of pages in pink, green and blue. There was even a little ordinary white on display. Crumpled wads in all colours dotted the broadloom. Another table against the outside wall had been commandeered to make a bar. It was loaded with every bottle permitted across the border. My stomach was beginning to protest in advance against another onslaught of sour-mash whisky. But maybe Sayre had lost interest in converting me after that first attempt.

I took a seat in velvet splendour and so did Adela. I could see that under her banter she was troubled by what had been happening, and I didn't blame her.

"You heard about poor Miranda?" she asked. I nodded. I didn't offer any details, since she didn't seem to know that I'd known first. "She was a good friend. One of the best. We go back a long way. It still hasn't completely hit me yet. I keep thinking the phone'll ring and it'll be

137

her. Tonight I'm coasting on a prescription and pure nerve."
Adela lit a cigarette from a black butane lighter and sent
the blue smoke skyrocketing to the hotel ceiling, showing
off her long, attractive neck. I helped myself to a Player's
from my pocket. Adela leaned over, lighting the cigarette
herself. This close I could see age in her face, but she had
the kind of bones and carriage that go on forever. I heard
a rumble from the next room. Jim Sayre was having a good
hack in private so he wouldn't cough in public. Then in
he came with a nearly empty glass in his hand. There was
something about the way he held it that told me the ice
had melted. He took it to the liquor table like a caddy takes
a ball to the rinse bucket.

"Well, young fella, how are you feelin' in this cold?
'Course you're used to it. I used to be, but I can't take it
any more. Remember one time I'd been thrown out of
school and my father sent me up to Montana for the winter.
Old friend of his in the cattle business. Boy, I learned about
frostbite that winter. And about hard work. The best lesson
I ever had. Went back to school in the spring like a lamb
to a ewe." He looked back to see whether I was holding a
drink, collected Adela's and topped it up.

"Damnedest thing, this Miranda business. Can't even
say the word: death, suicide, hanging! Ugly!" He started
this as a mutter between his big false teeth, but the force
got away from him, surprising all of us. His eyes were on
his drink or the carpet or maybe on the liver marks on his
wrists. Then he caught my eye: "Would you ever get stuck
so bad you'd hang yourself, Ben?" His expression seemed
to reach inside me for the right answer. Only there isn't
one.

"I don't know. Hope not. I guess she must have been
stuck worse than I've ever been."

"But don't forget courage," said Adela. "It takes courage to tie a curtain cord around your neck."

"I guess," Sayre said. "I guess." He sipped at his bourbon for a minute. Then the phone rang. Jim told somebody
named Austin to fend off calls for the rest of the evening
but to give him a list in the morning. Then Austin was

putting his own oar in and Jim had to hear him out. Adela let an electric smile pull at her features for a second then ignored the rest of the telephone conversation.

"We had a nice old talk the day before yesterday, you know," Adela said. "Just two old bags letting their hair down. She was so full of fun. We were in her room across at the other hotel. She slipped through the connecting door into Neil's suite and came back wearing a waiter's jacket, one of those room-service jobs with the logo on the pocket, and gave a wonderful impression of a sleepy waiter rolling in breakfast on a trolley. She had everything. She was so quick in her observation of people's quirks. A wonderful eye. But . . ." She waved her hand hopelessly and we nodded and listened to Jim saying "Yeah . . . Yeah . . ." to Austin and to the sound of the falls on the wind.

Jim got off the phone, freshened his drink and sat down.

"What will her death mean to the picture?" Adela put her drink down hard and got up to look out the French windows.

"Pictures are bigger than people. That's the first fact of life. Why should it change anything? Oh I know Raxlin is having kittens, but it's more because of the bad publicity and delays. The part was just a supporting role. Even she knew that. Nothing will have to be shot over again. No, the picture is going to roll, it's going to roll on over everybody. That's the way it is. It's pictures."

"I finished up one of the *Sally* pictures one time. Charley Oakley'd been taken off to do a picture in Santa Rosa, and I wasn't doin' anything much but collectin' my pay. I was on contract then. Miranda was a little winner in those days. Bright as silver dollars fallin' into your hat. I was lookin' forward to working with her again. Damnedest thing." His eyes were shining and he squeezed the bridge of his nose. Then he came up grinning: "I saw you out there today, Ben. Now you've seen how we do it. Did it take away the magic?" I smiled and shook my head. Sayre reached for a cigarette and Adela watched him carefully. He looked at her through the space between the burning match and the cigarette in his other hand, and then brought the two together. He blew the smoke in her direction.

"Those the only clothes you brought with you, Adela? I swear I can tell what underwear you're wearin'."

"Jim! We've got company."

"I know that. So do you. Tryin' to vamp him, Adela? Tryin' to tie him up and put your brand on him?"

"Jim, shut up. Please," she said, turning to me, "I'm sorry."

"Don't say you're sorry. Ben's okay. You don't need to apologize. Not for me, anyway. I just thought you could have picked something a little more suitable. For tonight especially."

"If you want me to change, Jim, just say it."

"Drink your drink, Adela. Pay no attention to an old man."

Adela got up, looked at me with a head tilted ironically, and excused herself.

"I'm an old prude, Ben, in my home life, I guess. Age does it. Maybe it's a reaction against the tits-out kind of business this is. A man needs a private place where you can't see everythin' for the price of admission. Sometimes it takes me worse than usual. I'm upset about Miranda. I know that. Don't have to be a shaman. We're all involved in every death, like the poet says." I nodded. It wasn't from *A Midsummer Night's Dream*. I was sure of that.

"What was she like, Jim?"

"Oh," he screwed his face up and worked his mouth from side to side while he thought. "Miranda was a bundle of talent when I first knew her. She had a funny, out-of-breath way of tellin' lies to me on the set, like she'd just run around the sound stage. Sometimes beauty's a trick, an illusion; but she had the real thing. I don't know what started her on narcotics. She still had her looks, her figure, talent to burn. I think Neil was good for her. The last of a long line of men that could all wear the same suits. She liked writers. Never actors. Once . . ." he looked me in the eye ". . . for five and a half days, she liked a director. In recent years she got to be the clingin' type. She watched a man so close he squeezed out the drain. Joe Gillis got out from under just in time. He was the one before Furlong.

"Let's see, what else is there? She could be funny. She could handle her money. That's rare. She didn't run around much. Took people one at a time. Sort of settled, but jealous, if you follow me. She was the makin' of Neil, you know. He was just a television writer when she met him. Didn't know what a screen credit was. She took him around, showed him off, opened a few doors. I guess there wasn't anybody in town she didn't know. And lots owed her favours. Neil harvested most of those favours over the last half-dozen years. Now he's comin' to be the best-known writer around. What with the Broadway plays and the movin' pictures being made from them. Funny, I saw him on the coast a month ago. A young writer was pesterin' him about somethin' and over the noise I heard him say, 'Send me the book.' Said it like the bottom had never been out of his pants. 'Send me the book.' Like books grow on trees and he was born to the grand manner." He took a pull at his drink, then seemed to sink deeper into the sofa he was sitting on. "I'm sorry for his trouble, as the Irish say."

Adela came back into the room and we both got up. She was wearing a dinner dress that was suitably modest. Sayre said nothing, but I could see he approved. "We're goin' out to dinner," Sayre said. "Marilyn and her beau have invited just the two of us."

"He calls Peggy . . ."

"Ben's sorted that out, Adela; don't spoonfeed him."

"You know who her beau is? Beau! Jim, you begin to date me. I'm going to have to stop listening to you. Tonight you said 'vamp'."

"I did not. Hampton Fisher's been takin' her out, and I think they want an old couple like us to show we approve."

"And do you?"

"Well, he's a crank of the first water. He hates crowds, doesn't like publicity, parties or surprises."

"Has his water flown here from California."

"Carries a thermometer in his pocket. But, hell, he's young, and from what I hear he's puttin' those papers back where they were in his grandfather's day. Increased circulation, all that."

"I think he's kind of cute," Adela said, with a broad smile and wink.

"Well, he's not a toad in the road. He'll give Marilyn a good home. He's not one to run around once he gets settled."

"It's pretty serious, then?" I asked.

"I know Peggy likes him. She told me."

"Well, if she likes him, that's all that matters," said Sayre with finality. "She's a fine girl, just the opposite of all the publicity bumph. I don't think she'd have a mirror in her place if she didn't need it for her work."

"Jim, what a lot of nonsense. Peggy's a normal, healthy girl with a normal, healthy vanity." Jim joined our laughter, although a little after it had started.

"Well, if you're going out to eat, I'd better let you get ready." I put down my half-empty glass and made movements to leave.

"Have another drink. No rush." Sayre got up and collected my glass while Adela took a quick look at her jewelled watch. Her mouth made a straight line. But I don't think it was personal.

"You have to finish dressing, Jim," she warned.

"Won't take two shakes. Lots of time." He poured a drink for each of us, a bourbon for him and Canadian rye for Adela and me. He added water and a couple of ice cubes to the glass as an afterthought. "Ben's practically family, aren't you, Ben? I don't know what I'd have done without you that first day. He saved me from the demon hoards, like Cúchulainn against the forces of Madb."

"What?" Adela said.

"The *Táin Bó Cuailnge*, the great Irish epic, the greatest cowboy story of them all."

Adela laughed: "Is that the book you got Paramount to option?"

"I sent them an outline while I was workin' on *Donnybrook*. Changed the settin' to Arizona in the nineties. Madb became a cattle baroness. Claudia Horlick put me up to it. She just typed up my drunken ravin's from the previous night. And damned if they didn't option it. I turned the money over to Claudia. She'd done the work. One of the decent things I've done. One of the damned few."

The doorbell rang. Adela put her cigarette out, and got up to answer it. "That'll be her. She's right on time, too." In a second a dazzling Peggy O'Toole was in the middle of the room. She seemed to sparkle all over in a cool blue dinner dress and a fur wrap cut like a fluffy white bomber jacket. I could hardly bear to look at her, it was like she was giving out light and I had to shade my eyes.

"Hello, everybody. I'm sorry I'm late. Hamp said he's expecting us for . . ." She shook her wrist. "Damn it, I think it's stopped. I can never remember to wind this." She was turning the jewelled bracelet in her hand. "All the others have batteries."

She sent her electric smile my way, but the batteries were going on it too. There was something of the actress in her manner tonight, something I hadn't seen before. "Adela, Mr. Sayre," she said, taking Adela's elbow and pulling Sayre into a small circle of three. "Please promise we won't talk about it. I won't be able to stand it if we talk about it when we get over there. I'm ready for a strait-jacket now."

"Of course, my dear. Leave it to us."

Jim took a last gulp from his glass and made a loud satisfied sound. I put my half-finished drink down, got to my feet and wished them all a pleasant evening. On the way down in the elevator, I wished that I had only a dinner to look forward to.

sixteen

I was still early for my eight o'clock meeting with Noonan, so I took the elevator from the heel of the Pagoda up to the TV station where Wally Skeat hung out. He'd asked me to look him up more than once and this was a good time to take him up on it: I could use all the experience of the Pagoda I could get.

The elevator was one of those plastic affairs with a wrap-around view of the falls from the best angle. With the coloured lights shining on the water every view was a tinted postcard. In fact, as the car rose two hundred feet in the air the panorama widened, but the spectacle shrank.

The reception area of the TV station tried to make a contemporary statement with its furniture and decor. The trouble with contemporary statements is that you've seen them before. There were giant blow-ups on the wall of American television stars appearing as characters in series carried by this station directly or through the network it was affiliated with. I recognized most of them, but I must admit I was feeling a little strange. It had been nearly a week since I'd spent a quiet evening with my feet up and a box of potato chips on my lap. The receptionist's desk was empty and her typewriter covered. I walked by her desk and through into what I found was a busy newsroom, with men in shirtsleeves and girls in T-shirts and jeans either leaning over teletype machines or sweating out copy of their own. The windows here, under the bright fluorescent ceiling lights, were black bands that half surrounded the room. Wally Skeat was sitting at the desk examining some copy that had just been handed to him. He read each page carefully, placing each sheet when he'd finished behind the sheaf in his hand. When he got to the bottom of the last page he smiled at the editor who was standing by his shoulder making reading difficult. "Can't you squeeze in a clip from the interview she did with me? There's good stuff in it."

"Wally, we don't have the VTR time to edit it. But I'll see what Hester says, okay?" And off he went. Hester was a woman in a lively print dress with a high forehead and glasses perched in her hair. Everything was being referred to Hester. Hester was in charge.

"Benny! For the love of Mike! Where have you been? I've been trying to get you since this Miranda thing broke. Hey, Ralph!" he called, and introduced me to Ralph Fosdick, a senior editor, as the man who'd discovered the body. Fosdick shook my hand like he didn't want to get too close. He and Wally excused themselves for a short conference with Hester, who looked at me under her glasses, like I was a geek in the circus, and then crisply shook her head. Wally returned by himself having shifted into a lower gear. "Boy, are we busy with this suicide story. We've got all the US networks taking feeds. I'm going to be on CBC News with a clip. I did a phone interview with a bevy of her co-stars long distance. It's been one of *those* days. You want coffee? They can struggle along without me for five minutes."

I followed him into one of a string of offices on the edge of the news area. This reduced some of the noise of the room and with the door pulled shut you could almost think you were in a changing room in a department store. Wally had wired up a coffee maker on a crowded bookshelf, which I looked through: review copies with slips of paper in front asking him to send two copies of the review to the publisher. The wall was decorated with pictures of Wally under the lights reading the news, different angles, different studio sets, but it all looked like the same news. I took the other chair, and could feel the back wall behind me and his desk pressed into my knees.

"Tell me, Benny, what do you make of the suicide? I hear there wasn't a note."

"Wally, I just find bodies, I don't theorize about them. I just told the cops what I found. I didn't see any of the usual fake suicide things at the scene."

"What faked stuff?"

"Every time a murderer tries to cover his tracks by making a crime look like suicide, he slips up in ways that are easy for an expert to spot. If you've spent a day in front of the television, you know some of them. In a hanging, for instance, if it's faked, you can tell when the body has been strangled first and then hoisted into place. If you pull a heavy weight over a beam, friction will wear a groove in the beam and also worry fragments of hemp off the rope. That's the first thing the cops look for. You've got to be a forensic specialist to see the fine points, but any experienced homicide man looks for obvious things like notes, access to the windowsill, the length of the fall. That sort of thing. No, Wally, it looks like poor Miranda did herself in after settling a score with David Hayes." Wally handed me a cup with the station logo on it while I was talking.

"I've got to get back in a minute, Benny."

"Sure, sure. Wally, tell me, is there a blueprint or a chart of this place around somewhere?"

"You mean the Pagoda?" He knew I meant the Pagoda, so he paused for a second then jerked his thumb in the direction of one of the other offices. "Greg has his office littered with that stuff. If you want to see his albums, he can show you pictures all the way through construction."

"Unnecessary. But I would like to see the architect's drawings, if I may." Wally gestured "Help yourself" and finished off a mug of what looked like cold coffee. While I studied the visible part of Greg's collection, he went back on active service. I saw where the stairs went, and how the rooms and offices branched off the central stem. The whole structure had a hollow core and up it ran most of the service conduits. It was all very instructive.

On my way out, I passed the control room, which looked through a double-glass window onto the familiar desk and cut-out skyline of the news set. I took the elevator up, past the observation floor, to the dining-room. I'd booked a table for two in Noonan's name. All heads turned when I came into the room. It gave my ego a pleasant boost, but later I noticed that all heads turned when anybody came into the room. It was that kind of crowd. All their conversations looked bright and trendy. I was a few minutes late, but the maître d' didn't remind me as he showed me to a table with the famous view. It was still lit up like a ten-cent postcard, and from this height it was no more animated. I could see the crack in the floor which separated the revolving part of the room from the stationary part. I watched the view change minutely through the window. After I'd travelled about six feet, I changed places with myself. I hated riding backwards. Another fifteen feet went by and Noonan was standing beside the table. I offered him the other chair and he took it.

"You get a great view from up here," Noonan said, and I ignored it. He was panting like a bird dog in August.

"You talked to your pal?"

"Look, you didn't give me much time. And with this Pride thing coming out of left field . . ." A waiter brought us huge menus. I hadn't counted on having to cope with distractions, so I asked what the special was and ordered that. It seemed the simplest way, even if I didn't understand the French. Noonan ordered steak, and a double rye before the hors d'oeuvres arrived.

"It doesn't matter. It's not a mystery any more. You can relax and enjoy your meal. Furlong's got other headaches tonight. You can come out of the closet without surprising me."

"I didn't say that."

"That's right. I didn't hear it from you. You want it in writing?"

"Well, I . . ."

"Cut it short, Noonan. You aren't protecting anybody. The battle line has shifted and you're left waiting at the gate alone. This has all got more complicated than you can imagine. Billie's become too popular for one man. This is an international convention. What did Furlong tell you?"

"The truth of the matter is . . ."

"I said cut it. Do you want this girl's blood on your hands?"

147

"Look, I'm only acting as an agent here."

"I know, I know. Your gloves are clean. Nobody's going to bring suit against you. Don't worry. So, let's hear what he said."

"He told me to stonewall you if I could."

"But you can't. So then?"

"And if I got stuck, I'm to tell you that, yes, Neil did see Mrs. Mason a few times. It seems that . . ."

"Yeah, I know. They're old friends. Just catching up for lost time."

"That's right."

"Meanwhile, where is Billie Mason? When did he see her last?"

"I don't think he saw her after Wednesday night."

"I was with him on Wednesday night and he was alone."

"I mean for dinner. They went over to the Patriot Volunteer on the road to Youngstown on the American side."

"I saw him beginning around 11:30 or 11:45 and I was with him until he left to talk to Raxlin about script changes. So he left Billie around eleven. That checks out with what I have. How is he taking his wife's death?"

"I left a pretty broken man, I'll tell you. He was just limp with grief. Couldn't even talk about it."

"I see. This afternoon you said you'd call him. Why the change? He had something for you? Something on account, for services rendered?"

"You've got a filthy mind, Cooperman. I couldn't even imagine anything that low."

"Well, you've got an envelope sticking out of your inside breast pocket." Quickly he moved his right hand to his pocket, his heavy brows nearly joining for a second, and then when he found I'd been bluffing he put his hand on the table: a fat little hand with short fingers and untidy nails, but useful for picking things up and then forgetting where they'd been stashed.

"Tell me all about Hayes. The whole story this time. The time for fiction is past. I spent this afternoon with the cops and they aren't finished with me yet. So far I've kept you out of it."

"Okay, sure. There's not much to tell. They came to see me together, Billie and Hayes. I took their names, did all the routine things, put them in the file. Then . . ."

"Then you decided to get Billie on her own. Up to your old tricks."

"A man's only human. You don't see a girl like that twice. Sure. I called her up, invited her out to eat. We were in the main restaurant of the Colonel John. I was trying to impress her, I guess. Furlong was sitting at the next table. Sitting alone. Miranda was still in New York. I invited him to join us."

"Still trying to impress her, only it backfired."

"He told me later that he knew her from a few years ago. They did plays together or something. They didn't even notice when I got up to go to the john. They were like a couple right from then on. Neil gave me a look and I excused myself. If I said I had to go talk to my dead grandmother, they wouldn't have noticed anything off-key. So I beat it. The next day Neil called and told me to cover for him in case Hayes came looking for Billie. He seemed to be sure he would, and he was right. Hayes came in asking questions and said she wasn't at the boarding house any more. I told him I'd keep my eyes peeled and he left. I only saw him again once more. He called every day, though. I had Estelle take the calls after the first day."

"She's a good-looking girl, your Estelle."

"She can do eighty words a minute."

"Old Incorruptible."

"Hey, wait a minute. Estelle lives with her mother."

"I never breathed a word. Tell me about that last time you saw Hayes. When was that?"

"It was on Tuesday morning, two days before he was killed. I was having breakfast at the Colonel John. Neil was sitting behind me, must have arrived after I got there. He would have joined me if he'd seen me, since I was by myself. Anyway, I heard two voices being raised. Not loud, you know, not an argument, but just a smidgin louder than the hum of breakfast conversation."

By that time, the hors d'oeuvres had arrived and I stayed close to the tried and true, things I recognized like grated raw carrot and hard-boiled eggs. There was a lot of other stuff on the platter too, but I couldn't look at most of it. Then, when dinner came, Noonan got his steak: it was fresh-killed and bleeding. I got a thin piece of veal with a lemon sauce on it. It could have been worse. Over the years I've found that my expectations go down the higher off the ground I'm eating.

"Back to business. You were saying?"

"So I looked over my shoulder, and there was Hayes standing talking to Neil. I thought, 'Oh God, he's found out about Neil and Billie, and Neil'll blame me.' But, in a minute, Hayes sat down with him at his table and they were talking more friendly like. When I got up to pay, I pretended not to see them, but I listened a little. They were talking about *Ice Bridge*. I thought that Neil was a cool customer to talk Hayes down so fast."

"Do you remember anything specific from what they said?"

"You don't want much for nothing!" Noonan snorted, then ate another piece of dripping steak. "Hayes was saying 'We don't need the Pagoda. We can bring in hoods from Atlantic City.' Then Neil stopped him and told him that was out. There had to be another way. Hayes started to laugh at that, but Neil said that if it wasn't changed either or both of them could end up dead."

seventeen

I made some excuse to Ed Noonan and got off the
elevator at the TV station again. He looked much relieved to see the last of me. I didn't go into the newsroom. I didn't start looking for Wally Skeat, who by then
would be sitting under the lights doing a pre-broadcast
run-through.

At the end of a short corridor, I found the fire-door
that led to the central core of the tower. The Pagoda stacked
a few exclusive offices one on top of the other beginning
about eight storeys below the TV station. Through the core
ran all the electrical and plumbing conduits that served
the offices, a dumb waiter that serviced the restaurants, as
well as an emergency stairway and an elevator which stopped
at the office levels. The tourist elevator rose on the outside
of the tower from the ticket hall to the TV station, the
observation level and the restaurant at the top. To get to
the offices it was necessary to take the elevators at the core.

In the centre of the pylon I got for the first time a
feeling that I was high above the ground. There was something about the raw concrete floors and stairways, the marks
in the concrete left by the forms of the builders, the sound
of running water in the conduits, the lack of windows. I
can't put my finger on it. Maybe I was just a little scared.

I walked down eight flights, stopping to correct the
dizziness that comes from circular staircases, and the echo
of my steps kept rebounding far below as I stood there
catching my breath. I didn't look. No good at heights. I
didn't like the echo and I fought against turning back. I
sometimes think that I'd like to skip over a few pages in
my life, the way you skip descriptions of the dawn coming
up over the rain-washed landscape in a novel. I felt like
I'd arrived at a good place to move ahead.

The fire door opened on a carpeted hallway, curving

gently with the circular shape of the tower. I passed a trolley of green garbage bags and mops belonging to the cleaning staff as I carefully moved along the corridor. I came to a glass door: *Syndicated Securities*. That wasn't it. Neither were *Martin, Morrison, Nunamaker and Duffin*, or *Salter-Price Associates*. But I hit pay dirt with *Cataract Vending*. According to Norman Baker, that was the door behind which Tullio Solmi operated.

There was a light burning under the door of Solmi's inner office, although the reception area was dark. The inner office had a blind door to the corridor, a very useful device, especially when it comes between the main entrance and the emergency stairs. It seemed that Solmi had thought of everything. I tried the outer door. It was open, maybe left that way by the cleaning staff. Dark shapes of pinball machines jumped up at me out of the gloom of the reception area. There was a hall stand with a coat and hat hanging from it; no windows, but one curved wall was covered with heavy draperies. I walked to the inner door and put my ear against the wood. I could hear voices, but I didn't believe what I heard Billie Mason say:

"And no anchovies. I hate anchovies." On second thought, I decided that it was a good thing to hear. It told me that she was not only unmurdered but that she was reasonably comfortable and in something of a bargaining position.

"Don't get too lonesome," said another voice moving in the direction of my ear. I skipped over the broadloom, nearly tripped on a raised electrical floor outlet, and dived behind the curtains. I could hear his key in the door. Then I could feel him come into the room through the soles of my feet. I couldn't see a thing until he switched on the lights. My breath was holding itself. He locked the door from his side. "You want single cream or double?" he yelled at the closed door. The answer came back:

"Double. And I'm nearly out of cigarettes."

"Okay. Double. I'll be right back. In case of fire write 'Help' on a note and slip it under the door." I heard a drawer open and the sound of keys landing in a clump on other keys and paperclips. "She's got matches," the voice said to itself as I heard noises of the man climbing into his coat. "Her funeral," he concluded and closed the outside door behind him. I didn't move for a minute in case he forgot his hat. I was about to come back into the world of light when I heard Billie, on the other side of the inner door, testing the lock.

"Shit!" she said when nothing happened. I tried to find the right desk drawer for the keys and got it first time. Desk drawers of the syndicate, the Upper Canadian Bank or the Anglican Church of Canada are all filled with the same junk: paperclips, a staple remover, a dusty roll of cellophane tape, odd tops to ball-point pens, thumb tacks, elastic bands, empty typewriter ribbon spools. It was a free-masonry that was bigger than morality or the law. And there were the keys I wanted at the back. Most of them were for cabinets with refills of more paperclips and rubber bands, but three were for the office doors. The second one worked. I turned the knob and walked in.

Billie Mason sat curled up on a dark leather chester-field with a French magazine on her lap. She looked like she had given up waiting for her date who was three hours late; the silk dress she was wearing had lost some of its crispness. On the marble-topped table, the colour of hal-vah, six other magazines were piled, all expensive and ei-ther French or Italian. She was smoking and by the look of the ashtray she'd gone through more packs than a few. She didn't look up at once.

"You forget your wallet?" That was when she saw me. "Benny! Oh, Benny! How did you get here? Are you trying to get yourself killed? Angelo will be back in a few min-utes." She had jumped to her feet, shaking the magazine from her lap to the floor with a rustle of the lively Liberty print material. She came at me with both arms. It was a nice hug. I can't say I didn't like it. Billie knew all there was to know about hugs.

"Exactly how long have we got before he gets back?"

"Twenty minutes, maybe just ten. Oh, I'm so glad to see you." I pulled her head off my shoulder and her hands away from my tie.

"We can get out of here right now. Do you trust me?"

"I don't want to get killed."

"Me neither. But you'll certainly get yourself killed if they find out you've been playing games with them. They'll want something for their time and effort, even if it's only your head for a trophy. And if Pritchett finds out you've been here without a chain holding you to the wall, he may stuff what's left. So either side can write your epitaph if you stick around here any longer. Your only chance is to walk out of here with me right now."

"All right, if you say so," she said, like I'd asked to cut her grass or something. I grabbed her coat, wrapped her in it and pulled her wrist, hoping the rest would follow. I went to the door to the corridor and peeped out. The coast was clear.

"I hope your friend Angelo likes double cheese and all the trimmings." Neither of us drew breath until the fire door closed behind us.

Once again in the core of the Pagoda, the echoes of footsteps trampled on my ears. Our enlarged shadows climbed the eight flights ahead of us, and the wall wrapped around us like an overgrown piece of sewer pipe stuck on end. I was glad when I could shove Billie ahead of me through the fire door into the TV station's hallway. The smiling photographs of the TV stars on the walls applauded our deed and for a minute made me think we'd finished. But I didn't even dare to catch my breath. This was only a half-way house for safety. I pushed the button to summon the outside tourist elevator, watching Billie's face as she tried to smile assurance at me. She didn't say anything. She couldn't. The elevator arrived and we got in. The doors closed us into the view of the falls slowly moving up to our level.

"Benny, my car!"

"Never mind your car. We're saving your neck."

"But it's here in the Pagoda. I parked it here days ago because it was central."

We dashed to the stairs. It was wet and chilly going down that last few flights. In a couple of places water actually gushed out of the side of the concrete: an underground spring or a sign of early thaw. Elsewhere columns of ice tinted with rust held up parts of the wall. The lighting that followed us down the tightly wound spiral of stairs looked like it had been designed not only to withstand the dampness but to work underwater. There was enough light for me to make out the little French car when I saw it parked up against a fat squat pillar.

Billie found her keys and opened the door on her side, then she leaned across and let me in the passenger side. I hoped her driving was going to be good enough for the ride I was imagining. She got the car started on the first try and backed expertly into the exit lane for a fast getaway. She handed the attendant a two-dollar bill and he opened the barrier.

"They didn't take your keys?" I asked.

"I told Angelo they were duplicate keys to Lowell's car. Are we going to be all right?"

There were two ramps, the east and west. The east one led down the hill toward the falls and the other led toward the residential and industrial side of town. Billie took the ramp heading west. A good choice, I thought, for avoiding the ravenous Angelo with his hot pizza pie. The ramp curved around coming up to ground level just to remind me again of the echoing tubes at the core of the Pagoda. At ground level I could see a long main-line freight train was stalled under the two great legs that held up the tower. While traffic on Clifton Hill, the east-west street, stood idling waiting for the freight to move further along the track, the engineer totally ignored the artery he was temporarily severing. With the Pagoda and the tracks behind us, Billie turned west. We had a clear road; it was the other lane that was stopped.

We hadn't gone very far when I heard Billie groan.

That's what it was, a real groan. I followed the look in her frightened eyes.

"Benny," she whispered, "it's Solmi!"

"I looked straight ahead. One of the cars waiting in line for the train to move was filled with five men. For a minute it looked like they hadn't seen us, then the car nosed in front of the Renault and stopped. The back door opened and a man started to get out.

"Back up!" I said through teeth that had frozen together. Billie shifted the gear and turned to look out the rear window while racing the car back to the tracks. We narrowly missed clipping a Ford, coming down the ramp from the Pagoda behind us. Nice, I thought. He'll block Solmi from coming after us on wheels. "C'mon," I shouted, only it came out a strangled rasp. We both got our doors open, and Billie followed me up the incline to the Pagoda's upper entrance. "We've got to get up to the ticket hall!" Billie looked at me as well as she could as we pounded up the hill to the western leg of the tower. She followed, but I never took my hand from her wrist. When we got up to the ticket hall, right on top of the shunting freight, Billie stopped, as though I had some fool notion to buy a ticket to view the sights in all their glory.

"This way," I croaked, out of breath, and feeling my lungs pinch. I dragged her down the steps leading to the downhill leg, the eastern leg that was on the other side of the tracks. From the entranceway, it was a short run to the parking lot where I'd left the Olds. Billie was an extension of my arm. Thank God, I thought, she doesn't have one of those ankles like they have in the movies. I was in no mood for a scene with Billie limping after me shouting: "Save yourself! Don't bother about me!"

By the time I could see figures standing in the entrance of the Pagoda, I'd bailed us out of the parking lot. The freight train had started shunting back through the tower again, like a thread being withdrawn from a needle. The men stood on the steps with their arms, as they used to say, akimbo. By the time we had turned into Falls Street, with a clear road back to Grantham, the train had stopped again.

156

eighteen

"Cooperman! What are you doing banging on my door at this hour?"

"Martha, I want you to meet a friend of mine, Billie Mason. Billie, this is Martha Tracy, my best friend in all the world, a girl you can trust in an emergency and depend upon completely."

"Cut the blarney, Benny, what's going on? I just got rid of a house full of people and I don't have strength left to empty the ashtrays."

"Martha, there are some people who are trying to find Billie. If they catch up to her it won't be pretty. Can she bunk here in your spare room until things blow over?"

"Hell, why didn't you ask straight out instead of buttering me up? Sure she can stay, but I got no time for you, Cooperman. Banging on a maiden lady's door at this time of night."

I'd driven a fast but complicated route from the Falls to Grantham and headed straight to Martha's. Nobody would think of looking for Billie there, and nobody would link Martha and me. Martha always pretended to spit nails, but she was all peppermint cream inside. I handed Billie in through the storm door to Martha, with some relief on both sides I think, then I headed for my parents' house off Ontario Street.

I let myself in with my key and tiptoed unnecessarily on the tangerine broadloom down the stairs to the TV room. I could catch some sleep there before heading back to the Falls.

"Benny! I thought it was your father. What are you doing here?" My mother was wearing her wine-coloured robe and sitting in front of the colour television. In her lap lay a Chatto & Windus paperback. By craning my neck around I could read the title, *Time Regained* by Marcel

157

Proust. The television set was flickering, but the picture had gone out of phase or something.

"No good movie tonight?"

"Oh, I've seen them all about fifty million times. I'm enjoying this. I like family stories and this is the end of eight of them. I get hooked on these complicated series things. I guess it started with *Upstairs Downstairs* and the *Forsyte Saga* on television. Then I went through Trollope and Balzac and now this. Did he do any other books, Benny? I'd like to get them." I shrugged. She told me a bit of the story, and then we went upstairs to put the kettle on. My coming home like this unexpectedly meant that we were going to have a talk. And you can't talk without tea.

As the kettle came to a noisy boil, Ma asked me if I'd enjoyed meeting Linda Levin the other night. I told her that, yes, I'd enjoyed the evening.

"I didn't ask you about the evening, I asked you about Linda. I wasn't fishing for compliments for the way I make Campbell's soup. You and Linda seemed to be talking nicely together and getting along without too much pushing from your father and me, so I was just wondering, you know, whether . . . whether, you know . . ."

"Ma, it's still a secret. We don't want anybody to know until we're sure. But when we are, you'll be the first to know. I promise."

"Always joking, Benny. They'll remember you as always joking and going back to a hotel room. You can joke too much, Benny. It's like the boy who cried 'Wolf!' You can't expect to be taken seriously if you are always telling jokes. Do you want some lemon?" I nodded and she got the plastic lemon from the refrigerator. I gave the teabag a bash or two with my spoon and removed it to the saucer. A squirt of lemon, two spoonfuls of sugar and I was in business.

"Do you mind if I catch some sleep on the couch downstairs? I don't want to bother going back to my place tonight."

"The couch? What do you think the guest room's for?

We don't have that many guests and I think the sheets are clean from when Sam was here at Christmas."

"The couch will be fine. I'm going to have to make an early start back to the Falls."

"You can start early from the guest room too. But suit yourself. I've finished reading for tonight anyway. I'm not going to wait up for your father. He went out to see what was going on downtown at ten o'clock. I guess he found a card game. Who knows?"

We talked for another ten minutes about family things, the birth of twins to a cousin that I still imagined as an eight-year-old, the story of Aunt Julie's forty-four day visit to her rich brother, my Uncle Irv, whose wife counted the days herself, and reported the tally by phone not ten minutes after Aunt Julie's plane left for Miami.

"Well," she said, as though she'd come to a momentous decision, and hoisting herself out of her chair at the round table, "I'm going up. I'll put a pair of your father's pyjamas in the guest room. If you hear a noise in the night, it'll be your father. I've given up sleeping with one eye open for him a long time ago. Benny, you'll turn the lights out before you come up?"

I decided to stay in the guest room. It was an independent decision based on the fact that I could have a morning shower without waking everybody up. After all the running I'd been doing it was no secret I'd been doing a lot of running. I found the pyjamas, pulled down the bed and got out of my clothes. I decided that the shower couldn't wait until morning.

At the green marble counter in the United Cigar Store on St. Andrew Street, I braced a copy of the *Beacon* against the menus and sugar shaker. It carried an impressive spread about the death of Miranda Pride. Dawson Williams mourned her passing and recalled happier days. James A. Sayre did not go on at length, but a brief, formal statement had been issued, probably written by Adela. They'd tried

159

to lure Peggy O'Toole into it, but she was out of reach visiting Hampton Fisher in his guarded enclave atop the Colonel John. A spokesman for Neil Furlong said that he was under a doctor's care and would not be making any statement for some time. Savas was keeping his beak clean: "No comment." I wondered whether he would comment over the telephone.

It was a short walk from the United to my neglected office. The curved pavement of St. Andrew Street looked wet instead of cold. Icy patches had become puddles. It was warming up. On a bench, waiting for a bus, a woman in a fur coat was sitting, trying to keep what looked like her grandchildren calm and out of mischief. One of them was rubbing her face into the fur of the coat, the other was blowing patterns in it and rubbing them out again with her mittened right hand.

Nobody was waiting for me on the stairs, but the toilet was running at the top. I jiggled the lever until the tank began to fill normally. Once I got behind my desk I placed a call to Niagara Regional and waited.

"Savas?"

"Christ, Benny. Don't you knock off on weekends? Who is it this time? Or is it more than one for a change?"

"Nobody's dead. Relax. Would you rather have me tip-toe away from the scene of the crime and let you stumble across your own bodies? Maybe you like them when they get sort of ripe? You want me to send you a postcard next time, routed via Honolulu?"

"Okay, I get the general idea. What's the commotion?"

"Do you have the post-mortem results on Miranda Pride?"

"Sure I have, but that doesn't mean I'm going to sing them over the phone to you. Singing telegrams are nearly extinct."

"Chris, we're both on the same side."

"Benny, whenever you're playing, you're a side all by yourself. The woman hanged herself. That's what I say, that's what the coroner says."

"So, what's the harm in reading me what he says?

You've already given me the pill; all I want now is the glass of water."

I heard him sucking at his teeth for a few seconds, vacuuming the crannies with his tongue. Then: "Okay, hold on to your shirt while I get the report of the examination." He left the line for a while longer than I was prepared for, and I could imagine three cops looking through the doorway at him, each with his own problems, each waiting for him to stop talking long enough for them to get a word in. Then he was back: "Okay? Here it is. This is what we found. The subject tied a running noose in the centre of a twelve-foot nylon cord, put two silk scarves around her throat and fixed the noose over them, then tied off the two ends of the cord to the bracket and jumped off the windowsill, not the chair that was standing nearby. We've got latent footprints on the chair and windowsill. That's the circumstantial stuff, now here's the gist of the medical examination."

"Wait a minute. What's with the scarves?"

"Vanity of vanities, Benny. She didn't want to leave ugly tell-tale deep impressions around the lovely neck. A cord like that would leave nasty discoloration, you know, lines running under the cord. A thin cord like that would have left a very deep impression."

"So with the scarves she's just as dead."

"Benny, you got no class. We're talking about a lady, a movie star, not some wino with debts to a loanshark. She didn't want to get marked up. So what?"

"I wasn't criticizing her, I just wanted to be sure I understood what you were saying. Remember, I only saw her for a few minutes and, to tell the truth, I wasn't focussing very well."

"You were a little green when you let us in. I remember. It helped soften the blow. You missed all the carrying on. First Furlong, then Raxlin, the producer. Benny, you want to hear this thing or not?"

"Shoot."

" 'Subject well nourished, evidence of balanced diet, normal care and attention. Height, five-foot four. Weight,

132 pounds. Muted impressions around neck of noose with suspension point about one inch in front of the angle of the left lower jaw. Vital changes locally and in the tissues beneath as a consequence of sudden constriction. Ecchymoses in the face. No marks of violence or restraint. Time of death . . .' Are you still with me, Benny, or did I lose you at 'ecchymoses'? 'Time of death sometime between eight o'clock and ten in the forenoon.' You want more technical stuff, Benny? 'Air passages constricted. Substantial engorgement and asphyxial changes.' Is that enough? You want food residue and other stuff?"

"Any sign of illness?"

"Good try, but it doesn't lead anywhere. 'No organic disease . . . subject was a healthy woman at the time of death.' Apart from needle marks on the left arm, that's it. 'Cause of death: strangulation caused by hanging.' "

"I don't get it."

"Don't get what? You want me to send you a medical dictionary?"

"No. What I don't get is 'why'. Why didn't she leave a note? Why didn't she say why she bumped Hayes?"

"Why don't people phone us before robbing banks, why don't they write out their own parking tickets? It's the same thing."

"Needle marks. What does your guy say about that?"

"Ancient history. We did find cocaine, but not much of it. There was some diazepam and he thinks there was an anti-depressant in the picture. He's doing tissue and blood analysis."

"Did you find anything unusual in her suite?"

"We went over her place and her husband's suite next door."

"Anything odd or out of place?"

"Nothing but the coke and the straws she used to sniff it."

"Nothing peculiar in the wardrobe line?"

"Clean bill there. Furlong must own fifty pairs of shoes. Got to go, Benny."

"Wait a minute, not so fast! I want to know what Miranda

told you about the Hayes case. She knew enough for you to pull her in but not enough for you to lay a charge. Are you happy with Miranda as the one who shot Hayes?"

"In a nutshell: right."

"Well? What did she say? Did she kill herself to square things?"

"That's all privileged stuff, Benny."

"What are you talking about? You've got the goods on a corpse. You think the crown prosecutor's going to give you an indictment? There's no case, Chris; your suspect's dead."

"All the more reason to keep quiet."

"Okay. Don't tell me anything that hurts. Do you think I'm going to phone the *Beacon* when I'm through with you? Come on. When's the last time I got my name in the paper?"

"Yesterday, and then again this morning."

"Yeah, well . . . But I wasn't shooting my mouth off. At least tell me what your witness saw. That's fair."

"William Blacklock, of Detroit, identified her as the woman he saw coming out of David Hayes' room. We showed him some pictures and he picked out Miranda right away. The night clerk saw her coming through the lobby from the other hotel."

"How'd she take that?"

"He was alive when she left him, she said. So then she goes and kills herself. You can't tell me, Benny, that she did that because she was innocent, or in order to shield somebody."

"What about the affair with Hayes?"

"In the end she admitted there'd been one. That's when I took her in. First of all she didn't know him at all, and she worked her way up through all the stages until we had her telling us all about how and where and when. The only thing that didn't happen, she insisted, was that she killed him. I might have bought that, or at least rented it, if it weren't for the fact that when last seen together they were having an ugly fight. That's from the bartender from the bar at the top of the Tudor."

"You were in a spot. It's not proof positive, only an

indication. If she wasn't the stuff headlines are made of, you might have held her. As it was . . ."

"Don't rub it in. I'm only a cop, remember."

"Chris?"

"I'm still here."

"Miranda killed Hayes."

"Check."

"Miranda killed herself."

"Double check."

"The neatest package that ever comes across your desk: murder and suicide. Pawn takes pawn. Pawn takes pawn. The one balances the other."

"That's right. It's all balanced on the books."

"You know what, Chris?"

"What?"

"You know it stinks to heaven as well as I do."

nineteen

*T*he Saturday paper was lying tucked up into itself
on the porch of Martha Tracy's bungalow. I collected
it under my arm and banged on the door. I could
soon hear footsteps padding down the long hallway. Billie
was wearing a rust-coloured corduroy dressing gown that
was obviously borrowed from Martha's wardrobe, and as
she fumbled with the unfamiliar door to let me in, her
trim figure played lost and found in the fabric whenever
she moved.

"Benny! Am I glad to see you! Martha's gone for the
weekend's groceries." She watched while I slipped off my
galoshes and put them on the streaked rubber mat. "I want
to thank you for . . ."

"Catch your breath. Let me catch mine. Have you
phoned anyone? Does anybody know you're here? If you've
been near the phone, I'll skin you alive." Billie took my
hat, and looked around for someplace safe to leave it. She
made a nervous hostess.

I followed her into the kitchen. She carried the kettle
to the sink, filled it at the tap like she'd never done it before
and set the promise of coffee going on the gas stove. We
sat down at a chipped white enamel-topped table. Billie
took a tug at the sash of her robe and made instant.

"We didn't get much chance to talk last night. Can
you tell me what happened? Were you a prisoner or having
pizza with the boys?"

"I thought I was finished talking. That's all I did since
they grabbed me outside the hotel the day before yesterday."

"Do they know about Furlong?"

"Of course not. They . . ." She stopped and looked
confused for a second, then frowned. "That was a trick
question."

"You'll give yourself wrinkles. They what?"

"They don't know very much about that. They wouldn't take it seriously. They think I came to the Falls on business. I tried telling them the truth, but they had their own story and were going to play rough until I went along with it." She rubbed her wrists just thinking about it. "I've been talking since I saw you in the coffee shop."

"As long as you haven't done any talking on the phone since last night."

"Benny, I haven't spoken to anybody. Honest."

"Billie, if you're not straight with me . . ."

"Well, I called Ed Noonan to tell him I wouldn't be available for a scene. That's all. If I had my way for a change, I'd be shooting the scene right now instead of cooling my heels here."

"Oh, that's perfect! That's fine, just fine. If Noonan knows, then Furlong knows. If Furlong knows, it's probably in the script by now. You take a lot of looking after, Billie. It's a wonder your old man wants you back at all."

"I didn't say where I was. Give me a little credit."

"Between us, it's cash and carry from now on." She sipped from her mug and I sipped from mine in silence. What she'd said about having her own way for a change kept echoing in my head, making me cross. I unbuttoned several layers of clothing and laid them on the seat of a pressed-back chair.

"Tell me all about Furlong, Billie. It's time I heard." Billie gave a deep sigh while ripping a strip of the folded newspaper on the table.

"I guess you already know quite a lot?" She looked at me like I was a magistrate and she was in the oldest instead of the second oldest profession. The smile on her face looked like it was going to blow away.

"I have to know it all. From the beginning." Billie began to spindle the newspaper strip around her fingers.

"Well, I saw him first when I was still in high school. I'd won a prize for acting in a one-act play. He phoned and said he'd seen my picture in the paper and wanted to know if I could be in a revue he was working on. My parents didn't give a damn, so I thought I'd meet him and talk to him at least."

"Was that here in Grantham or in the Falls?"

"Here at first. We did that show here, then there were others, and some of those we did in the Falls."

"And at the Patriot Volunteer over the river?"

"Hey! Yes, we did a smashing revue there. Where did you find out all this?"

"I read tea leaves. Did Furlong write it?"

"Wrote, directed and played in. Monty Blair gave Neil professional pointers. Monty had polish and style. Neil had energy and guts."

"Afterwards, you all went drinking at the Surf Lounge?"

"Fairly often. I was a young terror, I guess, in those days."

"And fondly remembered by Hatch."

"Hatch! Is he still alive?"

"Cut it out, Billie. You saw him New Year's Eve." She bit her lip and made a face. "How close were you to Furlong?"

"I was jailbait, but I can tell about it now. It doesn't matter. We were as close as we could get considering that I had parents, he was living in a furnished room with no visitors after ten and we were with a gang most of the time."

"Was Dulcie Osborne part of the gang?" Billie crossed her legs and frowned at the name, like I'd just rubbed her hand on the gum on the underside of a restaurant table.

"Yeah, Dulcie was there, toward the end, anyway. Neil said she had talent. That was his word for it."

"Tell me about her death."

"He'd somehow — through Monty, I guess — got a summer job in Toronto working on a TV show. While the regular actor who played the mute clown was away, Neil got a start. That was his launching pad. He got in with the writers and producers of the show, then he started writing a TV game show, then he wrote his first TV dramas. Next stop Hollywood fame and fortune."

"But he came back to the Falls before he left for good?"

"Sure. He had bridges and matches."

"Go on." Billie stretched her arms out straight and bent them back as far as she could.

"Well . . ." Then she suddenly folded both arms across her chest, leaned her elbows into the table top and turned pink around the cheeks. "He told me it was all over. Said that he would always remember me. He tried the same song on Dulcie, but she wouldn't buy it. She wasn't quite as ready to cut the cable as I was. She told me that he couldn't just leave, that if necessary she'd find a way to make him stay. They went off to the Patriot Volunteer. They were both drinking. They had an argument. She drove off in his car and on the way down the road she drove off the pavement into a tree."

"Did you ever hear from him again?"

"Not even a postcard."

"Wasn't he worried about your being under age? He could have got into a lot of trouble."

"Oh, he knew I'd never pressure anybody and I knew I'd had my time with him. How can I describe the way it was with Neil? With him people were temporary. Every so often he had to clear the decks of his old friends and start over again. And the new friends were always able to help him in his career in some way. His wife's the best example of that."

"You knew that you were going to see him in the Falls when you left Lowell?"

"I knew and I didn't. I knew he'd be there, but I didn't know exactly where or when. I ran into him the second day after I arrived. I hadn't even begun my hunt. It was like some romantic movie of the forties. We pretended that we'd never met; Noonan introduced us and we shook hands. Later he gave Ed the high-sign to push off, and he did. Neil's wife was going to be away for the holiday, so I stayed with him until New Year's Day. I let him book me into a room at the Colonel John under another name. He said there'd be no difficulty getting work as an extra, but getting a bit part would take some doing. He told me to stay close to the telephone and called a few times, came up a few times. He looked worried to death most of the time: paced the carpet like a hungry grizzly. I think he was scared Tullio Solmi or one of his boys would pay a visit."

"Solmi? What was his connection with Solmi?"

"When Neil first came to the Falls from Port, his old man was in a jam. He'd beaten up on Neil's mother — not that that was unusual — but this time he really hurt her and the police were involved. Solmi knew a lot of powerful people and so Neil went to see him. I don't know what happened exactly but his father didn't go to jail and Neil became palsy-walsy with Solmi. For a while he enjoyed driving around in Tullio's big car and tried talking out of the side of his mouth. But he soon dropped all that."

"But he could write quite a lot about Solmi if he wanted to?"

"About those days, sure. With authority."

Inch by inch the front of Martha Tracy's housecoat had fallen open. Since it was Billie Mason who showed through, I found it hard to concentrate on my work. Billie discovered the source of my distraction, blushed and then covered herself with a businesslike pull at the lapels. It was just as hard to think afterwards as before.

"When did you see Furlong last?"

"The night before David was killed. He said his wife was in Toronto, so he came up and we had drinks and then went out for dinner over the river."

"At the Patriot Volunteer. Right. Let's see . . . There's always the important last question and I usually forget to ask it. Try this. Last Wednesday morning you telephoned David in his room at the Tudor."

"And you answered."

"Did you talk to him before that? I mean after you ditched him?"

"I didn't . . . Oh, what's the use? I called him on Wednesday, about an hour earlier than when I spoke to you pretending to be David." She let her lip curl on the word pretending. "I told him that I had to see him and he wanted to see me. I suggested late Wednesday night, but he begged off because Miranda Pride was coming over.

He told me she'd been making a pest of herself and that all he wanted was to see me again. I told him that I'd call him back when I'd cleared some time, and when I did, you took the call."

"And you mentioned this to Furlong?"

"What if I did? They were long past the honeymoon those two. They couldn't even share a suite."

"I see. Well, Billie, if you want my advice, I would forget all about getting into this movie."

"But . . ."

"It's not worth getting yourself killed even if you have lines and a close-up. Do you want to be one of those people who show lots of promise but die young? Keep clear of the Falls until this mess is sorted out. Meanwhile you can stay here."

"Eventually I'm going to need some clothes."

"Good. You won't show your face in the Falls in one of Martha's mother-hubbards. Perfect. I like it. Print it."

Back in my office again I dialled long distance for Information in La Jolla, California. In less time than I would have guessed I was the proud possessor of Claudia Horlick's phone number, and I put it to work right away.

"Hello?" said Peggy's mother in a voice that sounded like I'd got her out of bed.

"Mrs. Horlick? This is Ben Cooperman. I'm a friend of your daughter."

"Marilyn? She's up in Canada."

"I know. That's where I'm calling from."

"Is something wrong? Is she all right?" Her voice was quickly waking up. "Has there been an accident?"

"No, everything is fine. Peggy's fine. She sends her love."

"You gave me a fright." She asked who I was again and I told her.

"What I wanted to know — it's for an article I'm doing about Hollywood in the heyday of the fifties — is about the Writers' Building at Paramount in those days."

"You should talk to the writers: Herb Schaffer, Joe Gillis, people like that. I was only a secretary."

"But you worked with some of the big ones?"

"Sure, I even did the weekly shopping for some of them. I helped Mr. Gillis buy a car once. He took me over to Lucey's a couple of times. He liked Gibsons." She went on about different writers she'd been assigned to, and when she showed no sign of coming to the part I was interested in, I interrupted.

"Did you work on *Donnybrook*?" There was a pause.

"Yes, I did." Silence.

"When was that exactly?" I tried to put a smile in my voice.

"What's this article for?" The smile didn't get across the Mississippi.

"It's for one of the serious movie reviews." I tried to think of a name, but all I could think of was *Silver Screen* and *Modern Screen*, so I didn't offer a title. I let her prate about a few more of the directors and writers that she'd been typing for and made appropriate noises whenever she paused for breath. Finally, she began to slow down.

"I don't know that there's much more I can tell you. I wasn't as young as a lot of the girls there then. And there were a lot of good-looking girls, and some hanky-panky going on between the girls and the people they worked for. But I was married, so I wasn't involved." She sounded like she was reasoning backwards. "You should talk to some of the younger girls. *Girls*, I mean they're old women now. Although I don't think of myself as an old woman. There were some crazy times what with the carrying on and the drinking."

"Did you work closely with Jim Sayre?" Another silence that reached across the continent on my seventy-six cents a minute.

"Mr. Sayre finished *Donnybrook* early in 1954. I didn't see him after February of that year. I was reassigned to work with Mr. Geller, and after several weeks I went on to work with Emmett Lynch on *Walk East on Main*. Then there were a few odd jobs lasting a few months, and then I said goodbye in December. I didn't go back after Marilyn was born. But some of the girls kept in touch for a year or so."

"So you left the studio in December of '54, right?"

"That's what I said. Just before Marilyn was born."

"What was Mr. Sayre like in those days?"

"You're very interested in Jim Sayre, Mr. Cooperman."

"That's right. He's one of the great directors of our time. I should do a book, not just an article, about the era of his first important work. It must have been wonderful being in on everything."

"He was a perfectionist. He wanted everything authentic. We all worked very hard. You could go out for a drink with him and he's as friendly as pie, then the next day he'd work you like you just came in as a temporary." She paused, taking a second to lick old wounds.

"Not much of a man for sentiment?"

"No, it's not that. He was a very warm man. He just tried to keep the work moving steadily. He loved making pictures."

"Could you have fallen for a man like that, Mrs. Horlick?" Another pause.

"If I'd given him any encouragement, he might have come on to me very strongly. But I never did." This time I started the silence. But there was nothing further coming on that subject.

"I see. You said you weren't like some of the other, younger girls. The other girls were less stand-offish?"

"Some of them. But I had a few good friends: Erica Tilloch, for one. Blanche Tyler was another. We lunched whenever the men went off in a gang. They didn't want us around then. But usually we'd be working too hard to fool around. Blanche did very well for herself in the end. Her sister married Joseph Kindall Hurwitt's agent. You know, the mystery writer?"

"Basil Simpson, 'the internationally-known lawyer-sleuth'."

"Well, Blanche became the executive producer of the TV series. It ran for years and years."

"Any message for Peggy?"

"Oh, she calls me pretty often. We keep in touch. I tell her about my aches and pains and she tells me about, you know, what she's doing. Oh, yes, she keeps in touch.

She's a typical Libra in that way: easy to get along with, gentle. I never had cause to be ashamed of my daughter, Mr. Cooperman. She's a good girl and she came out of a God-fearing, church-going family. She was a happy child. My late husband took her everywhere with him. Have I answered all your questions? We got off the subject of the Writers' Building. We sometimes worked in relays around the clock. Oh, we had some wonderful times."

"I want to thank you for your help, Mrs. Horlick. I've taken up a lot of your time."

"That's all I've got now, since Mr. Horlick passed on. Say hello to Marilyn when you see her. Tell her to be careful. Somebody told me there's rattlesnakes up there."

Before heading back to the Falls, I closed the office door and put it on the spring lock. I didn't want a client for the next five minutes. I slipped off my right shoe and sock, leaning back in the chair behind my desk. I then pulled the lace out of the shoe, tied a slipknot in the middle, slid the noose over my big toe and pulled. I tried it several ways, and shortly before gangrene set in I'd learned quite a bit about hanging toes and other things.

twenty

I parked the Olds in its familiar corner and walked over to the Colonel John. The lobby was alive. Half the newsmen in the country were making themselves at home on the dozen or so chairs and couches in the place. The other half were keeping watch near the locked door of the street-level beverage room, waiting for the first stroke of noon. How often do you get an international story like this with so many side-bars? All-star cast upset by suicide of time-honoured superstar. Peggy O'Toole pursued by America's most eligible bachelor. I wondered whether Fisher's own papers had orders to ignore that part of the story. Probably. He hated to be in the headlines, unless it was for one of his deep-sea diving stunts. At twenty the guy led an expedition to the North Pole, where he tested some warm suits for the US Navy in the water under the ice at 90 degrees north. Then he took off for the South Seas to dive the wrecks of Truk. It was just my luck to lose Peggy to a guy like that.

I pushed my way through the crowd and took my chances with the weather outside. Across the park from the gift shop and the hotel a crowd of tourists were gathered, not to look at the falls, but at something in the river gorge. I crossed the wet street — the falls had been spitting again, but it hadn't frozen — and bent over the parapet. Down below, arranged like a latter-day nativity scene, the tiny fixed figures of the film crew were standing under arc lights, reflectors and behind the camera. Four versions of the *Maid of the Mist* were drydocked just out of reach of the intruding ice. In front of the cameras two figures were moving — Dawson Williams and Peggy O'Toole — I could pick them out even at this distance. Behind was the piled-up mountain of ice, a dramatic backdrop even from where I stood.

I felt somebody looking over my shoulder, and I turned around. Nothing. Then I glanced up to the balcony of the penthouse on top of the Colonel John Butler and got my first sight of Hampton Fisher, boy publisher. It wasn't much of a look, foreshortened as it was, but it was the only view of him most people ever saw. There he was, with a poorer view of the proceedings than I had. I wondered if Hampton Fisher, with his phobias, his highly controlled escapades, could ever engage in anything so unrehearsed as a human relationship. I tried to imagine him with Peggy. It wasn't easy. So I blew a few germs in his direction and stepped out into the street to cross back to the hotel.

What further thoughts I might have had about Peggy's beau evaporated. The reason, a speeding dark blue Duster came down the street at me at sixty miles an hour. It sailed right through where I'd been standing and kept on going. I felt like a matador when the bull takes the nap off his suit of lights. This Duster almost had my lights and my darks as well. I have the sound of that speeding motor in my head still. And not a hint of the screech of brakes.

"That was close!" A short man at the curb grabbed my arm and pulled me across the road and onto the sidewalk. "They never even stop. I tell you, it's some kind of world where you can get killed just crossing the street." I was busy dusting off invisible paint marks from my coat and wondering which of the current crop of acquaintances was trying to write me out of the script. "What you need is a drink, my friend." The little guy led me by the arm into the beverage room at the back of the Colonel John.

"We don't open till noon," the bartender said. "Oh, I'm sorry, I didn't recognize you, Mr. Cohn." I took another look at my rescuer. He had a chirpy brown moustache under horn-rims, thick lenses, and not very much hair. His ears looked like rabbits had nibbled at them and his skin was pink the way smoked salmon is pink. He was looking me over.

"Mordecai Cohn?" I asked.

"That's right. You'd think Mordecai or Cohn, wouldn't you, but my mother thought it should be both. But things were different in those days. People had values, standards."

Cohn leaned on the table with the elbows of his fine navy-blue overcoat. A white silk scarf with his monogram was tucked under the collar. He pulled at himself to make himself more comfortable as we sat there sizing one another up. For a long time he kept his eyes locked on mine. It was the kind of eye-contact stuff that made me nervous, as it was supposed to do.

The bartender had brought a teapot and placed it with two teacups in the middle of the round table. The teapot wasn't steaming.

"I'm not that hard to meet, Mr. Cohn. You didn't have to go to all that trouble."

"I wanted you to think that I'm your friend. I *am* your friend, you'll see. At the moment, Mr. Cooperman, you don't have a better friend in the world. Believe me. What you did last night has made a friend and colleague of mine, a very calm and relaxed businessman, very impulsive and vengeful. He could get into a lot of trouble he's so mad. So, like a good friend, I tried to calm him down, get him to see reason, only the only thing he sees is blood, Mr. Cooperman. Now in the old days we both saw a lot of that. We're both experienced. We're old surgeons. Once you've seen one gall bladder, you've seen them all. Know what I mean? So, when my friend gets mad and starts yelling for blood, I know right away he's annoyed. In fact, he hasn't been so hot since his kid was turned down for West Point. I mean he spends more time over the river than he does here. Anyway, like I was saying, I know it's dangerous to stand between an angry man and his wrath, but I'm basically a peacemaker. A peacemaker is what I basically am. So I asked my friend if I could have a shot at you first, so to speak. But we've got to talk fast, because my friend can only smoulder so long. I don't have that much influence when it comes right down to it. So let's see if we can find some sane, reasonable way out of this."

"That Duster, was that the way of reason?"

"That was to get your attention, that's what that was."

"Okay, you've got it. What's on your mind?"

Mordecai Cohn examined his fingernails; they were neat, clean and manicured to within an inch of their lives. His shirt-cuffs were crisp and white, held together by cuff-links with amethysts. His tie was of the same washed-out violet, pinned to his shirt with a sterling clip. He smelled of talcum, just like my father.

"I was thinking of this country, Mr. Cooperman. You know, the seasons we get up here: spring, summer, autumn, winter. Down south in Florida, or Havana in the old days, it was all the same. Every day the same thing. Here we go from season to season. I like the contrasts. I suspect that you like them too, or you wouldn't be working up here. Am I right?"

"They're okay. Go on. Speak your piece."

"Well, it would be a shame never to see the spring, Mr. Cooperman, that's what I was thinking. You know, with the daffodils, the robins coming back, the eternal renewal, that sort of thing. Well, my friend has probably eaten as many robins as you've looked at. He's not big on sentiment, although I will say this for him, he's a great family man. He's got a wonderful wife and kids you wouldn't believe. But right now, with a nod, my friend could fix it so you don't see the spring. No more daffodils, no more robins. Right now, I'm the only thing stopping him from fixing that this morning. Funny, I left him eating Rice Crispies half an hour ago, and he could have fixed it between spoonfuls."

"I'm not going to tell you where she is, Mr. Cohn. That's not something I'm going to bargain about."

"I understand your reluctance. Look, I've got finer feelings too. I had to look the other way when Solly Minden got it. Solly and I went back to prohibition days. We were like brothers, used to date the same girls, bet the same horses, fix the same fights. But he was caught creaming the top off the profits that he was supposed to be putting away for my business associates and myself. So Solly was creaming our cream. It was open and shut. I went to see him, but I couldn't talk any sense into him. Where was I?

So, what I'm saying is that in the end you've got to decide whether you want to see the robins again or whether you don't. It's up to you."

"I see. What are you going to do with her?"

"You don't have to worry about that."

"What do you think she's done?"

"Again I'm telling you, don't get involved. You don't want to carry around useless information. You want your mind clear to see the big chance when it's looking at you."

"I guess I'm not going to get time to break that idea in?"

"Uh-uh."

"And there's no use telling you that it's all a terrible mistake?" He shook his head, and seemed to see the teapot for the first time. He poured out mine first. These hoods are clever. It even looked like tea. "You don't want to hear about how my friend is interested in getting a break in the movies. She doesn't want any more to do with her husband or his business, especially his out-of-town business."

"I think my friend would like to take this up with her himself."

"He had over twenty-four hours."

"She was starting to see things our way."

"Did Solmi tell you that? Do you really believe that it took your pal a full day to get that girl to see a money-making proposition? Come on. I thought you said you'd been around."

"Talk broken English. I don't follow you."

"I'm saying that I happen to know a deal was settled between them as soon as they started talking." I tasted the tea, following Cohn's lead. It wasn't the best rye whisky I've tried, but probably the best I've had before noon from a teapot. Cohn was thinking about what I'd said. I decided not to push it. When you sow a seed, you don't overwater it. Cohn shook his head.

"I don't believe it. I don't believe it."

"Suit yourself. You don't think he was acting mad just to put you off?"

"Be quiet a second. I know him like a brother."

"Just like Solly Minden." Cohn's moustache began to tremble under that nondescript nose.

"How would you know? We've had peace between us for ten years. Nobody'd believe a Jew and a Gentile could do business together like we do. We had sneers on both sides, but I've been at his christenings and he's been to my bar mitzvahs. There hasn't been any of that rough stuff on the Niagara frontier for all this time. Why would he throw that away?"

"You know that Tony Pritchett is here, don't you? Maybe your friend is looking for another partner. Did you know that Pritchett has money invested in this movie, or did Solmi forget to tell you? Try out the sound of it: Solmi and Pritchett. It has a nice ring to it." Cohn pushed himself away from the table, nearly upsetting his teacup. His mouth was moving while he got up, but he wasn't saying anything. I expected at least a final glare from those large distorting lenses, but he looked right through me, then stormed outside.

I don't quite know what I hoped to achieve by putting Cohn off like that, but in my position, I couldn't see how I could make things worse. Better to have Cohn hunting Solmi than Solmi hunting me. Anyway Cohn deserved it for nearly running me down in the street. As for Solmi, even without meeting him I didn't think much of his methods.

I cut through the kitchen of the Colonel John to get from the beverage room to the lobby without running into any of Tullio's friends. Nobody noticed me, and I liked that. A big fight was going on, a battle in black and white: the chef was arguing with the maître d' about whether or not it was part of his job to heat Campbell's vegetable soup for Hampton Fisher. Coming into the lobby, I nearly ran into the stringbean of Thursday night. The chefs were still at it as I scooted out the back.

With unaccustomed warm weather fanning my face I returned to my room at the Clifford Arms. From the pay phone in the malty lobby, I tried to reach Captain Jim Loomis of the New York State Police. I'd heard Savas mention him once or twice and my head holds on to things like that like my pockets collect fuzz. I caught up with him in the Lewiston Detachment. He sounded friendly enough, with a voice that could have sold breakfast cereal on television. I gave him some invented regards from Chris, then told him what I wanted. He said he'd do what he could, and I told him I'd check in later.

Ned Evans was holding court on his adopted ground in the beverage room. It was early, but Ned and Jack and Will must have been on a party. Ned's eyes were half-shut and red-rimmed. He was wearing that secret smile that gave him a superior look. I didn't want to get sucked in, but I couldn't see a way out.

"That fellow Noonan's on the take. He can be bought," Ned said. "He's looking for loot, not talent. I showed him my review in the *Beacon*, Benny. Remember my Romeo?

"That was a bit before my time."

"The *Beacon* said that I brought a spirit of professionalism to the Niagara Peninsula. Professionalism! It went on to say I no longer had the figure for Romeo, but no matter. They wouldn't have appreciated Henry Irving or Martin Harvey either. Bloody provincials."

"Ned, did you direct that one, or was it in Monty Blair's day?"

"It was Monty's triumph, my boy. When I say I was good, it is no better than faint praise. I was brilliant!"

"Not on opening night," whispered Will.

"No more of that."

"What happened?"

"I was brilliant throughout the run. On opening night I was also brilliant, until the tights split, then I was inventive. The facts are a matter of public record. You can read all about it among Monty's papers at the Library. Part of the historical record of our times, Benny."

"Not on opening night," repeated Will.

"Tell me, Benny, what do you say to *The London Merchant*?"

"What is it? It's not Shakespeare, is it?"

"George Lillo, eighteenth-century, cast of nine. I will

play poor Barnwell myself, and you might make a possible Trueman. It's a play that takes hold of the stage and shakes it." He spilled some beer on the table for emphasis. "Ah, but who will we get to play the incomparable Millwood?"

"Well, what about Jack, here, or Will?"

"Millwood, my boy, is a woman. She's a woman of great beauty, but a savage siren. The incarnation of evil. She tempts the innocent Barnwell into a life of crime because he's in love with her. It's one of the great parts and requires the most perceptive of actresses..." Ned went on and on about this play, and eventually I put down a few bills and excused myself.

It was eleven miles to Grantham from the Falls, and I'd covered that piece of road so often in the last few days that I felt like a bus driver. This time, though, because of Ned's tip, I felt that I wouldn't be making the trip too many more times. That gave me a light feeling in the heart and added an ounce or two to my foot on the gas pedal.

twenty-one

E lla Beames was in her usual place in the Special Collections Room at the Library. Ella and a few other token human beings had been brought over from the old Carnegie building when it was destroyed to make way for an empty lot. She had helped me on more cases than she knew about. In fact I've pocketed a lot of change for work Ella looked up for me for nothing.

"Benny Cooperman! My, it's good to see you. I was just thinking about you the other day."

"What have I done now?"

"Oh, nothing like that. I just remembered I haven't seen you in a couple of months. How's your mother?"

"No change. Still glued to the television."

"In the old library she used to come in and clean me out with her novel reading. She ran through Faulkner like grain through a goose. Then she went on to Hardy. I saw her through Trollope and Balzac, Dickens and Thackeray. Even Meredith. I could understand George Eliot. She put me on to Mary Webb, you know. And now she watches television?"

"She still reads a lot. She's found some Frenchman now."

"That would be Proust. She called me about him."

"Ella, Ned Evans says Monty Blair left his papers to the Library. Could I have a look at them?"

"I don't see why not. You're a member. You were even in some of his plays. I remember you in a green hat."

"Ned gave me my big break in *A Midsummer Night's Dream*. Monty only let me do bits in one-acters. I did the Guard in *The Valiant* six times. All he ever says is 'Yes, sir.' "

"Well, I'll have one of the girls bring you the boxes. Monty's sister sent them over a year after he died. I don't suppose they've even been properly catalogued. You're the second person in here asking to see them. A young reporter with the *Beacon* was in here not long before Christmas."

"David Hayes?"

"A tall young man with a nose like the Cutty Sark."

"David Hayes."

"Shouldn't take more than ten minutes to fetch the boxes. Meanwhile, why don't you get us both a coffee? Not the stuff they sell downstairs. Go to Stewart's on James Street. They make the best coffee around. I've tried them all."

When I got back, Ella had cleaned a place for me at one of the bleached maple wood tables that fanned out from her desk. Monty's papers looked more like Monty's effects. When your whole life is put together, you hope it will amount to more than two cardboard boxes. I pried the lids off the boxes and then off the coffee. I saw Ella watching me, so I didn't mix business with pleasure. Then, when the cup was empty — she was right about Stewart's — I began to pull things out of box number one.

There were a lot of books, mostly books of plays with pencil lines drawn through many passages. Sometimes Monty had used different coloured pencils to keep track of two or more versions of the same play going at the same time. Occasionally there would be slips of paper with a part written in for a narrator.

Under the books, I found scrapbooks with clippings of reviews from all his productions. There were photographs included: a cast picture in colour with twenty people smiling with identical pink eyes from the camera flash, pictures of Monty presenting awards or accepting them. Some of the photographs were familiar. I was even in a couple of them, holding a spear, well to the back. Under the first scrapbook was another and another. There, during the Second World War, was Monty in uniform, shaking hands with John Masefield, the poet laureate. He'd never said anything about it.

Then came a series of small diaries. There was one

for each year for twenty-eight years, the last one left incomplete on his death. In this, another hand — it must have been his sister's — had written on a blank page at the end of several weeks of blank pages, that Monty had died on this date. Four pages later, the time and date of the funeral were noted. I started to flip backwards in that last year looking for familiar names. He had commented on Ned's drinking, the stinginess of the city council's donations toward a summer of Shakespeare in the park, and the difficulty of finding good local scripts.

This wasn't any good, this flipping backwards. It wasn't a magazine. So I reached for the first of the diaries and slowly worked my way through nearly thirty years of twisted dreams and frustrated ambition in the life of Grantham. At once Monty's writing voice seemed stronger. There were fewer moans and complaints. He seemed to be full of life's juices and having a good time. Occasionally his sister butted in and put an end to a promising affair. Lucia was a demon for the straight and narrow. Here she was attending every rehearsal for *Salomé* and not paying much attention to *Stalag 17*. No women in that. There she put an end to a flirtation with Pamela McKeon, and later with Monica Bett, both of whom had shown real promise. She didn't object to men showing promise, though:

APRIL 2. *Young man tried to impress me with a piece of "original writing". Familiar echoes. Turned out to be Salinger dressed up so it would fool no one. I had a talk with him. I told him that I recognized the original in his pastiche. He brazened it out, saying that it was experimental. I've never met anyone so ambitious. He's hungry for fame the way I've never been. His name is Neil Furlong, works as a garage mechanic, and comes from Port Richmond. He can read and write, barely. Elspeth has stopped writing to me . . .*

That was in the early 1960s. A month later he wrote:

MAY 16. *Neil has some excellent ideas, but most of them come from comics or movies. His deceptions are so childish they are charming. And when I catch him out, he pouts as though I had been the deceiver. I've given him a reading list and have tried to tell him about singular verbs and plural subjects. What is at the bottom of this naked ambition?*

Later still:

> JUNE 20. *I've decided to let Neil act as my stage manager for* The Shrew. *Since he is always around it would be folly not to make use of him. I'm quite flattered when I hear him repeat one of my sayings . . . His father was in court this week for beating up his mother . . .*

The entries went on and on like that. Neil appeared to be working out well. That first awkward plagiarism was forgotten. Neil turned Monty into a one-man university. A move from Port Richmond to Niagara Falls was noted along with a change from mechanic to public relations man at the railroad. Toward the end of the decade Furlong was absent for long periods, then back for an intense week or two connected with a play or revue. Then silence until the beginning of the seventies:

> DECEMBER 23. *A card from Neil in Toronto. Very friendly! Does he imagine we don't have* TV *here in Grantham? His play was very well received by the critics, and I don't see him making any statements about his debt to* Angel on My Rooftop. *I've talked to Lucia about it, and she wants me to speak to Hollis.*

> DECEMBER 24. *Drink with Hollis in the back office. He told me to forget the play. He sketched for me the costs involved in bringing a suit of this kind to court. I hope Neil has a merry Christmas. Imagine the cheek of sending me a card! I always said he was an extraordinary fellow.*

From then on — still in the early seventies — Furlong was mentioned only in passing. In 1975 Monty noted that his most recent TV play was based on well-known facts of a case involving people from the Falls. Later he noted that he had a play due to open on Broadway.

> OCTOBER 25, 1976 . . . *He's taken the thing straight from Thomas Heywood!*

I flipped over the pages more rapidly. Billie Mason's name came up under her maiden name. Again Lucia steps in. Again Monty dives into another theatrical production. I was tempted to linger over his accounts of meetings with Monica Bett, Elspeth Trail and the others, but decided to save them for a rainy day. It was five years ago when he first recorded meeting David Hayes:

> 2 MAY. *Tall young man came in to watch rehearsal and afterward asked for work as anything from stagehand to extra. Educated fellow by the sound of him. Name of Hayes.*

> 19 MAY. *David Hayes is working out well as ASM, unlike Jack Ringer, who prefers the sessions in the Harding House after rehearsals. David caught me in a blunder: I'd shortened a scene so that now Jessica will not be able to make the costume change. I've had to put the cut lines back. He suggested interchanging act III, scene iii and iv. That way we will have a main scene separated by two in front of the curtains . . .*

> 30 MAY. *Long talk with David. He promised to show me some stories he wrote at university. I told him to try writing a play.*

> 12 JUNE. *Finished the last of David's stories. Nice touches to all of them, but he hasn't been able to push them beyond nine pages, so development and characterization suffer. Says he's got a play in the works. Monica Bett is expecting! . . .*

> 9 AUGUST. *After the show, David handed me a manuscript and rushed away. I spent all night reading it. It's a very accomplished comedy. He has a genius for laughter.*

12 AUGUST. *David has sent the play to Neil Furlong! He knew that I had helped him start off, but nothing of my problems with him. I'll write to Neil to explain who David is. He is well-enough established, so he can afford to be kind to a beginner.*

3 OCTOBER. *The worst has happened. Never, never, never, never, never, did I believe anyone could be so utterly low. Last month Neil phoned me to tell David that he had talked NBC into doing his play. He explained how he had worked on it himself to transform it to fit the format of a series, so the network would buy. I gave him David's number. I wanted no further role in this. Last night David came over and announced that this was to be a "learning assignment": he would be paid a small amount, but would receive no credit. It was* Angel *all over again. Why are we condemned to repeat our mistakes? I'll write to Neil, try to appeal to his better instincts, but I fear he is beyond reasoning.*

Then we were in Monty's last year. David was obviously on his conscience. Every mention of Hayes was tinged with sadness, every mention of Furlong laced with disgust. But there was no hatred. He was like a sprinter talking about a non-starter. There was no resentment in his tone. David's ability somehow made him the winner no matter what had been stolen from him. Monty's was a strange kind of pride and I respected him for it. But as I walked out of the Special Collections Room and toward the burnt-orange stairway to the main reference section, I wondered how David Hayes had taken all this. Had he been as passive about it as Monty?

In the Reference Section, I looked up the Zodiac and was told to "*See* Astrology". I found a book and spent half an hour reading up on the Sun signs. They were all there, except Pistachio.

twenty-two ────────

From the lobby of the Library, with its bubbling fountain and babbling brook, I telephoned Martha Tracy. The line was busy. I hoped that it was Martha on the phone and not Billie. I wasted a handful of change trying to locate Savas. I left a message with Pete Staziak, another sergeant in the department and an old high-school friend. "Tell Chris that I think I can see daylight and green fields in the Niagara Falls business. Suggest to him that he keep an eye on Furlong. I think he has some explaining to do." Pete said he'd pass the word, but didn't promise results. I shook the phone and told him I was a taxpayer and he laughed me off the line.

While I was standing there with little to show for my investments, and before the water music got to me, I put a few coins to work and dialled Captain Loomis in Lewiston to see whether he'd stumbled across anything interesting. When I asked him that, he said he'd leave the interpretation up to me. "Let's see," he said, and I could hear the crackle of paper over the wire, "it was a 1959 two-door Ford, registered owner Joseph Furlong of Port Richmond. Ontario plates and . . ."

"That made the car ten years old at the time of the accident."

"Yeah, according to this the body was rusted out. It wasn't worth much even before it hit that tree."

"Witnesses?"

"Two. Peter and Eva Wheeler of Rochester were passing and say they saw the car, travelling at high speed, fail to slow down at a sharp curve. The car went into it at top speed, jumped the curb, went through the guard-rail and into a fat oak tree. That tree's claimed about a dozen fatalities in as many years."

"Did they check the brakes after they got the wreck back to the garage?"

"Sure. But it was impossible to tell whether the brake fluid line separated as the car went through the guard-rail or before. The bottom of the car was scraped clean by the metal railing."

"So, you were looking for mischief, were you?"

"It didn't smell of roses, I'll tell you that. Did you know the girl was pregnant?" That caught me like a punch in the mid-section.

"No, I didn't. That's in the post-mortem?"

"Yeah. The girl wasn't married. Under-age, you know. She was living at home with her father. We figured that she couldn't face going on or being found out, so . . ."

"She did herself in in a borrowed car?"

"That's about the size of it."

"How pregnant was she?"

"The fetus was about three, three and a half months old."

"Did anybody tell her father?"

"No. We didn't think that would make any difference. Bad enough the girl was dead. No need to break her old man's heart a second time."

"Right. Well, thanks a lot for your help. I'll give your regards to Chris Savas when I see him."

"Thanks, but to tell the truth, I've never met the guy. So long."

I tried Martha Tracy's number again.

"Cooperman, where have you been?"

"Two hours ago I was drinking coffee in your kitchen. Ask Billie."

"Ask her yourself, if you know where to find her."

"Isn't she there?"

"I walk in with groceries enough to last all week and discover your friend gone."

"Martha, are you sure? Maybe she went out for cigarettes or to get some clean clothes. Let's not panic."

"She left a note that said thanks for everything. Shall

we panic after all, or does your twisted little mind have another idea?"

"It means trouble, Martha. I'll be talking to you."

"Somebody better. I'm not running a theatrical boarding house, you know." On my way down the stairs, I thought of six ways to wring Billie Mason's lovely neck.

The Falls had continued to warm up while I was away and the wind had come around to the south. I left the Olds in a lot behind the Colonel John and made it to the lobby without running into the mob or the syndicate. I bought a paper, feeling actually warm outside for January. The cops were growing everywhere again for some reason. I felt like I'd missed a chapter in a serial. I found a constable near the reception area and asked him if he'd seen the sergeant. He said he'd been called away suddenly on another case, but he'd left word for me to wait for him here. All the way from Grantham I'd been having a meeting with myself at a high level. It was time to talk to Savas.

The hotel dick left off reading his detective magazine long enough to let me use his phone to call Lowell Mason in Grantham. He was the guy who was paying me and I'd let his wife get away from me twice. The least I owed him was an explanation. I could make a preliminary report. After he was sure that I charged the call to my office number, the hotel dick went back to his reading.

"Mason Real Estate. Can I help you? It was Mason himself trying to sound like a receptionist.

"You could have, but now it's too late. This is Cooperman. Remember me? I've got a report for you if you want to hear it."

"Cooperman! Where is my wife? What have you done with her?" He sounded like the same bastard who'd hired me, but the concern in his voice sounded genuine.

"I think I can promise a full recovery, Mr. Mason. But if you want it to last, I'd cast off from your business friends. I don't think they help the relationship."

"I'll ask for advice when I need it. Right now I want

my goddamned wife back. Do you hear?" He didn't wait for an answer. And I didn't have one anyway.

I took the paper to the Guard Room and ordered an egg-salad sandwich and coffee. The headline in the Falls paper grabbed me at once:

GANGLAND WAR HOTS UP: CLAIMS FOUR

The story continued:

> Shotgun blasts killed four men today in what has been described by police as a "gangland style" war which has suddenly exploded in the Falls area. Dead are one of the alleged underworld dons, Tullio Solmi, and three of his business associates. The shootings occurred in Mr. Solmi's private office at Cataract Vending in the Pagoda Tower. There were no witnesses to the murders, described as "executions" by a police spokesman. With Mr. Solmi on the blood-spattered carpet were the bodies of Frederico Pacifico, president of Old Pal Juice Company, Sean O'Feeney, a director of the consortium that owns and operates the Pagoda Tower, and Vic Bertolini, of the Ben Nevis Trucking Company of Fort Erie. A special Niagara Regional task force is being established to deal with an increasing number of incidents that can be linked to organized crime . . .

And so on. It was clear that the writer, crime reporter John Pozzetta, was aiming for a National Newspaper Award with his prose, but he got the essentials where they belonged. Now it was the turn of the heirs and assigns of Tullio to blast away at Mordecai Cohn, who, for my two dollars, had his name written all over this job. I wondered whether Tony Pritchett would then just step in and take over the pieces of a buckshot-pitted empire after the smoke cleared. That would be playing it smart. But you can never tell about these guys. Maybe next spring Solmi's Cadillac will show up parked next to Al Capone's bullet-proof limousine in the exhibition around the corner.

Savas shoved in beside me, moving my coffee cup aside with his big elbow. Sergeant Pete Staziak, a fellow-sufferer of Harry Croft's geometry class in Grade 13, plunked down opposite me. Both wore grey faces, daring me to lighten the moment with a witty saying. Savas glanced at the paper. He'd been working too hard to have seen it. Nor did he see the rehashed story about the Pride suicide, which had now been moved to the bottom of the front page. The Chamber of Commerce wouldn't like having two major deaths on page one. Editors can't unmake the news, but they'd managed to lose poor David Hayes among the advertisements toward the end of the first section.

"Benny, Savas and I are dead beat," Pete said, rubbing the red mark on his forehead where his hat had been sitting. I waved down one of the gingham-dressed waitresses and she brought two fresh cups and a Silex full of coffee. Chris blew into a spoonful of hot blackness and sipped it, looking at me from under his generous eyebrows.

"Benny, where are you in this thing? I'm going nuts." I could feel my brain trying to draw breath. There comes a time to bring out into the open the facts that are known and the speculations which might be harbouring facts under the ivy.

"Okay," I said, "let's talk about it. Question number one?"

"Who let the mob out? They've been quiet for years; now, suddenly we're back in the twenties. What gives?"

"It's like launching a boat."

"What are you talking about?"

"You know how they knock out the last wedge to coincide with the bottle of champagne? That's what's been happening. The wedge is gone and look out below."

"Who knocked out the wedge?"

"The short answer is: me. I did. But I was just the dull immediate cause. The deep, underlying cause was more complicated. One gang was moving in on the other; it was inevitable. Pritchett and his crowd, mostly centred around Atlantic City, are crowding the syndicate which has controlled vice in this area for the last ten years. The explosion was unavoidable."

"Why can't everything be as tidy as Hayes and Miranda

Pride," Pete said, almost under his breath. "At least some things obey the rules of probability."

"That's where we went wrong," I said. "Miranda didn't kill Hayes and she didn't kill herself either." Four eyes looked at me with dislike. I was supposed to make things easier for them, not more complicated. I repeated it a different way, but their eyes didn't change.

"Pete, take hold of your tie and pull."

"Not now, Benny. No time for . . ." I leaned over and grabbed Pete's tie which was hanging like a blue tongue down his yellow shirt.

"Hey!"

"Just watch a second. Look, if I pull this side, the knot gets tighter and the end gets longer. If I pull this side the knot gets tighter, but it doesn't slip. Now watch when I pull both ends together as hard as I can: nothing happens."

"You've wrecked this tie!"

"What's going on, Benny?"

"Why did Miranda tie a noose in the middle of the curtain cord?"

"She wanted the cord doubled; didn't trust a single strand."

"Yeah, but it was single around her neck, wasn't it?"

"That's right. I don't know."

"Tell me, were you there when she was cut down? I'd been taken to another room for questioning, you remember." Usually Chris would take this as a cue for a wisecrack, but he let it slide by.

"Yeah, I watched the whole thing. What about it?"

"Well, when I saw her I don't remember seeing two separate strands of rope. Were they twisted around one another?"

"Maybe half a twist, not much for the length. She didn't turn on the rope because her legs were touching the wall."

"The noose worked like Pete's tie; there were two ends to it, one pulled, the other didn't."

"Check. So?"

"So, why were both lengths the same? If she'd tied off the rope and jumped, the slipping side would have tried to cause strangulation and death. But the other end would have virtually remained fixed and would have prevented the slipping side from doing its job."

"What are you working up to?"

"The rope we saw was holding the body with equal tension on either side. I'm saying that she can't have achieved that by tying off the ends and jumping. If the two ends are tied off even, that doesn't allow for the slack needed to kill Miranda. So, what I'm saying is that she was strangled first and then hung up behind the curtains. Otherwise the . . ."

"Hold on, Benny. Drive this by me again." I demonstrated with Pete again, showing how the non-slipping side prevents the other from slipping.

"So let me put it this way: if you tie off a slipknot so both ends are the same length, it isn't a slipknot any more." I put the stretched ends of Pete's tie in Chris' hand. "Try it out, you'll see."

"But we've got latent prints from her bare feet."

"It's that clever bandit you were talking about."

"What are you going to tell me about the scarves? How do they figure? You're going to surprise me again, right?"

"The scarves look right. Honest. If she did it herself, she would have tried to protect herself from unnecessary marks. And they certainly were used to prevent our finding more than one set of marks. The scarves blurred the impressions, so that on the basis of marks alone the coroner couldn't say she was hanged after she was strangled."

"Let's see if I can jump a step ahead of you. If Miranda didn't kill herself, that means she didn't kill Hayes, right?"

"In a roundabout way, right. I mean she could have killed herself for reasons that had nothing to do with Hayes. Also, she could logically have killed Hayes and in turn been murdered herself." Both policemen got that look in their eyes again. So I added, "But my bet is that both of them were killed by the same person." They relaxed a little at that and Chris began to sip cold coffee.

"This is getting to sound like one of those English murder mysteries. Our training says look for the simple explanations first."

"And it makes sense. Let me show you a couple of things I've found out and see what simple pictures develop."

"Movie time, eh?"

"Reel one. For this we have to go back nearly thirty years."

"Oh, God," said Chris, "one of those."

"Monty Blair was in his heyday putting on plays in Grantham. Monty befriended a young mechanic named Furlong. Furlong paid him off by stealing a play Monty wrote, changing a few things, then passing it off as his own. By that time Monty's spent a lot of time knocking the rough edges off Neil; nearly ten years. Monty didn't squawk about the play because he didn't have enough beak and claw to make it hurt. Time moves on, you can see the calendar pages blowing away, and it's the late seventies. Monty takes another writer under his wing, maybe boasts a little about 'knowing Furlong when'. The young writer fires off a play he's written; and sure as rent day, Furlong doctors it and passes it off as his own work. He pays Hayes a little, but gives him no share of the credit. Hayes isn't like Monty: he's mad, and just as ambitious as Furlong ever was. Call that reel one.

"Reel two. For this we go back to the mid-sixties. We meet a Furlong with more poise. He's living and working in the Falls and has two girl friends. One is Dulcie Osborne, the other you know as Billie Mason. He puts both of them into his shows here, in Grantham and across the river. When fame calls from Toronto, Neil decides that he wants to cut his losses around here, so he tells both girls that the fun and games are over. Billie takes it like a pro. She's as ambitious in her way as he is, so she's not hung up on anybody. He's not so lucky with Dulcie, who is thinking of rose-covered cottages and meeting Neil at the door with news of how baby's cut a tooth. Neil doesn't buy the idea of married bliss with a girl from the sticks, so he tries to shake her, but she's made of glue. Eventually he gets her drunk and stages a phoney accident. She kills herself on that bad bend on the Lewiston-Youngstown road."

"The burden of proof, Benny. I hope you know about that," Chris said, and I nodded. It was true, but with what we knew we could build up a pretty good circumstantial case.

"Let's change to a fresh reel. Our third. It's announced that a movie is going to be made here in the Falls. The author is to be none other than the home-town kid himself. Two people who are still living in the area hear about it and decide that there's capital to be made from it. They happen to know one another, but neither knows the other's hold on Furlong. Hayes has the better hold. He can make a lot of trouble. Billie has only old times to drag up. Or maybe she just wanted to say 'Hi!' and then turn to the cameras.

"Billie finds that Neil is glad to see her. His wife is away and New Year's Eve is coming up. They shack up for a few days for old times' sake. Out of it, Billie wants a small bit in *Ice Bridge*. That's not a lot to ask from an old friend. Not when you look like Billie Mason. Hayes is a more serious pest. He can spoil things. He has a grievance going back to Monty's day. Hayes doesn't just want to get his face on the screen, he wants his name in the screen credits: 'Written by Neil Furlong *and* . . .'

"When Furlong is convinced that Hayes won't just go away, he puts his mind to getting himself out of a corner. This time he can't simply put his own name on somebody else's work. Things are more complicated. Pritchett spots Billie talking to Neil, and wonders whether Billie has gone on a talking spree with his whole operation spelled out for the matinee audience. Meanwhile Solmi and Cohn have more than suspicion to go on. They have the script and they don't like what they see about themselves in it. They put the gears to Raxlin, who insists on big changes. Hayes wants to help with the changes, but for credit. Hayes has had five years to get his act together, so Furlong can't buy him with promises. He's back in the same corner he was in when Dulcie Osborne told him how happy they'd be in a little two-room flat over the fish store. That required cool thinking and steady planning, and so does this.

"By the time I'd traced Hayes to the Falls, he was on Furlong's personal payroll and he was busy making changes. Meanwhile Miranda returned to the Falls on New Year's Day. Dear, superfluous Miranda. She began asking questions about Hayes. She'd fallen for him. She'd seen Furlong take advantage before, but probably never with someone so young, attractive and green. She knew where to find all of Furlong's pressure points.

"Furlong had had good mileage out of Miranda. He'd used all of her connections and walked through the doors she opened for him like he'd opened them himself. By now Miranda knew all about his funny business with scripts. She was capable of dragging that out when they fought. But even when things were placid on top, there was always the chance that she'd tell. It was like sitting across the breakfast table from a blackmailer. Of course most of it was in Furlong's own mind. He knew what Miranda *could* do, maybe what she threatened she *might* do. But as far as we know, she wasn't doing it. All she wanted was for things to go on as usual. She wouldn't want to hear about separations or divorce, would she?

"So, Furlong hits upon the idea of getting rid of both headaches at once. Supposing, he figures, that Hayes is shot. Supposing Miranda is seen leaving the scene of the crime, and then commits suicide. Murder and suicide, the tidiest package that ever comes through your mail slot.

"As soon as he was convinced that Hayes was not going to back down on his demands for credit, Furlong put his plan into operation. Through Billie he knew Miranda was meeting Hayes in his room at the Tudor Wednesday night. A few hours after Harvey Osborne clipped him, Furlong put on a white busboy's jacket that he'd picked up on one of his many trips through the two hotel kitchens. From outside a door he picked up a room-service trolley, and from there on he was invisible."

"Hold your horses. You're going too fast. Where'd you dream up the room-service angle, and what about Raxlin?

He swears he saw Furlong take some sleeping pills he gave him. These were powerful prescription pills. How do you account for that?"

"Furlong was clever there. He simply palmed the pills, just pretending to take them. As for the jacket and trolley, you told me."

"I told you! I've never seen a room-service jacket."

"Exactly. Adela Sayre told me that she'd seen Miranda do a little act with a jacket from one of the hotels. It should have been in Furlong's suite when you searched it. Since you didn't find it, one explanation is that it was used in committing the Hayes murder. With trolley and jacket the murderer was part of the hotel decor. Who notices the comings and goings of room-service help in big hotels? He knocked on Hayes' door, and, when he was admitted, shot David Hayes. He left the way he'd come, losing the trolley and jacket before going back to the Colonel John. Then he took the pills and had a long and undisturbed sleep. It went like clockwork, just the way he'd planned it: the first half of the perfect crime.

"Miranda was the second half. He watched her go to bed on Thursday night. He made sure she took her pills. She was on coke; we both found the straws she used. Maybe Furlong went to sleep too. Maybe he could sleep. In the morning, though, he was up early. He took a cord from the curtain track and fixed a running noose in the middle of it. He wrapped two scarves around the sleeping Miranda's throat, and placed the noose high up over them. He tied off the non-slipping end of the rope to the bedframe. Then he strangled her by suddenly, with all his weight, and using the bed as a fulcrum, pulling at the sliding end. He did it so violently and quickly that there was no struggle. It was about as efficient as a bad hanging, but it probably brought about sudden unconsciousness if she wakened at all. When he could be sure she was dead, he carried the body to the curtains where he carefully lifted her to the windowsill, left a set of bare footprints, tied off the rope and then dropped her over the edge. The noose didn't change position, or if it did slightly, the scarves masked any new impressions on her neck. There were no friction marks on the rope except those that should have been there. He retired behind his side of the door and waited until the body was discovered. The second half of the perfect crime, and end of another reel.

"Now we come to the part that ties all of these pieces together. Someone was watching Furlong. Someone who may not have seen what he did to Hayes or his wife, but who had a good idea about the sort of fellow he was."

"Harvey Osborne. I told you that . . ." said Savas.

"No, not Harvey. Harvey shot his bolt when he slugged Furlong. When I saw him he looked like he'd just done fifteen rounds with him."

"Who then?"

"What do we know about Furlong? We know that under his charm he wasn't very nice, and we know that he used people to climb on. He used Miranda that way, but his beloved Pye had slowly dissolved in the pills and drugs she became addicted to. We know that Miranda had a tight hold on him, and wouldn't willingly let him leave her. The fact that he chose to get rid of Miranda strongly suggests that he wanted to move on to a new woman."

"You don't kill somebody just for that," Pete said.

"Right, and why would he kill Miranda just to climb into bed with Billie Mason?"

"You're both right. Furlong wanted his freedom from Miranda. He also wanted her silence. And he couldn't get both. But you're right, Chris: he wasn't after Billie Mason. He'd been there before and he had her telephone number. No, he was after bigger game."

"Who?" they said together.

I let them run through the cast for a moment.

"Peggy O'Toole."

"But she's engaged to Fisher. Anybody who reads knows that."

"That's right. But Furlong, as we have seen, plays dirty. For instance, he knows more about Peggy O'Toole than she knows herself."

"That's two mysteries you're holding in the air," said

Chris, while Pete turned to see what the commotion was at the door of the coffee shop. "Stop looking so smug, Benny. What doesn't she know?" Three police officers came toward our table. Chris turned on the leader:

"What is it, Russ?"

"It's Furlong and Sayre, sir. Agnew went to tell Mr. Furlong that you wanted to see him. He'd said he was going back to his suite, but there was no answer. Agnew looked and he was nowhere. Culp and I then checked to see if anybody else was missing. That's how we found out that Mr. Sayre was gone too."

"How long ago did this happen?"

"Furlong has been out of sight for about twenty minutes. And we've no way of knowing when Mr. Sayre left his suite at the Tudor. His wife's still there."

"I'll want to talk to her. Meanwhile, close the international bridges to both of them. Get to taxis, buses and the airports. They won't get far, and they won't cross the border." Chris glanced at Pete and me, caught his breath, then told Pete to call his New York State opposite number.

We all got up at once, Chris still talking like a teletype machine at Pete and the three men in uniform. Pete and Chris separated and went off from the coffee shop in opposite directions leaving me without a backward glance and with the tab to pay.

twenty-three

Outside it was dark once you got out from under the bright marquee of the hotel entrance. Melt-waters were running from crevasses in the frozen snow near the fire hydrant; the gutter was moving water and silt to the sewer grating. It spoke of glaciers and drumlins and eskers, and I kicked a dam of slush across the flow, a peevish gesture because I was in a hurry without knowing where I was going. I crossed Falls Avenue to the entrance of the Rainbow Bridge. It was business as usual, with the guards asking the same familiar questions. I turned right and walked along the damp sidewalk toward the falls. The park, twinkling with a filigree of coloured lights caught in the trees, smacked of left-over Christmas pudding. By now I could hear far-off police sirens moving away from the hotel in different directions. The only quiet place seemed to be right where I was standing. That's the way I liked it. I looked over the parapet and down into the gorge below. The ice was grey except where the illumination from the falls painted it. I noticed that the spray from the falls was reaching further downstream than it had all week. And it wasn't freezing. There was a thaw in the air. It had been there all day.

Traffic was thin along the Niagara Parkway. What there was of it came out of or disappeared into the sticky mist. I watched a taxi slow down and stop at the curb near a shuttered souvenir kiosk. Before it was properly halted, a figure came out of the shadows by the *Maid of the Mist* ticket booth. It ran up the slight rise to the cab and was opening the back door when I caught up to Ed Noonan and piled in after him.

"Cooperman! Get the hell out of here! I got no time." He was flushed with running and he shouted in short bursts.

"Not before you tell me where you've been," I said,

201

cocking my head toward the river, as though I already knew some of it.

"I want no part of this, Cooperman. I'm getting as far away from here as possible. They can kill each other as far as I'm concerned. It's none of my business. Now, clear out. I'm not joking."

"You mean Furlong and Sayre? Where are they? The whole town is looking for them. You'd better fess up, or it'll bite you where it hurts. Furlong's wanted by the police for murder and you don't want to aid and abet a fugitive, do you?" Noonan's mouth dropped and I got a look at some surprised tonsils along with a whiff of stale rye.

"Oh, so that's what it is. Furlong asked me to get the gate unlocked, and no sooner had I done that when Mr. Sayre came after him. He had a gun in his hand. Furlong took off down the hill toward the *Maid of the Mist* landing."

"How long ago was this?"

"Five minutes, maybe ten. Did I tell you? Sayre had a gun."

"Who called the taxi?"

"I did. I called from the hotel twenty minutes ago. I didn't know how bad I was going to need it. Close the door or get the hell out, Cooperman. I don't want any part of this."

The driver had been watching us in his rear-view mirror. He wasn't in a hurry and the meter flag had been engaged. To him this was just another rear-view melodrama. I climbed out of the car and Noonan nearly slammed the door on my coat-tail.

The *Maid of the Mist* ticket booth was stone like the kiosk, built to harmonize with the rest of the un-commercial look that had been decreed for the view leading up to the falls. Stone baffles and steel pipes were arranged to handle the heavy summer crowds past the ticket window and forward to the incline railway that slanted steeply down to the boarding dock. The red and yellow cars looked hung up to dry. The crowd-control devices made the place all the more desolate tonight. Not quite parallel to the funicular, and upstream slightly, a narrow road pointed down toward the power plant at the foot of the Canadian falls. It clung closely to the wall of the gorge and sometimes was overhung by it. I started down that unilluminated black line.

The high wire gate was standing open. A padlock hanging unfastened on a plastic-covered chain didn't stop me. A few yards more and there was a sign that warned pedestrians like me to proceed no further. The ice underfoot was still frozen in irregular lumps. I skidded a few times and came down with a crash that took the skin from the heel of my hand. As I worked my way down, I could feel the temperature moving down beside me. I realized that on the Parkway it had been almost balmy. Very strange weather for January. Once under the lee of the cliff it was easier to see the way ahead. The lights from the town above and behind me lit up the edge of the gorge, but didn't help much down here, except for reflections from the surface of the ice below.

There was no snow on the roadway, only frozen slush that had hardened in the shape of bootprints and tire treads. It was slippery going and I was beginning to feel a little silly, when I thought I heard something almost directly below me. I tried to see where the sound was coming from, but I saw shapes all over the place. Under me I could make out the form of four *Maids of the Mist*, mounted on frames. I kept moving down as fast as I could, leaving the shapes behind me. By now I was feeling pain in the front of each shin. Downhill does that to me. A few hundred feet beyond the ships, the road divided: one fork continued straight ahead under the cliff toward the power plant, the other made a sharp descending hairpin aimed back toward the dark shapes of the ferries. I cleared the *Maid of the Mist* office and came out toward the ice between that and the dry-docked ships.

Then I saw it. A black shape moving out away from the ice-jammed boarding area. It was climbing up on the ice bridge.

"Sayre!" I shouted. I heard the echo play around with the sound, and thought I heard the ice begin to growl where it touched the shoreline. I thought that the silence was going to settle back in place when I heard another voice out on the ice. It was far away and sounded like the parting shot from a dead battery. About a hundred yards ahead I could see another figure making its way across the ice. It looked like all the other shadows on the ice, except that it was moving diagonally across from me toward the far abutment of the Rainbow Bridge. If there was any place where a man might be able to climb out of the river gorge, it was here. I watched the shape move, Sayre moving quickly after it. I called to Sayre again.

"Cooperman! Go back. Don't come any closer! I've got a gun!"

"To hell with your gun. Are you crazy? This thing isn't safe. You can't go out there!"

"Get back, Ben. This is between me and him. He's out there and I'm going to get him. I've been studyin' this ice for a week now."

"I can see him from here. Let him go. Come on back." I hadn't stopped moving. By now I was able to see Sayre more clearly, moving steadily out across the river on the packed ice. At the shoreline the snow and ice were firm like in the Christmas carol: deep and crisp and even. But from there the bridge slowly mounted, like a vault over a gigantic sports palace, running from the up-river side of the American falls to beyond the Rainbow bridge. It had the shopworn reflection of a grey and threatening sky, with darker shadows like coal sacks marking gaps and crevasses. Attached at the up-river and down-river ends, cleaner ice was visible. These sections looked newer than the band that ran from shore to shore in front of me and were formed of ice more recently swept over the falls. Downstream, this less dense flotilla had been forced under the ice bridge by water power difficult to imagine.

I could see a gap where Sayre had jumped from the boarding dock to the bridge. He was moving forward ahead of me, steadily and without looking back. I called again, but he didn't turn. I thought a moment then jumped after him. By now Furlong was about half-way across. He'd reached the high point of the bridge and from then on I could only see him as he rounded some high eminence. His path took him to the edge of the older ice, dangerously close to the smaller, less compact floes that stretched down toward the international bridge. My eyes were becoming cleverer in the dark, and my feet, though both freezing and soaked, helped me move safely over the unreliable surface. Twice a solid-enough path gave way under my weight, which taught me to look closer before investing all one hundred and sixty pounds of me in one place. Ahead, and to the right, I could see the pale ghost of one of the wonders of the world looming straight as a wall and going up two hundred feet in the air. I knew the American falls were less than that, but you try being precise from where I was. From time to time I could see movement in the newer ice to my left. One floe jumped eight feet in the air and came crashing down in a shower of fragments on the floes that had already moved to fill its place. I felt like I was walking on an eggshell with hobnail boots. Over my shoulder I could see how far I'd come from the ice reaching up to touch the sterns of the four *Maids of the Mist*.

By now I was nearing the top round of the ice bridge vault. Below me, Sayre had been shortening the distance between himself and Furlong. I tried calling again.

"Sayre, don't be a fool! He's not worth it!" Fifty yards ahead of me Jim Sayre looked back over his shoulder.

"I'm going to get that son of a bitch!"

"If you're doing this for Peggy, you're crazy."

"You just don't know what it's all about. Stay back!" Sayre was looking ahead, trying to find the dark shadow in front of him. The falls were getting to sound like the biggest broken air-conditioner on earth. I couldn't make myself look up at them.

"I talked to Claudia in La Jolla," I shouted. "I figured it out from there." He was leaning on a piece of timber, part of a broken log-boom that annually attempts to control the ice from Lake Erie. It looked like it had been through a shredder; one end was rounded like the top of a bullrush. He levelled the gun at Furlong, then changed his mind, starting on again down the sloping roof of ice toward the American side. I climbed, slipped and crouched my way after them. We were all walking on the down-river edge of the old ice. Suddenly I heard what sounded like a shot over my shoulder. More like a cannon than a revolver.

"What the hell was that?" Sayre called. I looked ahead to see whether it had been Furlong. Sayre saw me and shook his head. "It's not him. This is his gun." Both of us were puzzled and paused. Then I saw it.

"It's the ice, Sayre. It's breaking up!" To my right a long fault ran parallel to the edge of the ice. If the whole ice bridge wasn't falling apart, at least it was shedding the piece the three of us were crawling over. The gap was widening. Between the two parts, I could see a strip of black water many feet below. The huge piece of ice we were on was very slowly moving away from the main mass. I yelled again: "You crazy old galoot, you'll never stop him. He can't get across. The ice is breaking up. The river will get the two of you!"

I felt like I was standing on a huge slice of meatloaf that was being slowly tilted over out of the pan and onto a plate. I could see the crack getting bigger. I turned and ran back to the break. By now it was too wide to jump. Back in the direction of the ferry landing, the crack was less pronounced. The ice was still locked together. I took a run and leaped across the gap. Below me it felt like the ice was actually pulling apart beneath me, like a seam was being ripped out and I was trying to jump at the point where the material was just letting go. One leg landed safe and dry. The other pulled me down toward the water reaching up for my galoshes. I had to roll up to the other side.

I lay there, not even feeling the cold, my face resting roughly on the scratchy surface of the ice below my cheek. When I'd caught my breath, I stood up. Sayre had almost caught Furlong, who had come to the end of the disengaging ice cake. They both stood about ten feet above the level of the flotilla of brighter ice floes that told where the water level was. Furlong had got about three-quarters of the way to the American shore. Between him and shore ran a curve of looser ice running close to the main mass. He was standing at the edge when Sayre got to him. The older man reached out and pulled Furlong around to face him. Neil punched out awkwardly at Sayre who doubled up. Going down, he grabbed Furlong's knees. Now they were rolling over one another. I couldn't make out who was on top. I couldn't hear anything above the roar of the falls. It was like watching television with the sound turned down; even wrestling looks like ballet. A dependable feeling in the back of my knees told me to get back to the Canadian shore. The ice bridge was deceptive. It looked like it would last a thousand years. It already looked at least a hundred. But it was slipping away whenever you were distracted for a minute.

Furlong was standing over Sayre. I could see that the yellow Anorak was spread out on the ice. That had to be my last look, because I thought I could hear the ice growling a warning. I turned around and ran, skipping and skidding, back to the *Maid of the Mist* dock. The ice was now further from the shoreline. It meant a jump of about two yards. It wouldn't stand thinking about so I did it at a fast clip. I felt myself falling, then landing flat against the shore-side of the broken-away bridge. I seemed to be sticking on the slanted surface by invisible suction cups. For a moment I was suspended there, holding fast with my face and fingernails. When the slide began, it was like all my contact points were being rejected at once. Down I went into the water of the river. Luckily, there was more ice just under the surface, and the second after I felt that, a hand reached down over the shore and caught my flailing arm.

"Easy does it," a voice said, and up I came suddenly eye to eye with a rough, weather-worn face with a mariner's wool cap over grey hair. I squeegeed water from my shoes and trouser cuffs and looked back across the river. It was good to feel solid, if frozen, ground underfoot again. I couldn't make out anything on the ice bridge. Both Furlong and Sayre were on the side sloping away from us. I could see more ice coming over the falls. The rest of the ice was holding fast. Above Goat Island a new noise joined the parade: a helicopter was throbbing and blinking its riding lights out in the dark. For a moment we listened to the noise, then I let myself be led up the steps and into the *Maid of the Mist* office by the man who had grabbed me. It was warm inside, and I saw the makings of coffee before I began to shiver.

twenty-four

I remember sitting with Peggy in a waiting-room at Niagara Regional that Sunday trying to get some idea of when they would be finished with Sayre. Dawson Williams turned up for an hour or so, went out to get us coffee and replenish our store of cigarettes, but then moved off after wishing us and Jim Sayre the best of luck. He walked awkwardly to the glass doors, embarrassment showing even in the familiar smile. Peggy sat close to me and kept asking questions which led closer and closer to quicksands I preferred to avoid. I could see she found me maddening, but what could I do? It wasn't my secret.

"I keep coming back to what you said, Benny: Neil killed Miranda and the writer, Hayes, in order to be free of both of them. And it all has something to do with me. But that's where I lose you. I sometimes think I've got mothballs for brains. Tell me again, and I promise it'll be the last time." She gave a big smile to a policeman who was standing opposite us staring at her. He looked like he was trying to remember whether it was permitted to ask for autographs while in uniform. Peggy killed her smile when she thought I might imagine the mothballs weren't concentrating again.

I explained what had happened just as I had to Chris and Pete back in the Falls on Saturday. She followed me with nods and short exclamations at all the right places until she had the main lines of the plot.

"But why didn't he just divorce Miranda? Surely that would have been simpler."

"Miranda knew too much about his *borrowing*. He couldn't be sure that during the cut and thrust of a divorce, Miranda wouldn't use her knowledge against him. Besides, she was part of the perfect crime. He needed her 'suicide'

209

to halt the investigation of Hayes' murder. That's how he saw it, anyway."

"But why did he choose such a bizarre way to get rid of her? I mean, well, wouldn't pills have done as well?"

"I guess Furlong knew, as most writers do, that a faked suicide by hanging is very rare. The cops wouldn't expect it."

At that moment I saw Savas cross the corridor from his office. He didn't look our way. A moment later Jim Sayre walked into the room.

"Well, that didn't take as long as I thought," he said. "I once spent six days in a Mexican jail for drinkin' with some students." Sayre sounded like his old self, but you had to look at him twice to make sure it was Sayre and not a reasonable facsimile. His face looked caved in under his cheekbones, the way he'd gone pale under his tan when he got coughing and couldn't stop. He glanced at Peggy, then shot me a worried look. I shook my head, and tried out a grin, like I was smiling with a learner's permit. We'd got up and were now standing around. I felt a little like I did the time I picked up my grandfather at the hospital and took him home. He had that look of sickness about him, like he wouldn't be able to stand up much longer. Peggy saw that and said she'd go to get the car. When she'd gone, Jim followed her with his eyes, which were beginning to shine in the semi-dark of the waiting room.

"You know, Ben, I've done a peck of stupid things in my time. But she's one of the good ones. Where's Adela? At the hotel?"

"She started packing, then she decided to talk to Raxlin."

"Raxlin? Why Raxlin?"

"Well, I guess she assumed that he'd want a new director, then she decided to talk him out of it."

"Talk him out of it. You're pullin' my wooden leg."

"You were pursuing a fugitive. You haven't done anything criminal. You should get a medal."

"Isn't she the damnedest? That woman's always wet-nursin' me. And I treat her sometimes like . . ."

Peggy beeped the horn from the curb in front of

Niagara Regional and Sayre and I walked out to the car. Sayre shook my hand and said, "Damn Furlong and damn mendacity." Peggy had rolled down the window on the passenger side and looked up at me smiling. Sayre thrust his head next to hers so they looked like a royal couple on an old coin. "Listen, Ben," he said, "I'm goin' to finish this picture and when I do I want to see you at the première. You hear? I'll save tickets. Won't take no for an answer. Marilyn here'd never forgive me if I let you just disappear."

Peggy leaned her head out of the window. I pushed my cheek at her and she planted a good one.

"So long, Pistachio," she said. She put the car in gear and drove off down Church Street heading for the highway and the Falls.

Gradually the cast was thinning out. I'd checked out of my room at the Clifford Arms, leaving Ned and the boys happily talking about extra jobs they'd been promised. I saw Raxlin talking to the man in the wool mariner's cap. By then I knew that my rescuer was Captain McCool, the supervising skipper of the four white ladies of the mist. Raxlin reported that the ice bridge was going to hold and that the production had a lot of time to make up. His last word was a lament that everybody but him was on golden time.

By Monday I had clean clothes and a tidier office. But I still didn't have a line on Billie Mason. So I was right back where I started. I promised that I would take up Lowell Mason's problem first thing Tuesday.

But that wasn't to be. Chris Savas and Pete Staziak followed me out to my parents' condominium off Ontario Street. I was soaking in the tub, trying to get rid of the chills that had moved in to stay when I got off the ice bridge. My mother answered the door. I could hear their voices downstairs as I pulled the plug.

"Is Benny here?" Chris asked in a polite tone I'd not heard before. I could picture them standing in the hall, slipping out of their rubbers. I got dried and into my clothes without catching a draught. When I got downstairs, they were all sitting in the tangerine front room. Ma was still wearing that fuchsia wrap because it was still early, not even noon yet. The boys wore their civilian clothes like they were in uniform. Maybe, once you've been in uniform, it's hard to get out. After a chat about the break in the severity of the winter, I led the way down to the rec room. The TV was cooling off from early morning duty and we all made ourselves comfortable in the imitation leather chairs. Pete admired my father's bar with the light-up displays that he'd collected from bartenders of his acquaintance.

"Nice place, Ben."

"Yeah. They're comfortable. Pa's gone to get some smoked salmon and a loaf of rye."

"We've just come from the Falls," Chris explained.

"Just cleaning things up," added Pete. I nodded my approval.

"Next time you go chasing wanted men, let us know where you're going."

"Hey! What are you talking about? I didn't know that Furlong was going to try to beat it across the border the hard way. I don't even think he planned it that way. Sayre was talking tough with him and took his gun away. He didn't have much choice. He didn't know how much Sayre knew or how badly Sayre could hurt him."

"So he got Noonan to open the gate to the *Maid of the Mist* landing."

"Sure. Noonan had been letting the cast and crew up and down all week."

"It was a damned near run thing for Sayre. He caught the ladder from the helicopter seconds before that chip off the ice bridge turned over. Lucky Furlong hit him and went on across the slob ice. You couldn't see that, could you?" I shook my head. "From up top, he was seen fighting toward the American side. Only that slob ice was as steady as ice in a rye and water."

"Yeah, the end wasn't pretty. They still haven't got the body. They're still dragging at the whirlpool, but they've got their own ice problems down there. No, we won't see Furlong till spring, if then."

"Benny, I want to hear how Sayre fits in. He had a

part to play, but he wouldn't say why he played it. He just told us about how they'd fought and so forth."

"You got to the point where Peggy O'Toole came into the story."

"Does she have to come in?"

"At least as far as the three of us. Whether it goes any farther depends on what it changes," Chris said looking me in the eye.

"You said that Furlong knew more about her past than she knew herself," Pete prompted. "Sounds like blackmail to me."

"Right. And that sounds like Furlong."

"Okay, let me get my facts straight," I said, attempting to focus on things I'd already tried to forget. "Right. Peggy O'Toole is Peggy's stage name. Her real name is Marilyn Horlick. Her mother, Claudia, worked in Hollywood in the old Writer's Building at Paramount. She was a secretary with some seniority in the early winter of 1953–54. According to the official story, Peggy was born in December 1954, the twentieth to be exact. That makes her a Sagittarian in the Zodiac. Only when I talked with her mother last week, she told me that she was a Libra. She said that being a Libra made her easy to get along with. To be a Libra she would have had to be born between 24 September and 23 October. I looked all of this stuff up at the Library. Everybody seems to agree that Libras are easy to get along with. Now why would Claudia Horlick get the sign of her only daughter wrong? My guess is that she didn't. I bet Peggy's birthday is October 20, not December 20.

"Why make the change? What difference does it make? The only thing that I can think of is this: if Peggy was born in December, and not October, there is no way that her real father could have been James A. Sayre."

"What?" Savas looked really surprised. I didn't often see that expression of sincere incredulity written on his face.

"That's right. Sayre finished work on *Donnybrook* in the early winter of '53–'54. He told me he was gone by

February '54. He could have fathered a child born to Claudia in October. When I talked to her long distance in La Jolla last week, the subject of Jim Sayre was still a sore one. But apart from that slip about her sign of the Zodiac, she didn't drop her guard. She said that it was the younger girls who played around not her. By disguising the birthday she was able to keep the truth from Sayre. But I think he found out about it years later. That's why he has stood up for Peggy, that's how she got her start in his movies. He probably felt rotten about not being in on the birth of his daughter but he tried to make up for it.

"Who else knew about Sayre and Claudia Horlick? Not her husband. Not the studio brass. But the other girls knew. They could count backwards on their fingers faster than a cash register can ring up No Sale. One of these girls, Blanche Tyler, became the first wife of Neil Furlong of blessed memory. Is it likely that Blanche would keep a juicy piece of gossip about the origin of one of the youngest and brightest stars in years a secret? She knew that Furlong lived on gossip, filled his plays with it. Maybe she thought that it would bind him to her for a little longer. I don't pretend to know that.

"Sayre is a gentleman of the old school, in spite of his tough-guy front. I think he enjoyed playing a secret role in Peggy's life. He wanted to be her Daddy Warbucks, her Daddy Longlegs."

"But why? Why did he want to keep in the background?"

"Because Peggy'd had a happy upbringing. She loved her supposed father and doted on the whole family connection with show business. He didn't want to rain on her strawberry festival. He was glad to see her getting on in pictures and happy to see her about to team up with Hamp Fisher. Sure, Fisher was known to be an eccentric, but nobody ever said anything low or mean about him. So what if he did have a peculiar fear of microbes? I don't care that much for them myself. A bit of an oddball, but solid in a business way, and, most important, nuts about Peggy. As a father, Sayre approved the match.

"But then along comes the spoiler: Neil Furlong. He knew all about the past and tried to get Sayre to help him with his own suit to Peggy O'Toole."

"That's plain crazy! He was still married for one thing."

"Yes. Just another good reason for including Miranda in his scheme to rid the world of David Hayes."

"You're saying Furlong tried to pressure Sayre into helping him with Peggy, or he'd reveal to Peggy that Sayre was her real father?" Chris asked carefully.

"That's it. He wanted Peggy so bad he couldn't wait. And the sight of Hamp Fisher on the scene meant he had to act fast. He asked Sayre to help him or else. Sayre saw red, and, not having a bull whip handy, drove Furlong to try to make a getaway."

"But why did the bastard think Sayre would help him?"

"He knew Sayre liked playing Dutch uncle to Peggy. He knew that Sayre wanted to suppress the real story of her paternity. He wanted to protect Peggy, her mother and her career. He didn't want to cause Peggy to feel any differently toward her early life or her parents. He carried a lot of guilt around with him. Furlong couldn't have touched a nerve more tender than that one. And he paid for it with his life."

"But Furlong didn't have a chance with Fisher around."

"Sure, and the choice would always remain Peggy's, but Furlong knew Fisher would run off like a startled rabbit if any story suggesting Peggy's promiscuity got to him. He is one of those guys who lives in constant fear of picking up a dose. All Furlong had to do was bring that kind of report to his attention, and then open out his welcoming arms to pick up the pieces. Also all Fisher needed to hear was the story that Peggy was a bastard and that would have queered any marriage. He was all heart, was Furlong."

"Pretty hare-brained all round," Pete said. "I guess he was getting desperate."

"It hadn't been his week. First Billie came back making demands, then Hayes made bigger ones. He killed Hayes and then Miranda. I think he was proud of his performance there: two perfect crimes, and one cancelling out the other. But he hadn't figured on Sayre. Sayre wanted no part of Furlong's scheme. Furlong was about to blemish the one thing in his life that he had tried to keep pure: Peggy. Sayre didn't want to see Furlong's shadow pass over her; he wasn't going to let the arch-spoiler claim another unearned victory. So he got Furlong mad and followed him out on the ice waving that gun around like a sheriff in a western."

I heard my mother's footsteps on the carpeted stairs. She came into the room with a tray of instant coffee which she'd poured into a Silex to improve its provenance. She was beaming.

"Don't get up," she said, and Chris and Pete began at once to climb out of their deep chairs. "I'll put the tray down on top of the magazines." I helped clear a place. "I'm getting used to having a house full of people again. It's like when the boys were young. The house was always full of their friends. I used to wonder, 'Don't they have families?' I think it was the Baked Alaska. I never got it right. But then they kept coming back just the same."

Ma had got dressed and was even looking glamorous for a change. She sat down and let Chris and Pete exchange awkward glances. When you could almost hear the clock ticking next door, she asked: "So, you are friends of Benny? You live in town here?" Savas and Staziak answered together so you couldn't make out what they said. I tried to get into the act:

"Pete and I were at the Collegiate together. I was in a play with his sister." She nodded the way she does when she's after deeper truths than the ones I'm relating.

"We're with Niagara Regional Police," Chris confessed.

"Oh!" she said with her eyebrows, and repeated the information as though that made it come true. "Benny's in that line too, aren't you, Benny?"

"In a way, Ma. But Chris and Pete are very high up in the Criminal Investigation Branch. They're working on a case."

"I see, I see. They're with the city. They get salaries,

and overtime and pensions. They've got the right idea." Turning to Chris and Pete she said, "Maybe you could talk my son out of being the lone ranger all by himself. A freelance policeman? What kind of life is that?"

With no luck at all I tried to get the conversation back to the weather. When I left them, they were all discussing a recent rash of hospital deaths in Grantham. Ma had her theory and I left Chris and Pete to hear her out.

twenty-five

I didn't honestly care if I ever saw the Falls again. The river-front felt like a relative you know better than you want to. I wandered around the trapline I'd set in the bars and coffee shops of the two big hotels, chatted with the house men, and gossiped with some of the movie people. Wally Skeat bought me a drink. Peggy introduced me to her intended. But nowhere in all my peregrinations from Table Rock to the Rainbow Bridge, or from the Surf Lounge to the Pagoda did I find a trace of the fine tawny hide of Billie Mason. After dark, I called it a day and came back along the familiar highway to Grantham.

In the United I was dozing into a daydream which featured me and a cast of refrigerated extras crossing the ice bridge. If I don't watch myself, I slip into fantasies so worn they have toe-holds built into them. In front of my coffee I could hear the voice of the waitress: "What's got into you lately? How come you stopped the back-chat?" I brought her into focus. The name "Irene" was clipped to the nicest part of her, and she was slipping a toasted chopped egg sandwich in front of me next to a tall glass of milk.

"Huh?"

"Never mind. You're just different, that's all. I get more conversation out of the mad scribbler than I do out of you these days. Never mind. Never mind." She walked down to the other end of the counter and another failure was added to those of the afternoon. I tried to think of something bright. All I got back were glimpses of Billie hiding between the napkin holder and the ketchup. It wasn't my day, and I slunk back to the office.

Ma phoned to announce that Linda Levin was seeing a computer programmer from Buffalo. She told me twice in the same five-minute conversation and was going around for the third time when I told her I had a client. It was a lie when I said it, but a rap of knuckles at the door made it true about thirty seconds later. I was looking at an offer to try handcuffs on a thirty-day-no-money-down basis when I saw Billie Mason walk into the room. I picked up my fallen cigarette and replaced it in my mouth.

"I guess you're mad at me," she said. Billie Mason was still the gorgeous woman I first remembered seeing in the eight-by-ten photograph her husband had shown me. Seeing her settle into the chair before my desk was an education in Technicolor. "For running away like that, I mean." She was doing her best to look contrite, and her choice of outfit for the visit achieved something like the effect of a young girl's communion dress. I noted the theatrical effort and decided not to be affected by it, then swallowed a lump in my throat.

"Not exactly mad, Billie. More like blind rage. Where the hell have you been?" She bit the nail of her right hand, while the snow on her open coat began to shine as it melted. I usually help clients off with their coats, but in Billie's case, she could manage or not manage. I was beyond caring.

"I had to go back to the Falls. I had to finish my business there."

"You haven't been near the Falls. What are you talking about?"

"I had to see Ed Noonan."

"I saw Ed Noonan. You didn't."

"I had private business with Neil."

"On an ice floe? Come on." She looked at me with her head cocked, shoulders vulnerable. She was pulling out all the stops, but it sounded sour. I offered her a cigarette, but she shook her head like I'd suggested we go for a dip in the Eleven Mile Creek behind my office. I watched her. The word that came to mind was pouting. She was copping a plea, but I wasn't buying it.

"You've gone back to Lowell, haven't you?" She examined the worn edge of my desk, running a finger along it, finding more dust than she'd bargained for, stalling. "Well?" The prickle behind my knees was acute. "Well, Billie?"

"Oh, he isn't all that bad. I mean, Benny, he's not a bad man. He's no genius, and he's not always been straight, but he's mine."

"He doesn't move in the crowd Furlong moved in. He won't ever be nominated for an Academy Award."

"I know. And maybe he won't end up like Neil did. We had a talk, Benny, a serious talk. We should have years ago. He's going to try to break with Pritchett. He doesn't need anybody else and it's no loss to Tony: he thinks Lowell lost his nerve. Real estate's not so bad . . ." I let her drift away for a few seconds while I wondered what the CBC documentary Norman Baker was putting together would do to the reunited couple. I'd know in less than three months. It would certainly give Tony Pritchett new things to worry about.

". . . It's a good living, really. And I'm pretty good at selling. I bet I could find you a better place than this office. And as for that hotel you're living in . . ."

"What did Solmi want you to do?" She frowned and I could see her face changing as she decided whether to tell me the truth or not.

"He wanted me to arrange a meeting between him and Tony Pritchett. I told him I would, just to get him to let me go. He thought that Tony was moving into the Falls area because I was there. He thought I was connected with money Tony'd put into the movie. I didn't even know about that. I didn't know it but Tony was planning to move into the Falls. I guess I tipped his hand. How was I supposed to know? People should be franker with one another."

"So, the English mob was about to push into the Falls and didn't want anyone connected with them to give the game away."

"Funny, thinking of them all now."

"Pritchett had money in the movie. You were seen with Furlong. Since he was the writer of the script, Pritchett must have thought you were spilling your guts out while he took it all down and divided it up into scenes. Did you know you'd been spotted?"

"Tony's man saw us at Hatch's place on New Year's Eve."

"Tall, lank-haired stringbean?"

Billie nodded.

"As soon as Pritchett found out he put the gears to your husband. That's how I came into it. You understand now why Pritchett was worried about you having anything to do with the movie?"

"People are so materialistic."

"There'll be more killed before this mob war you started cools down. Don't blame yourself too much. Things had been quiet for longer than usual. I played my nasty part in it too."

"Blame myself? I don't understand." Her eyes were round and big.

"Forget it. Just for the record, Billie, when was the last time you saw Dulcie Osborne? Do you remember seeing her the day she died?"

"Yes, I saw her. She knew I'd broken with Neil, and that Neil was planning to return to Toronto. She was in love with him."

"Did you know that she was pregnant?" Billie's face turned toward the light coming in from St. Andrew Street. It was one of those grey winter days when the light is blunt and hard as metal.

"Yes, I knew. What does it matter now?"

"Not much, I guess. I'm just tidying up my desk. So Dulcie had a better argument than you had for Neil to stay in the Falls. You couldn't see him doing public relations for the railway for the rest of his life, but she could."

"It would have finished him. Can you imagine him, stuck with a family?"

"A lot of people would still be alive if he had married Dulcie. But back then it seemed to Furlong that the best choice was to saw through the brake-fluid line. It doesn't take much of a mechanical aptitude. He worked in a garage for a while before he began to rise in the arts. He knew she'd kill herself driving at her usual speed along that road with no brakes. It was a lead-pipe cinch that he could remain unencumbered with a wife and family for a few more years."

"You mean he killed Dulcie?"

"Why not? Furlong didn't let people get in his way. He didn't even let his own lack of talent get in his way. He had drive and ambition all wrapped up in a cover of charm, and not a scruple or a damn for anything else. Billie, where do you meet these people?"

"Well, I won't meet any more like that, I hope."

"Tell Lowell I'll be sending him my bill."

"You can't take credit for my going back to him, Benny. It wouldn't be ethical. I went back of my own free will. I'm not a car or a horse. I'm not a child or a runaway teenager. I'm not a *thing* being returned to its rightful owner." She looked at me with her big blue eyes and her mouth turned down in a pout. I could have easily thrown her down my twenty-eight stairs without a pang.

"Billie, get out of here. Go home. Leave your husband's business to your husband."

"I won't stand by and see Lowell ripped off, Benny."

"I know where there is a fat part for the right actress that hasn't been cast yet."

"Benny, why didn't you tell me when I came in?" She lost that look of being the stout sentry at the gate. "What's the part? Who do I talk to?"

"Drop around to the Water Board and talk to Ned Evans. He's looking for a Millwood in *The London Merchant*. For you, Billie, it's the perfect part."

ABOUT THE AUTHOR

Born in Toronto, but raised in St. Catharines, Ontario, HOWARD ENGEL has been for many years a CBC radio producer. He now lives in downtown Toronto. His first Cooperman mysteries, *The Suicide Murders* and *The Ransom Game*, won him wide acclaim. A founding member of the Crime Writers of Canada, he is currently at work on a fourth Benny Cooperman novel.